ONCE UPON IN SUMMER

JESSICA CHABRILLAN

CONTENTS

1. Chapter 1   1
2. Chapter 2   4
3. Chapter 3   21
4. Chapter 4   36
5. Chapter 5   48
6. Chapter 6   61
7. Chapter 7   72
8. Chapter 8   83
9. Chapter 9   93
10. Chapter 10   108
11. Chapter 11   117
12. Chapter 12   134
13. Chapter 13   149
14. Chapter 14   159
15. Chapter 15   168

16. Chapter 16   179

17. Chapter 17   188

18. Chapter 18   197

19. Chapter 19   205

20. Chapter 20   220

21. Chapter 22   233

22. Chapter 23   247

23. Chapter 24   258

24. Chapter 25   267

25. Chapter 26   276

26. Chapter 27   290

27. Epilogue   294

CHAPTER 1

We were seated in the sand as a heavy cloud of summer heat around us.

Everett, who was covered with sand and salt, lay against my shoulder next to me. At this point, I had a sneaking suspicion that he was doing it on purpose because his head was hunched over me and his lips were caressing my skin whenever he laughed.

Under the bright yellow moon, the waves barely moved. Everett and Isla had left an illegible mark to claim our beach when the sea foam chewed into the sand as it lapped the coast. our isle.

I would be departing shortly because midnight was drawing near.

Fire turned our glum faces orange, and each of our laughs was hollow and eerie, like a phantom of who we once were.

Austin sat across from me, his legs covered in sand and his skin burned and red. He made a joke that only half of the group understood. Sky glanced at him and ran a hand over her freshly shaven head.

She pretended to be thrilled to graduate and leave Shellside Bay, but I could tell she would miss it by the way she regarded the water. All of us would.

With his smile just missing his eyes, Connor leaned towards River. His laughter, which are typically so casual and effortless, sounded flat to me.

River made no attempt to conceal it. He made an openly frowning fist in the sand a few centimetres away from Connor. Before raising his bottle to his lips and taking another big swig that I knew he would be feeling in the morning, he gave the earth two hard thumps as if making a decision. In front of the expanding stack of emptied booze near to the Nauti Buoy, he threw the can.

around some point in the afternoon, the Bennetts' boat—which had been dragged onto the shore around dawn—flipped on its side. As we repeatedly headed out to sea, our shirts and surfboards hung against it to swiftly dry out in the sweltering Australian sun. etching the waves' memory into our skin.

The day had flown by swiftly, with the afternoon being consumed by the glow of the sunset and melting into the evening. Pink-lined clouds teased us, reminding us that the day had to come to an end once the sun had dipped below the horizon and the water had gone a deep inky blue.

As if feeling my thoughts, Everett drew closer to me, stroking his hair across my arm. His black eyes were staring up at me as I looked down, and his hands were tightly clutching mine.

Under the crackle of the fire and the groan of the waves, he said, "You okay?"

My locks, which were heavy with salt and sand, flew loose as I nodded. Just put, "I don't want it to end."

He shifted in his seat and scowled while his eyes reflected mine. He released my hand in the same motion that he encircled me with his arm, drawing me in. I leaned in closer despite the fact that our skin was hot and the sand was scratching against our contact points.

He mumbled, "We'll get through it. "We've already done it once."

In an effort to convince myself that he was correct, I nodded once more.

We had previously completed it. Despite the vast differences in our life, we managed. We phoned. We text. He came over.

But summer couldn't last indefinitely.

I would be in Sydney tomorrow.

Everett would leave in a few more days.

And I would be alone.

The sand was being bit by the waves as they crashed at the coast in the dark. Despite the fact that I couldn't see it, I was aware that it was carrying our names out to sea and washing our imprint off the island.

And it would appear as though we had never arrived.

Chapter 2

The beginning of summer in December

Everett murmured beside me, "Shellside Bay is so much less fun when it's cold." Isn't summer supposed to be here?

I chuckled as I leaned more closely over the Shack's counter. "That doesn't mean it won't rain occasionally."

The Shack actually was what it said on the tin. Since I was fourteen, I'd worked there every summer for extra money in a little cabin on the edge of the shore. My last season at the Shack would be this one. I would miss it. I didn't think I'd be able to find a place like the Shack in the city where I was living.

Everett pouted, "We should relocate somewhere where it never rains.

I assumed you cherished Shellside Bay.

That was prior to my learning that it rains here.

Overstating it, it was raining. In fact, the rain was falling so lightly that not even the colour of the sand was affected.

Nevertheless, the sky had grown cloudy, and the sun was no longer visible. In this light, even Everett's browned complexion appeared duller.

He groaned and flipped his hand around to brush his fingers over my palm as he did so.

Why must you report for duty in the rain? Have you not saved enough money for college considering that all of your clients cancelled? River's stance on the rent hasn't changed, has it?

"University," I clarified.

He gave me a narrowed-eyed look. I continued, grinning sarcastically.

"River did not alter his position. In February, I'll be relocating to his home, I declared. "But don't push him. He's been so grumpy ever since we graduated in September. Like his acceptance to the university was a curse. He changed so much.

Everett joked, "Perhaps he doesn't want to live with you.

I smiled and rolled my eyes. More to the point of not wanting to leave Shellside. Here on Shellside, leave a special someone. Regardless, the money is fantastic. Next time, maybe I'll come see you in New York."

Everett's eyes shifted to our hands as his smile appeared to fade. Behind him, the clouds appeared to get darker. "Maybe."

I grimaced. His fingers were gentle on my flesh, and his eyes were fixed on our hands. He appeared to be dodging my gaze—and the prospect of my travelling to New York to see him. My skin suddenly felt ablaze.

I withdrew my hand, forcing his eyes to suddenly shoot up to mine as I swallowed. I grinned.

"Or maybe we can meet halfway?"

He repeated, "Half-way?" His lips curled back into a smile. What lies halfway between Sydney and New York?

"I'm not sure. Los Angeles?

He made a lip twitch. "I believe that is just over halfway," the speaker said.

Oh, Mr. Geography? Then, what would be a better substitute?

He made a humming sound. "I'm not sure. Hawaii?"

My grin spread. It's Hawaii, then.

□□□□□□□□□□

Now

Isla, get going and put your back into it.

I rolled my eyes as I lifted the last box from the lift and carried it inside River's flat via the door.

River wasn't a Shellside Bay native. He was born and reared in Sydney. Not to mention his wealth, which, despite his denials, was real. We didn't meet till he came to Shellside Bay when we were little.

Years later, here I was moving in with him.

I gave him a cold gaze and added, "You know, you could help." Just a thought.

That's what your boyfriend is there for, right? River fired back.

He leaned over the kitchen counter without even giving me a sidelong glance because he was still engrossed in his phone. He appeared to expect buzzed short but longer tresses to meet his fingertips when he ran a hand over his head. He scowled and lowered his arm to his side.

I dropped the box after saying, "You're right," and looked over my shoulder. "Ev?"

He yelled back, "Yep!" His head appeared around the door to my bedroom a split second later, his dark hair flowing over his brow. The golden streaks and his customary deep tan had faded because he had spent so much time in New York. He came over with ease and wrapped his arm around my shoulders. For you, I made your bed.

I jokingly remarked, "That's my man," and leaned in to give him a kiss.

River threw up. "If you don't stop, Isla, I'll start charging you rent."

I shot him a glance and leaned in for a deeper kiss with Everett, my hand slipping up to grasp his jaw under my fingertips. Everett's arm grew tighter around me as he moaned against my lips.

River sighed and headed for the couch after leaving the kitchen. I detest you, Isla, he yelled while burying his face in the cushions and muting his voice.

I just replied, "You love me," slipping out of Everett's grasp to get my box and take it to the kitchen. He could have threatened to do it, but I knew he wouldn't follow through.

It was rather surprising that he had ever been able to live here by himself. I was aware of River's wealth, but I was unaware of his extreme wealth. The most of the time, my teasing of him consisted only of jokes and banter. But now I was starting to realise how accurate my predictions had been all along.

It was a big apartment for the centre of Sydney. The living room itself was larger than my home in Shellside Bay and featured high ceilings as well as a wall of windows that provided a view of Sydney's skyline. On the opposite end of the room, a balcony reached out from one of the windows, and a hot tub was positioned in the far corner. A fireplace flashed in the marble wall.

I had the impression that I was a hotel guest. I mean, when I arrived at the building, a concierge greeted me. A doorman and everything else were present. It embodied luxury in all its forms.

Even worse, it was essentially deserted.

The walls were white and barren. The refrigerator was bare. The furnishings appeared to have never been used. Instead of a house, it felt more like a showroom.

That River sought refuge at Shellside Bay's inviting sands and friendly faces so frequently is understandable.

I had anticipated that his parents would at the very least investigate the girl who was moving in with their son even today. In an effort to create a nice first impression, I had done my hair and makeup, but they weren't there. I decided to ignore it since I was afraid to confront River about it. The next time would always come.

I laid the box down on the counter and started taking out the collector mugs I had brought with me from home.

I asked River, "River, where do you keep your mugs?" I yelled as I held a cup in the form of Spider-Man in my hands.

While still focusing on his phone, he waved at me. "I'm not sure. Simply place it anywhere.

I scowled as I opened each cupboard to discover cups strewn everywhere, sitting next to bowls, in the pantry, stacked on top of plates, and all over the place. This would have been a mission.

Everett wrapped his arms around my waist and rested his chin on my shoulder as I reached up to take a mug out of the cabinet that I had just decided to use as the plate cabinet. He pulled my jumper—his jumper—down to conceal my exposed waist by tugging at the hem.

"I really like how this looks on you." His speech carried a smile that I could hear. I backed up into his chest.

"Don't get too attached," I mocked. "By the weekend's end, I should have a replacement jumper," the speaker said.

the weekend's end. I would have only had that much time with him. After two days, he would fly back to New York, where we would only be able to communicate with him via sporadic texts and 3AM phone calls.

He grabbed me harder, letting his fingers go under my jumper and rest flat against my waist as though sensing my sudden change in mood.

I'm going to miss you, he said. But I'll be back soon, I promise. Then comes Hawaii. Additionally, River will be there to keep you company.

"Right." I wrenched out of his grasp and peered over my shoulder to see River prostrate on the couch with his face hidden by cushions. "Don't you think he looks like a little bundle of joy right now?"

He called from the couch, "I can hear you, you know.

Everett disregarded him and reached over my head to grab the mug I was trying to grasp.

As he returned to set it down on the counter, Everett said, "You sure have a lot of mugs for one person." I went over to the pantry, of all places, and pulled out a few mugs, which I grabbed and moved on the counter with the rest of the mugs.

"We might need to make some cuts." My collection was sitting in a box as I hummed. Where will I fit all of my cat-shaped mugs, I ask?

"Or your New York mugs," Everett continued.

I scowled as I remembered the unsightly New York mugs he had added to my collection. "Or one of my New York mugs."

He turned to face me and exclaimed, "Hey!" They are adorable.

I remarked sharply, "They're plain white with I heart NYC on them.

He smiled. "Classics."

"Fine. They may exit through the back.

After a year of long-distance romance, Everett grimaced, but I chose to ignore him as I started to take the "classic" New York mugs out of the box, one for each time he had come to visit me.

He always seemed to find an excuse to come visit, whether it was to celebrate his graduation, my graduation, or the tiniest festivals I had ever heard of. Knowing how much money he had spent simply to hold me in his arms for a week before taking a 20-hour flight back to New York made me feel bad to some extent.

However, I could tell he needed it more than I did as he hugged me tightly.

Everett barely mentioned New York at all. Since his father remarried last year, he has hardly ever acknowledged his new stepmother, and he didn't live with her for very long before leaving for college. If he ever mentioned New York, it would be in relation to his coursework, tests, tube rides, or anything else other than his family.

Even through a screen, I could see how homesick Everett was. It brought back memories of when I had just arrived in Shellside Bay from New York and had first met him. At the time, he appeared to have a perpetual frown on his face.

Everett pointed to the plain white mugs strewn over the cabinet and said, "At least they're better than those.

River jerked his head around to look at me and exclaimed, "Oh, you can throw those out." As I shifted to move his plain mugs over, he said.

I squinted. "These? However, there are a lot.

He made a shrug. Nothing matters. Not me, I didn't purchase them.

In my hands, I turned over one of the basic mugs. I questioned whether it had ever been used because it was still in mint condition. I carefully repositioned it on the counter.

I said, "I don't want to toss anything your parents bought." "After all, I get to stay here for free. Do they even realise?

They most likely aren't even aware that this flat even exists, River thought.

He quickly got up from his chair and made his way over to the kitchen counter. He moved across the kitchen, picking up the trash, and threw each of his mugs into it. He then put it back down and made an oblique gesture in the direction of the now-empty cabinet.

He remarked frankly, "See?" There is now enough room for your mugs.

He stopped, took one of my cat-shaped mugs out of the package, and scowled at its enlarged ceramic eyes. "Even if they're quite strange. I don't know why you came all the way here with your personal collection of mugs.

"I had to bring them, of course. Did you really think I'd be drinking hot chocolate from a plain white mug? I smiled and asked, snatching my mug from his grasp. Saying "Thanks, River."

Before River could escape, Everett swiftly cornered him and said, "And seeing as you're already here now."

He exaggeratedly rolled his eyes but nevertheless started to unpack the mugs. The kitchen was mostly stocked in a matter of minutes, and empty boxes started to outnumber filled ones. I grumbled and hurriedly scanned the final few boxes to unload before dusting off my shorts.

Now it's just stuff for my room, I remarked, directing a thoughtful glance Everett's way.

He raised an eyebrow and stepped closer after blinking. Should we start unpacking those now?

I gave him a flirtatious smile. Everett had a great idea.

"To your room then, then?"

River choked and said, "To my room."

I picked up a box and led the way, ignoring him. Everett followed following, taking the last two boxes, and we clicked the door shut behind us. Everett stretched and looked about the room as we set the boxes on the floor next to my bed, which was already made because this was once a guest room.

The question is, "What do you think?" I inquired as I jumped up onto the bed. My mattress shook under me.

He hummed, "I don't know," as he answered. "I'm missing your hot pink sheets."

Not daring to inform him that my old pink bedding were stashed away in one of the boxes, my face warmed and I rolled my eyes. Everett took a step back while pointing towards the toilet.

He answered, "I already removed all of your toiletries."

He laughed as he moved closer and gave me a hug as I smiled and held out my hands for him. He pushed me back into the mattress while dramatically kissing my neck, and I giggled as he did so.

Have I ever told you how much I adore you? I made fun.

He hummed on my neck, which only made me chuckle more. One or two times. You may nudge me once more.

"Oh?" I raised my arm, grabbed his chin, and pulled his face towards mine. He glanced at my lips with darkened, half-lidded eyes as I smirked at him. "How would you like me to kindly remind you?"

He mashed his lips against mine and whispered, "I can think of a few ways," before swiftly stopping. He gave me a slow, passionate kiss to start, and I slid my fingers up, up, up across his jaw, his cheek, and his hot skin against mine till I reached his hair.

Then he started kissing me quickly and hard. I had my leg over his hip while he was pulling me into the mattress. The blood in my ears raced.

My fingers dangled from his hair and landed on the t-shirt hem. He moaned against my lips as I pulled at it, my knuckles brushing against his chest. My tongue accidentally entered his open mouth as everything started buzzing and catching fire.

A knock on the door was then heard.

Both of us leaped. As we turned to face the entrance, Everett instantly withdrew, his eyes wide.

Say, "Keep it down!" River yelled in her voice.

My heart was thumping as I rolled my eyes and reclined against the mattress. Everett and I both began to giggle at the same time.

Everett said, "God," before backing away and slamming the door shut as though River were still inside. Even yet, "I wasn't even that loud, was I?"

I said, "You were so loud," even though I couldn't hear him over the beat of my own heart.

I stood up on my elbows to view him adjusting his shirt. His lips were bright and red, and his hair was untidy. He gave me a twisted smile while wiping his mouth with the back of his hand.

I suppose it means we should truly unpack, he speculated.

I exclaimed loudly. "Now? I much like to be engaged in other... more enjoyable pursuits.

Everett responded firmly, "My flight isn't till tomorrow. "We'll have the whole night to do other enjoyable things."

I complained, "I don't know how fun they'll be with River next door. The walls in this room were paper thin, even if we kept quiet. There is nothing like the traditional brick homes from Shellside Bay. The automobiles thirty floors below us, I reasoned, might be audible if I listened closely enough.

At me, Everett arched his brow. "I was discussing watching films and completing crossword puzzles. What were you envisioning doing?

Knowing he was making fun of me, I narrowed my eyes at him. Obviously, "exactly the same things."

I got out of bed and crouched next to the next box, ripping the tape off. It simply had the word "bedroom" written on it, and when I opened it, it was stuffed with various items, including phone chargers and a small snow globe my father had given me years before for Christmas.

That was the first thing I took out and gingerly set on my nightstand. Everett arrived and sat down next to me on the floor as he started to remove and lay everything out.

He pulled out a misshaped piece of teal plastic and asked, "What is this?" It resembled a shell in a way, but the plastic had melted a bit and had been chipped. It was in his hands when I grabbed it and set it down next to the snow globe.

I smiled at it and said, "Austin got it for me for my twelfth birthday." "He snatched it from an op store, I believe, where he worked all summer as a paper boy. The variation in Shell-side Bay is minimal.

Why did you have to bring it here with you?

I leaned over and gave him a shoulder bump. "It's emotion-al,"

Everett kept bringing out the remaining items from the box without saying anything.

My childhood best friend Austin was still on my mind when I first met Everett last summer. I had actually lusted after him for more than ten years. But he was always out of reach. Actually, I think that's the main reason I liked him in the first place. He was secured.

But that was back then.

Everett actually cursed his way into my life when he crashed into Shellside Bay. My fist rubbing up against his jaw and his fingers wrapping around my wrists were still fresh in my mind.

There were several disagreements between Everett and Austin that summer, but they looked to be getting along well now. Even if they didn't communicate much, the fighting had at least ceased. I occasionally questioned whether Everett was unsure of my feelings for Austin. If he did, he never brought it up.

This is now headed in a distinct direction.

When I looked up, Everett was holding a framed picture of the two of us taken in Shellside Bay.

When Everett came to visit over the Labour Day weekend a few months back, it perfectly timed with my high school graduation. So, with my eyes watering and my smile shaky, we smiled up from the picture frame, me wearing my cap and robes from graduation. With a smile, Everett stood next to me with a bouquet of flowers he had brought for me pressed to my chest and his arm slung carelessly over my shoulders.

We were both college students at this point.

Well, when he visited NYU back then, he had already en-rolled in college. He had even finished his first semester by the time he came to help me move into River's. He was returning to America tomorrow to begin his spring semester, and I was beginning my first day of classes a week from now.

My desired career has always been in marine science.

I smiled at it and leaned over to take the picture frame out of his hands, setting it on my nightstand next to my broken shell and snow globe.

"Perfect," I murmured.

Although it wasn't much, it was starting to feel more like home. I only needed a surfboard hidden in the room's corner and buckets of sand stuffed into every crack and pore of the floor at this point.

The thought caused me to frown. I had forgotten my little blue board at home. Here in the middle of the city, it was useless. Not when I'd be occupied with school. In addition, no waves could match those at Shellside Bay.

I shook my head and went back to the box. I retrieved the remaining pictures and lined them up beside my nightstand. My parents' pictures. Pictures of Austin and I when we were young and in lifeguard training. Austin was smiling as broad as ever, but I was wearing a terrible pout because I still detested him at the time.

I must also include a picture of my Nauti buoys. My best friend Sky, who had her arm around River's shoulders, was standing closest to the camera. They were still relatively new members of the gang, but they blended quite well. They seemed destined to be a part of us from the beginning. Originally intended for Shellside Bay.

I was smiling in the middle, with Connor and Austin at the back. We were still the same height back then. They were now taller than me by a full head. These days, I had to strain my neck to look at them.

Despite my want to accept and make the most of our last time together, I declined Austin's invitation to drive us up to Sydney today.

After our HSC examinations, he had just begun working at his father's construction company. I was unable to compel him to take time off for me. He and Connor, who both worked for the construction firms run by their fathers, were the only Nauti Buoys still present in Shellside. In Shellside Bay, construction was a booming industry, and the next time I went there, I wouldn't be surprised to see ten brand-new vacation homes.

The world was evolving.

Without me, Shellside Bay would change, and here in Sydney, I knew that I would also change.

I turned to look at Everett as he took out the few books and office supplies I had brought. He had dark hair. The freckles on his nose had disappeared, and his complexion had lost its brown. In New York, he changed. Without me ever noticing, he changed.

I hoped he wouldn't undergo a significant alteration while he was away.

Everett turned to face me as if he could read my mind. He moved the box aside with a lopsided, silly grin on his face and extended his arms to me.

I grinned as I climbed into his arms and relaxed while being held against his chest. I inhaled him as his hands caressed my back and gave me a hard squeeze. He still had the Shellside odour. similar to salt and sand. Fresh. When he first arrived in Australia, he often smelt different from the city.

He smelt a lot like Everett, though.

I was trying to remember his aroma. His contact. I had to commit Everett's personality to memory and hold onto it until I next encountered him. Who knew how different he'd be when I saw him again the following time?

This wasn't the same as the year we had been apart. That would be unique. Now that we were both in college. In Shellside Bay, I wasn't standing still anymore. The purpose of Everett's trips wouldn't be to take us back to the beach and the familiar sands.

I whispered, "I'm going to miss you," on his chest. He briefly tightened his hold on me before releasing his hold and turning to face me.

It won't take as long as you believe, he assured them. I leaned into his palm as he raised his hand to massage my face. "Time will fly by in college, and after my semester is up, I'll be coming home for vacation. It'll seem as though I never left.

"Uni," I rephrased. Who knows whether your trip will coincide with mine?

We'll work it out, he assured.

The question is, "But what if it doesn't match?"

"It will," he said. We'll have international holidays if it doesn't. Easter. Christmas. Fourth of July."

He laughed softly as I drew back to give him a frown.

Point is, we'll figure it out, he said. It will function.

I blinked. Then nodded once more as he leaned in and gave him a tight kiss. I stepped back and looked into his eyes.

"I know," I responded. It will seem as though no time has gone.

"None at all," he replied.

We both sounded unsure and unconvinced.

CHAPTER 3

Last Year

I sat on my bedroom floor, a blanket thrown over my shoulders and my phone propped against the screen of my laptop.

Everett's face flashed up at me from my phone. I could hear his gym's music faintly in the background. He was walking on the treadmill, his body shifting with every step he took. His face glowed with sweat, and it was hard to tear my eyes away from him to focus on my practice papers.

"So, explain to me again," Everett said, his breathing heavy. "You graduate in September, and then you have your final exams?"

"Exactly."

"Why?"

I shrugged. "I don't know. That's just how it works here."

"But that's not really a graduation then. I mean, you can't even celebrate 'cause you know you're not officially done."

"It's not really a celebration unless you're here anyway."

Everett frowned. Or at least he seemed to frown. It was hard to make out based on the pixelation of the screen.

"Isla, you're allowed to have fun when I'm not there," he said.

I sighed, dropping my pen and picking up my phone to hold closer to my face. "I know. It's just, it's not as fun when you're not around."

It was true. Since he'd left for New York again back at the start of the year, it was like something was always missing. No matter how many jokes Connor cracked, or how many beach trips I made with Sky; nothing seemed to fill that gap like Everett did.

It was like he'd barged his way into Shellside Bay and formed a permanent Everett-shaped hole in my life. And now that he was back half-way across the world, that hole was more obvious than ever.

"Isla," he sighed my name. He'd stopped moving, pausing the treadmill to chide me through video call.

"I know," I said quickly. I didn't want our call to be spoiled by this. It already spoiled most of our relationship, but I wouldn't let it have this much power over us. We could have a conversation without the distance ruining it all. I was determined. "I know. I think exams are just getting to me. How's university prep going?"

"College?" he corrected with a smile. "Good. I've got my things mostly ready. My room mate sounds nice. I don't know. I hope he's nice."

"It's so weird that you're going to be sharing a room with a complete stranger."

"You're going to be sharing a place with River," he pointed out. "In less than a year."

"He's not a stranger." I paused. Laughed. "Actually, yeah, no. I take that back. You're right."

I sighed, leaning back against my bed. Thinking about the future—about next year—it was like looking into the abyss. I didn't know what to expect. It caused a kind of sinking feeling in my stomach, the idea of an unknown future.

It was terrifying.

Growing up.

Leaving.

But it would be more terrifying to stay.

I only wished Everett could be with me.

"Maybe you could come here to study," I blurted. "Like, on an exchange?"

Everett was quiet for a long time. Eventually, I glanced at the screen. He smiled at me then, looking away momentarily.

"Yeah," he muttered. "Maybe."

My throat grew tight at his nonchalance. Everything in my body seemed to rush to a halt. He didn't notice how I'd grown silent.

I dropped the topic.

□□□□□□□□□□□

"Isla, are you listening?"

I blinked, looking up from my lab manual to see Sky frowning at me through the phone screen.

I had propped my phone up against my water bottle on the kitchen counter so that we could chat while I studied. Except, while she'd been chatting, I'd been completely zoning out, nonsensical numbers and letters floating in my brain.

"Sorry," I sighed, dropping my pen. "I'm listening."

She stared at me through the camera. She looked almost like a stranger without her long, thick curls that would frizz out into waves from the salty air of Shellside Bay. Her shaved head made her eyes seem like they sank into her head, and I had to do a double take every time I looked at her.

Sky's mouth opened, then closed again. She frowned. "Isla, how's uni going?"

I hadn't been expecting that question. I hoped the surprise didn't show on my face. I tucked my hair behind my ears, avoiding her eyes. Even through a screen, they seemed to pierce my skin. "Good. It's all good. Fun."

"Fun?" Sky echoed.

"Fun," I confirmed. She lifted a brow at me, and that was all it took for me to give in. I groaned, collapsing onto the table. "It's so hard. I mean—how am I supposed to understand all this by the end of next week?"

I lifted my manual to prove my point and Sky laughed.

"You're smart, Isla," she said. "You've got this."

I rolled my eyes and sighed loudly, just to be extra dramatic.

I never expected university to be hard.

Well, I expected it to be challenging. A little difficult. But it was like Sky had said herself—I was smart. At least, I was supposed to be. I'd done well in all my classes, topped most of them really, and even graduated as the school dux, top of my class. This wasn't supposed to be as difficult as it was.

"Yeah. I know. I'm just jealous of you," I said, changing the subject. "How's Cairns anyway? Or was it Darwin this week?"

"Darwin's next week," Sky said, smiling teasingly. "It's fun! It reminds me of Shellside Bay, just way bigger."

After graduation, Sky had decided to take a big road trip around the country with her cousins from Melbourne as a gap year. It was such a Sky thing to do, no one was really surprised.

The only thing that was keeping me sane was the thought of her coming back to Sydney next year to start university. I wondered if River would let her stay here. We had another room available, although I suspected it was probably his parents' room—not that they were ever here. She could always bunk with me, anyway.

Suddenly, someone shouted her name in the background. It was a male voice, and my eyes grew wide.

"Sky!" I gasped. "Is that a boy calling your name?"

"His name is Josh," she said.

"Josh," I repeated with a laugh. "Don't tell me you're dating a boy named Josh."

"It's not dating, first of all," she replied. She grabbed the phone, and it shook a little as she moved locations. Her voice lowered slightly. "It's just a summer thing. A summer crush, really. Unless he follows us up to Darwin. Anyway, you'd understand if you saw him."

"Summer's over, Sky," I said simply.

Without realising it, the words sent a chill of sadness through me, because it was true. Summer was over. We were a month into March now and Shellside Bay, and everything that came with it, was gone. A distant memory.

There were no more bonfire parties. No more morning shifts at the Shack. No more surfing, and beach tans, and sand beneath my feet. No more Nauti Buoys on the Nauti Buoy sailing to that distant island, where we'd dunk each other's heads beneath crystal waters until the sky turned purple.

No more Everett.

Summer was truly over.

"You're just saying that because you have a boyfriend," Sky said pointedly.

"I'm saying that because it's a fact. And, I mean, his name's Josh."

Sky laughed, rolling her eyes. "Not all of us can get a guy named after a mountain."

"His name is Everett, not Everest!"

"What's the difference?"

"Are you sure you're majoring in geography next year?" I teased.

"It's geology."

"What's the difference?"

Two hands planted on my shoulders, and I jumped, craning my neck to see River grinning down at me. I whacked him as he laughed, leaning over to look at my phone.

"Is that Sky?" he asked.

"River!" she squealed, waving both of her hands.

I rolled my eyes, shoving him off of me. "It's literally two in the afternoon, Riv. How are you just waking up now? Don't you have midterms too?"

"It's business," he said as an explanation, stretching and yawning. He pulled up a seat and slouched in a chair beside me, turning his attention back to Sky. "How's Darwin?"

"Darwin's next week," we both said simultaneously.

River arched a brow. He reached up, scratching his head. His hair had grown out almost completely now. It was strange seeing him this way.

He was no longer Summer River. His buzzcut was gone, black waves beginning to tickle the tips of his ears. He wore a hoodie. I'd never seen him in a hoodie before. I stared at him for a moment, trying to process this new side of River. A River outside of Shellside Bay.

This was Sydney River and I had no idea who he was.

"Have you spoken to any of the other Nauti Buoys?" he asked. It took me a moment to realise he was asking me, not Sky, because she was waiting for me to reply too. I nodded.

"Austin's still working, like, every day. His dad's trying to 'build character' or something," I said.

River stared at me, and I knew what he was waiting for. I decided to be kind and spare him from his misery.

"Connor's working too," I continued, "except he works on sites pretty far out from Shellside Bay. Spends half the day driving around. I don't think they even have time to see each other, much less come visit us anytime soon."

River released a tight breath and I noticed him sag into his seat. I wondered if he'd spoken to the boys at all since we left.

"And Everett?"

I blinked, turning to Sky. "What about Everett?"

"Oh, come on," Sky said. "He's one of the Nauti Buoys now. How is he?"

"He's... good."

Honestly, if I'd thought it was difficult finding time to video call him while in high school, university was a whole other issue.

We spoke here and there, but he needed to do well this semester, and I was struggling to keep up with all the content. It was tough.

And time zones were never helpful.

Back in high school, I finished classes by 3PM and had the rest of the night to talk. Now, my schedule was all over the place, and so was his. It was impossible to talk for more than thirty minutes at a time.

"How's college going for him?" Sky asked, slipping into an American accent with a giggle.

"Good," I replied. "He got an A on his last essay, and I think his spring break is coming up. Maybe he'll be here before we know it."

"I know he will," she said, grinning.

"Don't tell me he's staying here," River added. I looked at him sheepishly and he pretended to gag.

I knew he was joking, though. As much as he complained, he secretly liked the company. It was the reason he was always running away to Shellside Bay, back to us.

I nudged him hard in the ribs and he leaned closer to the screen, practically shoving me out of the way.

"Sky, your hair is shorter than mine now," River said, lifting a brow.

Sky giggled, running a hand over her head. "You never mentioned how much maintenance it was!"

"Oh, believe me. This shit's ten times worse," River replied, running a hand through his own hair.

"Why don't you shave it off then?" I asked.

He looked at me, like it was a stupid question, then shrugged and leaned even closer to the screen. I scoffed, nudging him with my elbow again.

"Shouldn't you be studying for your midterms?"

"It's business," he repeated, rolling his eyes as if that was an actual answer. He stood up straight and grabbed an apple from the counter before throwing himself onto the couch. "Besides, I'm tired. How will I concentrate like this?"

"You just woke up!" I called out. Sky giggled over the phone, and I almost shot her a glare for encouraging him. To her, I said, "He's really a hopeless case."

"I don't know how he made it through high school," she replied.

I didn't know either. He was always skipping school and barely spent any time studying, failing classes—and now he was acing university.

It didn't make sense to me. How could he be getting high distinctions in all his assessments with barely any studying?

A male voice called Sky's name again—Josh, probably—and she spun around for a second before turning back to me.

"I think I've got to go," she said with an apologetic grin.

I shot her a teasing look. "Ooo got to go back to Josh?"

"Shut up," she said. "I'll send you a photo of him."

I laughed, mostly because I did actually want to see what he looked like.

"Alright," I said. "Talk later."

"Bye!" she said in a sing-songy voice before hanging up. The line went dead, and I stared at the blank screen for a moment, imagining Sky having fun with her summer fling on the beach. Behind me, River was already beginning to snore.

I groaned and buried my head back into my lab manual, wondering if Everett was doing the same thing.

□□□□□□□□□□□

The next day, the numbers were beginning to make sense. I'd attended one of the optional lab revision sessions, almost ashamedly. When had I become the kind of person who needed revision sessions? But afterwards, I found myself glad I went. Things were beginning to make sense.

"So," Everett's voice came through my earphones. I was sitting on the light rail from university to Central station after the revision lab. "It helped, then? You think you're going to pass?"

Even hearing his voice sent shivers down my spine. My heart seemed to race at the mere thought of him.

I nodded, although he couldn't see me. "I think so. I mean, most of it is making sense now. It just depends on the kind of questions they ask on the day."

"That's good," he replied. "Have you made any friends?"

"I don't need friends, I have you. And the Nauti Buoys. You guys are my friends," I said.

I could hear his frown in his voice. "Is that a no, then?"

"It's a no."

"Isla!"

"Everett!" I mocked. "Seriously. I don't need friends. They're all... kind of stuffy anyway."

"Stuffy?"

"Yeah!" I sighed. "I mean, like, today for example. I made a joke to the girl next to me and she just gave me a funny look before going back to her work. Like, at least give me a pity laugh, right?"

Everett chuckled and I imagined him shaking his head, the way he normally did. I imagined him running his fingers through his hair. I wondered if it had gotten any darker since I last saw him, back to its natural dark brown that it was the first day I saw him.

"Isla, you're amazing. Anyone would want to be your friend," he said.

"Clearly not," I grumbled.

"You should at least try to make some," he pointed out. "College is more fun when you have friends to hang out with."

"University."

"Whatever," he groaned. He sighed and a second later asked, "Just try. Promise?"

"You're one to talk," I shot back. "I don't see you hanging out with friends every night, going out partying or whatever it is you do over there."

Unspoken words seemed to tag onto the end of my sentence. Everett's last friend had betrayed him, going behind his back with his ex-girlfriend. A part of me felt like he was avoiding making new friends because of that, but I couldn't imagine how lonely he must have been.

Since his mum had died, and his dad had moved quickly onto a new woman, I knew he didn't speak much to his family anymore. And I knew more than anyone how it felt to lose the person closest to you.

Except, I was all the way here in Sydney, and our conversations had dwindled down to scattered texts and phone calls at strange times of the day—whether he would admit it or not, Everett needed someone there for him, live and in person.

I wished I could be that person.

"I don't need friends, I have you," Everett mocked in return.

I scoffed, rolling my eyes with a grin. "Real original."

"Alright, look. Let's make a deal. You try and make friends, and I'll go out partying every night."

"I think I've changed my mind about the whole partying thing."

Everett chuckled. "I figured. Alright, you make friends and I'll stop being a hypocrite and talk to some of the people in my class, people other than my roommate."

I sighed dramatically, imagining his smirk across the ocean.

It wouldn't kill me to try and talk to people more but it was different from school. I didn't see the same people in each class, and most of the time, I'd only see the same people for an hour or two, once a week. And most of the time, they had already friends here in Sydney.

But if Everett was asking me, I could try.

"Promise," I said.

"Good girl," he teased. Despite myself, my face warmed. I realised then that his voice sounded raspy, and I frowned.

"Ev, what time is it over there?" I asked.

"Here?" he hesitated, the teasing tone immediately vanishing from his voice. "It's... not that late."

"What time?"

"Well, it's early if anything."

"Meaning?"

He exhaled loudly. "It's 3AM."

"Three!" I exclaimed. Some people turned to look at me and I clasped a hand over my mouth. "Three? You should sleep. Don't you have classes tomorrow? Isn't your roommate asleep?"

Through the speaker, I could hear some shuffling. I wished I could see him. A second later, he spoke.

"My roommate left yesterday." He paused. "It's actually spring break next week."

Spring break? Everett would be free for an entire week. My mind began racing with thoughts. We could video call more, we could talk. Maybe... maybe he could even visit.

"What are your plans?" I asked, attempting to sound casual.

"Plans?" he echoed with a bitter laugh. "Studying, studying, and, oh, studying."

"Seriously?" I frowned. "That's it? Live a little, Ev."

"Well, maybe I could throw a little partying in there," he replied. I could hear his smile in his voice.

"Because you're such a party animal all of a sudden," I teased.

"Really, I'd much rather spend my time talking to you."

My face warmed and I fought a smile. "You should go to a few parties. I don't want to hold you back or anything."

"You could never hold me back."

"You're just saying that."

"Because it's true."

"So, what? You're just going to study all week and call me at three in the morning?"

He laughed through the phone—a quiet, breathy chuckle that I missed with all my being. "Basically."

"Sounds like a plan." I pressed my lips together, hesitating for a moment before saying, "Maybe you could come visit?"

Everett was silent. My heart dropped into my stomach and I realised I'd said the wrong thing straight away. A flight to Sydney from New York was expensive. I shouldn't have mentioned it at all.

"Never mind," I said quickly.

"No, Isla, I could," he said.

I interrupted him. "No, it was silly. I mean, spring break is only a week, right? It's not worth it."

"Anything's worth it," he said quickly. His voice softened. "For you, Isla. Anything's worth it."

"Well, I'll be too busy studying anyway," I said. "We'd better save it for next time."

Everett was quiet for a moment before asking, "Are you sure?"

I wasn't. I wanted to see him. He'd left only a month ago and I craved him with every inch of myself. University was turning out to be horrible and I wasn't sure if I could manage this for three whole years without him. I wasn't sure how much longer I could go without seeing him.

And I knew, if I asked him to, he'd come. He'd say yes. He'd spend his last dollar flying here to see me if I asked him to.

I knew that, so I couldn't.

Instead, I nodded and attempted to make my voice sound cheerful.

"I'm sure."

CHAPTER 4

I sat in my chair with my lab manual open on the desk in front of me but my eyes decidedly far away. I slouched over the table, my gaze settling on a desk across the library.

A girl sat there, the same lab manual as mine open in front of her.

This was a sign, right? It was the universe telling me to go up to her—Talk to her! Make a friend!

And yet, I couldn't. How was I supposed to start the conversation? Hi, I'm Isla. I was watching you from over there and noticed we were in the same class. Let's be friends!

I sighed. This was all so pointless. Growing up in Shellside Bay, I'd been so focused on the downsides of knowing everyone in town that I'd completely missed the upsides—how easy it was to make friends.

It was like a town full of family friends. Back in Shellside Bay, I had a familiar face on every corner. I'd grown up around the same people. I knew every kid in my class—hell, every kid in my school, including the ones who had graduated years before me.

This—I was unprepared for this.

Suddenly, the girl stood from her desk and began walking towards me.

I started, sitting upright and smiling reluctantly. Maybe I wouldn't have to be the one to start the conversation after all.

She kept approaching me until she was right in front of my desk. I looked at her, lifting my hand to wave, when she kept walking.

I blinked, clapping my hand awkwardly over my mouth as she hugged her friend behind me.

I slumped further into my seat, covering my face with my hands.

Oh God, she hadn't seen that, right?

The pair giggled behind me, and I thought about getting up and just leaving. I'd decided to study in the library today instead of River's apartment on the off chance that someone would start a conversation with me.

That was a big mistake.

I grabbed my bag, tugging it towards me and shutting my lab manual. The blue cover was bright against the wood of the desk. I scooped up my pens and threw them into my bag without caring where they landed.

I was about to pick up my lab manual when a hand landed on the cover.

I blinked, looking up to find a boy with blond hair, longish, almost like Connor's, except a dirtier blond—almost brown. He wore a jumper with our university's logo sprawled across the front: UNSW.

I stared at him, half-expecting him to start marketing something to me, or start telling me off for something. Why else would he be approaching me here?

"You're in BABS?" he asked. I blinked again, speechless. He stared at me, his brow lifting, and I nodded quickly. "So am I. Which lab are you in?"

"Thursday," I said. I cleared my throat, forcing myself back into reality. "Thursdays at one. You?"

"Same!"

My eyes flittered over him quickly, taking in his lean body and casual outfit. He seemed familiar. I was sure I'd seen him in our lab before. He usually sat in the back, his face scrunched in confusion as he stuck his hand in the air every few minutes—questions always on his tongue.

His smile grew and he pulled out the seat in front of me, quickly sitting down across from me. "I'm Lachlan. Lachie, I mean."

A smile pulled at my lips. "Lachlan Lachie?"

"Oh, you know what I mean," he said, rolling his eyes. Up close, I could see how blue his eyes were. He was somewhat tanned, freckles staining his skin across his nose. I wondered if he was a Sydney native, or if he was from somewhere beachier. "And you are?"

"Isla," I replied.

"Well, Isla, I'm so glad I ran into you today." He reached forward, flicking my lab manual open to the page I'd been staring at moments ago. "Because I am really struggling with last week's lab questions."

I stared down at my page, blank of answers, and warmed. "Oh. Well, I haven't started yet."

It was a lie. I started hours ago. I just couldn't figure out any of the answers. They were basically just words on a paper, letters swirling beside letters, forming words I couldn't even pronounce. It was almost like a different language.

And based off the way Lachie was smiling at me, I felt like he knew.

My face turning hot, I slid the book back toward myself and slapped it shut. "I'm going to fill it out when I get home."

"Well, if you figure out the answers," he began, still smiling knowingly at me, "let me know."

Before I could say anything, he was holding his phone out to me. I stared at him for a second before lifting my brow at him.

"Are you trying to copy my homework, Lachlan Lachie?"

He rolled his eyes teasingly. "Obviously. Did I not make that clear enough?"

I laughed quietly, still aware of the library around us, and took his phone, typing my number in. "Alright, but if you figure out the answers first, then you have to text me, okay? Play fair."

"Got it."

I picked the book up, sliding it into my bag before throwing it over my shoulder and standing. Surprisingly, Lachie stood with me.

"Do you live on campus?" he asked, rounding the desk to stand beside me.

I threw him a sceptical look. Was this what making friends in university was like? I answered anyway.

"No," I said. A second later, I asked, "Do you?"

"No," he said. "I'm actually catching the light rail back to Central now. Do you want to catch it together?"

My smile grew. It was like—Oh my, God. This was it. I made a friend. I nodded wordlessly and we began walking together towards the light rail. It was only a two-minute wait, yet my stomach seemed to flutter with nerves—with the idea of carrying a conversation with a stranger in Sydney.

I felt like a fraud. Like, any second now, he'd realise I was from a rural town, or he'd mention some city thing that I wouldn't understand, and I'd feel like a sheltered idiot.

Luckily, Lachie was talkative enough for the both of us.

"I like your jumper," he said pointing at my chest.

I looked down, briefly forgetting what jumper I'd worn today. It was a baggy grey one with the letters 'NYU' embroidered on the front—a gift from Everett. Suddenly, my heart lurched, and I missed him more than ever.

He'd gifted me this jumper months ago now, and the smell of him had vanished completely. I tugged on the sleeves, fighting the memory of the day he'd given it to me.

And the day he'd left me here to fly back halfway across the world.

"Thanks," I said, finally. "It's from my boyfriend."

As the words left my mouth, I was hit with the realisation that Lachie might have only spoken to me to hit on me, and now that I'd mentioned Everett, the potential friendship was dead.

Except, he seemed wholly unaffected.

His smile didn't even waver. Instead, he seemed genuinely interested.

"Does he go to NYU?" he asked. I nodded and he whistled lowly. "Long distance then?"

"Not for long, though," I said, suddenly feeling defensive. "He's got less than three years left and he visits all the time."

Even saying the words, I felt entirely stupid.

Less than three years... and then what?

It wasn't like we'd talked about after university at all. What was I waiting for, really? Would we even survive three years like this? Talking through scattered calls and texts? University wasn't like high school. We were both so busy now.

Three years was a long time. A lot could change in three years.

I chewed my cheek, shooing the thoughts from my head. Whatever happened, it wouldn't help to worry over it like this.

"We're good at long distance, anyway," I added finally.

"Cool," Lachie said. For no logical reason at all, it felt like he didn't believe me, and I ground my teeth. "Tell him to bring me one back too next time."

And just like that, I was laughing again.

We talked the whole ride back to Central.

I found out that he went to school in Sydney. He'd never even heard of Shellside Bay before, but he liked the beach. He didn't even care that it was in the middle of nowhere—that this was my first time living in a city like this. He told me about a beach near our university and my smile grew—I hadn't swum in the ocean in months. I made it a mental note to visit as soon as possible.

But first, I'd have to figure out this lab manual weighing in my backpack.

When the light rail slowed in the heart of the city, both of us hopped off and I turned to him.

"So, where abouts do you live?" I asked, tugging on my bag straps.

He nodded back towards the light rail. "I live on campus."

I blinked. "What?"

"I live on campus," he repeated, laughing now. "So, I'll probably just catch the next light rail back."

"What? Why would you get on it in the first place?" I asked, shaking my head incredulously. "You didn't have to lie to me."

"But then you wouldn't have let me catch it with you," he said. "I wanted to get to know my new friend."

I rolled my eyes but couldn't help the smile that pulled at my lips—friend. I'd made a friend. I couldn't wait to brag to Everett.

"I'll see you at the next lab then, yeah?" he asked.

I nodded. "I'll see you there."

"Cool. Bye, Isla."

"See you around Lachlan Lachie," I teased.

He laughed and I waved, turning, and walking in the direction of River's apartment.

River lived just minutes away from the station, right in the middle of the city, which must have cost a fortune. As soon as I was around the corner and out of sight, I sprinted the rest of the way.

The lift up to River's apartment felt like it took forever. I fumbled with my keys, throwing my bag onto the couch as soon as I entered and pulling out my phone.

The first person I called was Austin, because I knew the conversation would be short since he'd have to get back to work. He didn't answer so I moved onto the next—Connor. After five rings, I realised that it was still four in the afternoon and both of them were probably busy working.

Back in high school, Austin and I would text and call each other daily. Now, it had been almost two weeks since we'd last spoken. And even then, our communication was mostly short texts full of irrelevant messages. A conversation between us could drag out across days.

I frowned, trying not to let it get to me. The boys were working, it was only natural. It was to be expected. We were growing up, after all. They had responsibilities.

Sighing, I typed in Sky's number. She answered immediately.

Before I could say anything, she said, "Isla! Sorry, I'm in the middle of something right now. What's up?"

I heard some rustling in the background and frowned. "Oh, sorry. If I'm bothering you, I can call back later."

"No, no," Sky said quickly. "What's going on?"

I smiled, Lachie's words coming back to me. "I made a friend!"

"Finally!" she squealed, giggling. "Who is it? Tell me all about them."

"His name's Lachie."

"No!" She gasped. "It's a boy? Isla! Does he know you have a boyfriend?"

"Obviously!" I said, laughing. "It's not like that. We're in the same lab so I finally have someone to sit with in class, I guess."

"Oh, Everett's going to get so jealous," she said. I could hear the grin in her voice.

"No, he won't," I shot back, although the idea of Everett jealous didn't sound too farfetched. "We're just friends. He came up to me in the library because he recognised my lab manual and when I told him I don't live on campus, he—"

"Oh, crap," Sky interrupted, her voice hurried. "I'm so sorry, Isla. I have to go back now. Will you text me about it?"

I frowned, trying to hide the disappointment in my voice. "Yeah. No, yeah. That's fine. I'll text you later."

"I'm so sorry," she said, and she really did sound sorry. "We'll talk later, I promise."

"It's fine," I said. "Really. Talk later."

I hung up before her and sighed, putting my phone down. This was our life now. We were all busy with our own things. Even talking to each other felt like something that needed to be planned weeks in advance.

It was like clipped phone calls, and messages left on read for days—weeks—at a time.

It was nothing like our days in Shellside Bay. Our spontaneous beach trips. Our boat rides to Isla. Our dives in the lagoon, crystal water surrounding us as we jumped from cliffs and dunked each others heads beneath the surface.

Those days were gone.

"Isla?"

I jumped, spinning to find River walking out of his room. His hair was messy, and I suspected he'd just had another afternoon nap.

"I thought you were studying at uni today," he said, yawning.

"I was," I said, lifting a brow. "It's, like, almost five now, River. Day's over. I finished studying ages ago."

"Oh," he said simply. If I'd thought River never cared about anything back in Shellside Bay, I clearly never knew him in Sydney. "Who were you talking to?"

"Sky," I said before pausing. "Hey, have you spoken to Connor recently?"

Instantly, his mood soured. He wrinkled his nose, narrowing his eyes at me.

"Why are you asking me about Connor? Why not Sky? Or Austin? I talk to them too, you know?" he said, instantly going on the defensive.

I didn't reply, only raised a knowing brow at him, and he scowled at me.

"No. He hasn't replied to my texts in three days." He paused before adding lowly, "Not that I'm counting or anything."

I sighed, leaning onto the kitchen counter. "Same. I feel like they've all been really busy lately."

River didn't say anything to that, but I could see on his face that he agreed.

"What about the American?" he asked eventually.

I blinked, suddenly remembering. "I was actually just about to call him."

River stuck his tongue out and rolled his eyes in a fake gag. "Keep it down, yeah?"

"Oh, shut up!" I shot back, laughing. "Not that kind of call!"

He gagged again for extra effect.

I grabbed my phone, walking into my room and shutting the door behind me. Everett answered on the third ring.

"Ev!" I exclaimed, my smile instantly returning.

"Isla?" he muttered. His voice was raspy, and my heart fell. I glanced at the clock.

"What time is it there?" I asked.

"It's two in the morning," he said. He paused to clear his throat before saying, "What's up, baby?"

I frowned. "I'm so sorry, I completely forgot. I'll just call you back later."

I moved to hang up, but he quickly interrupted me.

"No, no, no! It's fine, really. Let's talk," he said. "What's up?"

I released a tight breath. It was a Monday which meant Everett had a class at eight in the morning. Six hours from now, he'd have to be in class and ready to learn. I couldn't do that to him. He needed his rest.

"No," I relented, shaking my head. "No, I actually—I forgot. I need to go help River with something."

"What?"

"Yeah," I said quickly. "He's, like, really struggling with some business assignment that's due in a few hours. I'd better go help him before he has a complete breakdown or something. I'll call you when we're done though, yeah?"

"Oh," Everett said. "Are you sure? Because it seemed like you wanted to talk about something and I really don't—"

"Yeah, no, it's actually a really big deal for him. I'd better get going," I cut him off. "We'll talk later, okay?"

There was a deep pause before he finally said, "Alright. Yeah. Love you, Isla."

My heart leapt into my throat, and I fisted my sleeves into my palms—the sleeves of Everett's jumper.

"I love you more," I said and hung up the phone.

I sat on my bed for a moment, clutching my phone to my chest. My chest ached. Everything ached with missing Everett.

I wanted to talk to him. I wanted to tell him about my new friend. I wanted to tell him how hard uni was. I wanted to complain about the commute to class, and the birds that swooped for my head on campus, and River's terrible cooking, and any other little thing that would pop up into my head.

I wanted to hear his voice. I wanted him here, next to me. I wanted to hug him, kiss him, hold his hand.

I wanted Everett.

Except he was busy halfway across the world, and the other boys were busy at their fulltime jobs, and Sky was busy having the greatest gap year ever and I—I was here waiting all over again.

Always waiting.

CHAPTER 5

Last Summer

It was the last bonfire party of Shellside Bay before everyone was off to their futures.

Half of the graduating class would be staying in Shellside Bay indefinitely, taking over family businesses or jumping straight into working fulltime. The other half were mostly scattered off to different cities, secured into whatever universities and colleges would take them.

This was our final chance at one of our iconic bonfire parties—the last until nobody knew when.

We were intent on making the most of it.

Everyone had shown up. The entire graduating class, plus extras. Tourists, cousins, older graduates, younger grades. It was the entire young population of the town—plus some.

Everett's arm was thrown over my shoulder.

It was hot. The air was thick with sweat and heat. I couldn't tell the hot summer air apart from my panting breath. Apart from Everett's panting breath.

He leaned his face close to mine; not to kiss me or anything. He just smiled there, swaying tipsily as we danced to the music. I couldn't even make out the words over the sound of the waves and my heart in my ears.

I kissed him first.

I leaned up, pressing my lips to his—hard. Like reminding myself that he was here. That we were both here. And the bonfire beside us was real.

That this was all real, at least for now.

And now was all we had.

When I pulled back, he was grinning at me.

He leaned in close, his lips brushing over the skin of my neck. I didn't even think about the sweat that must have coated my skin, hot from the summer air and the heat of my hair sticking to my neck. Everett had learned every part of me now.

His lips moved higher, sliding over my ear.

"I think we should get out of here," he muttered.

I giggled. The alcohol was turning my bones fuzzy. "Where would we go? Your room?"

He shook his head. "My grandma would see us. Yours?"

"My mum..."

An idea struck me. I giggled again, grabbing his hand.

"Follow me."

We slipped away from the bonfire party, tripping over our own feet and the sand until the fire was a dot in the dark. We found our way across the beach off of muscle memory and the moonlight until we'd reached our destination.

"The Shack?"

"Tomorrow's a public holiday, they'll be closed all day," I replied. It took me three tries to unlock the door and let us in.

We collapsed on the floor, sighing in relief at the cold air that had been trapped inside the Shack, despite the heat that surrounded it outside. Sand stuck to my skin. I wondered if I'd taste like salt if Everett kissed me now. Salt mixed with tequila. The thought made me laugh.

Everett's side was pressed against mine. The ocean sounded far away from in here. It was muffled, like listening through a pair of headphones. There, and not there, at the same time.

He rolled over to look at me. Even lying down, the room seemed to sway a little. I was definitely tipsy at this point. We both were.

His hand lifted, tracing a path over the side of my face.

"You're so beautiful," he whispered. "I really love you."

I couldn't help the giggle that burst from my lips. "I love you too."

He smiled, sitting up to hoist me onto his lap. His arms tightened around my waist as I straddled his lap. "You mean that?"

"Of course."

"Even when I'm in New York? And you're here? And—and I can't be here for you when you need me?"

"Everett," I whispered. I leaned forward, pressing my forehead to his. His eyes fluttered shut. "Don't say that. You know that means nothing to me. We'll make it work."

He was silent for a moment. Breathing me in. And then, he kissed me hard.

His hands braced my face, his lips connecting with mine. It was a desperate kiss. And I knew, like me, he was proving this was real. That we were here, together. Sitting on the dirty floor of the Shack, covered in sand, and sweat.

His hands were all over me. On my face, then on my waist, sliding up beneath my shirt. His fingers were on my bare skin, over my bikini, then under. And I was gasping, writhing in his grip. He kissed me harder, leaning over me until my back touched the floor and I was breathing hard into his mouth.

I felt like I was sinking through the ground, and I wanted to pull him with me.

My shirt went first, and then my shorts. His lips pressed against my bare stomach and traced a path to the inside of my thighs. My bikini bottoms came off next. And he was whispering things against me, words I could barely make out over the buzzing in my ears, and my heart slamming against my ribcage.

I grabbed his hair, pulling him back up to my face. My fingers fumbled for his shorts in the dark, finding the waistband through pure touch. He moaned into my neck as I tugged them down, slowly, so slowly. Until he was groaning my name against my own skin.

The night faded around us. The dizziness from the alcohol quickly vanished, only to be replaced by the dizziness of Everett—of Everett on top of me, of his bare skin on mine, of his mouth tracing patterns over me, of him, deep inside of me and all around me.

We fit together perfectly.

And he kissed me like, in the morning, I would be gone.

□□□□□□□□□□

I sat in my biomolecular science lab, Lachie beside me as we stared, frowning, at my manual. My handwriting covered the page in smudged, ink scribbles, barely decipherable. I'd crossed out and re-written half the lines. Lachie narrowed his eyes, leaning closer to the page.

"You did the whole thing wrong," he started, "and yet you got the right answer."

"So... I'm right?"

"I mean—"

"Great!" I exclaimed, snapping the book shut and scooping my things into my bag. "So, that's settled."

"I'm pretty sure half the mark is in the working out," Lachie pointed out.

"What?" I pouted at him, and he laughed, closing his own manual and standing up.

"That's kind of the whole point of showing your work," he said knowingly. Sensing my disappointment, he rolled his eyes and said, "Don't worry, I'll send you a photo of mine later."

I beamed at him. "You're the best."

"Remember this the next time I need to copy your lab notes."

I cut him a glare, but my smile didn't slip. We walked together, waving to our lab tutors before exiting the room. The light rail was close to the labs, so Lachie tended to walk me there after our weekly class together.

And wherever we went, people waved at him, stopping him to say hello, inviting him places.

He was weirdly popular, which I didn't even know was a thing at university. I stared at my phone, pretending to text someone as he was stopped for the fifth time, this time by a dark-haired boy that I'd thought was Everett for one heart-aching second. It was truly incredible how many people Lachie knew on campus—and even more incredible how I saw Everett in every person I passed.

I scrolled through my phone, scanning my texts as if I hadn't read them all a million times. Everett was probably sleeping, but he'd texted me good night right before my lab. I'd already replied but I decided to text him that my class was over anyway. Not that it meant anything. By the time he woke up, I'd probably be asleep, and then he'd have his classes.

When was the last time I'd heard his voice for longer than ten minutes? A week ago? It felt like an eternity. I wanted summer back, where I could see him every morning until sunset, and even longer—without worrying about mid-terms and labs each day.

River had texted me hours ago reminding me to pick up some mixers for a party he was throwing tonight. I'd forgotten all about it. I frowned, suddenly realising I'd have to carry bags of heavy bottles up to the apartment now. Why couldn't he do it?

Ever since we'd left Shellside Bay, River had morphed into a sad lump that moped around the apartment all day, when he wasn't drinking himself half to death. A part of me wondered if he was always like this, for the eight months of the year that weren't summer.

I knew there was more too it than him missing the hot beaches and his board over the waves. No. It had more to do with the lack of texts he'd been receiving from a certain someone we'd left behind.

At least I could relate to him on that end.

"Sorry about that." I looked up to find Lachie stopping in front of me. He jabbed a thumb over his shoulder. "He's in my chemistry class."

I shrugged, pocketing my phone.

"It's fine," I said. Really, I was jealous and a little embarrassed. I wondered if he could tell that he was my only friend at university. I changed the subject immediately. "Actually, my roommate is having a party tonight. You should come."

"Oh?" A smile split across his face and he nodded eagerly. "Totally. Text me the address, yeah?"

"Of course," I replied. We'd reached the light rail now and I turned to him, tugging on my bag strap. "I'll see you tonight then?"

"For sure."

We grinned at each other and he turned, leaving for his dorm. I smiled to myself, pulling out my phone and popping my earphones in.

Tonight, would be good. I could feel it. After how horrible my start to university had been, it had to be.

□□□□□□□□□□

It was loud.

River never threw parties back in Shellside Bay. Those just tended to happen. A bonfire would appear and suddenly the beach would be filled with tourists, and teenagers, and alcohol, and it would be the greatest night ever to exist—until the next one.

Sydney parties were different.

They were music and lights and indoors. When was the last time I'd been to a party that didn't involve the sand and the ocean, with the moon glaring down on us from the inky sky?

These parties were crowded and stuffy. The air was sticky with sweat and the smell of vodka. I was choking on it. I sunk into the wall, a red cup clutched in my hands.

It was strange, going to a party without my Nauti Buoys around me. I missed having Connor with his massive, sweaty arm around my shoulders. I missed having Austin, rounding up the others when they got too drunk. I missed Sky—oh, I really missed Sky.

It had been a mission deciding on my outfit tonight without her around. It wasn't like I could wear my bikini like I usually did back home.

And of course, I missed Everett, for reasons that made me burn red in the face.

I'd settled on Everett's jumper and some denim shorts. It seemed good enough—until the guests arrived and all the girls were gorgeous in satin dresses and mini-skirts. Clearly, I hadn't heard the dress code. Not that it would've changed anything, with the majority of my clothes tucked away some-where back in Shellside Bay.

I tugged on the hem of my jumper self-consciously, scanning the crowd for the only Nauti Buoy left.

River. He stood on the other side of the room chatting to a boy with short hair. I couldn't tell what colour it was with the flashing neon lights. I stared at him, willing him to turn to me, and a minute later, he did.

I lifted a cup to him and the boy he was talking to turned to look at me. Then, they were walking towards me.

I cleared my throat, pushing off the wall as they stopped in front of me.

"Isla!" River shouted over the music.

It was weird seeing him like this. River without a buzzcut. River in a hoodie. Sydney River. River, eight months out of the year.

He nodded towards the boy beside him.

"This is Alistair!" he shouted. "We went to high school together."

Alistair nodded at me and I nodded back.

"Nice to meet you," I yelled. He only nodded again. Not the talkative type, then. A trait rarely seen among the Nauti Buoys.

"So," River shouted, leaning closer. His hair flopped over his eyebrows and I wanted to push it off—shave it all off. To see some semblance of the River I knew, of summer in Shellside Bay. But summer was over, and his hair was long, and he was yelling to me, "Why are you standing here looking so depressed? Get drunk! This is your house too you know?"

"I am drunk," I yelled back, lifting my cup.

"You're clearly not drunk enough!" he replied. He clinked his cup with mine before emptying his drink into mine. "You're not working at the Shack anymore, loosen up!"

I sniffed his drink and wrinkled my nose at the strong alcoholic smell. "What is this, straight vodka?"

"No, gay!" he shouted back with a wink. "It's actually all tequila. Enjoy!"

I raised my drink, taking a deep gulp and immediately gagging on the taste. "This is disgusting!"

He didn't reply, only winked again with a devilish grin before turning and making his way into the middle of the crowd. Alistair shot me a weak smile and followed him.

I sighed, leaning back against the wall. I could feel the dull thump of music through it. The crowd was growing, and I was only getting more and more bored, counting down the hours until Everett would wake up. Maybe we could talk before his morning classes.

I took another long drink from my cup. This time, the mixture of alcohol didn't sting as much.

"Isla!"

I spun, finding Lachie standing in front of me. I gasped, bouncing on my toes.

"You came!" I shouted.

He nodded. "Of course! I wouldn't miss it for the world."

"Oh, I have to introduce you to—"

I paused midsentence as I turned to find River pressing Alistair against the wall, their mouths attached. I blinked, stunned.

"Introduce me to who?" Lachie shouted.

I shook my head, still staring in absolute shock. River's hands were all over him—over his hair, his shirt, his chest, his arms. And Alistair's were all over River. I wanted to gag but I couldn't look away. I could have sworn that River liked Connor.

And based off the way that Connor had pouted when River and I left, I'd thought something had happened between the two. I almost thought...

I blinked hard, finally ripping my eyes away and looking back to Lachie.

"No one," I replied. "Never mind."

"That's a shame because I genuinely don't know a single person here," he said, laughing.

I laughed back. The room was starting to sway slightly, and laughter came easily. I took another drink before raising it to him, as if toasting to his words.

"Me neither!"

"But this is your party!'

"No, it's not!"

"It's your place."

"It's not the same thing," I said wisely, wagging a finger.

Lachie laughed before he glanced towards the kitchen where the drinks were lined up. He touched my elbow and said, "I'm going to grab a drink."

I nodded and he left, pushing through crowds towards the drink table. I leaned back against the wall, silently observing the room, watching everyone dance, watching couples lean into each other, and strangers pressing their bodies together. River still had Alistair pushed up against the wall—just how drunk was he?

It was like I'd blinked, and everything had changed. There was no more summer, no more Nauti Buoys, and worst of all, no more Everett.

That summer we'd first met, Everett had been by my side at Shellside Bay's bonfire parties. He'd taken care of me while I drank. He'd kept me company while the rest of the Nauti Buoys vanished—while Austin vanished, leaving me behind for Mia.

And now he was back in New York and I probably wouldn't see him for months to come. Even when he did visit, the days seemed to slip past, and he'd be gone again before I knew it.

I took a large gulp from my drink, trying to ignore the pang in my heart.

Everett wasn't here but that didn't mean that I couldn't have fun. Tilting my head back, I swallowed the last of my drink and turned to the kitchen, trailing after Lachie.

When I found him, he was already surrounded by a group of girls. I walked right into the middle of them.

"Lachie!" I shouted over the music. "Want to dance?"

He gazed at the group around him before smiling at me and nodding. Minutes later, we were in the middle of River's trashed living room, screaming to some Post Malone song and jumping on the coffee table.

Lachie was next to me, teetering on the edge of the table. He was absolutely and completely drunk, and I was too. The room swayed and spun around me. If I stood still for too long, I began to tilt off the edge of the table and I knew I'd fall.

So, I kept moving, jumping, bouncing on my toes, and screaming to the music. Sometimes River would appear and pass me a cold drink, sometimes I'd find myself in the kitchen pouring one myself, alcohol sloshing all over the counter.

My shoes vanished and then my phone and by the time the sun had begun to rise, the room was completely tilting.

I paused for a moment, staring at the walls in wonder, feeling my head spin and my stomach churn. And then, just as I'd suspected, I began to fall.

Chapter 6

"**I**SLA!"

My eyes strained open, harsh light stabbing at my head, turning my pounding headache into a deep migraine. My stomach churned and I groaned, turning on my mattress, trying to keep myself from vomiting.

"Isla!"

I held a hand to my head. I must have still been drunk because that sounded a lot like—

"Sky?" I mumbled.

My bedroom door flung open, and Sky walked in, her eyes sparkling and a wide smile splitting across her face. I shot up in my bed, immediately regretting the decision when my head spun, and bile rose in my throat.

The sheets were tangled between my legs, and I hadn't changed since the party. I could only imagine what my hair and make-up must have looked like. I could feel my curls matted at the back of my head. When had I even gotten into bed?

"Isla!" she squealed, pausing at the doorframe as her eyes landed on me. They trailed over me, and her lip curled into a grimace. "Oh, you look horrible."

"Thanks," I muttered. I patted the bed around me searching for my phone. When I couldn't find it, I turned back to Sky. "What time is it?"

"Like, one in the afternoon," Sky said, snorting. Lifting her hand, she threw something hard at me. My reflexes were still slow with my hangover, and it landed in my lap. I squinted down at it, realising it was my phone. "Exactly how drunk did you get last night?"

"Too drunk," I replied. I turned my phone on and was instantly greeted with missed calls and unread texts from Everett. "Shit. Everett."

He'd texted me the usual good morning texts at first, which quickly evolved into questions about River's party, and then questions about why I wasn't responding. We'd planned to talk when he woke up, and I always texted him good night—until now.

I quickly began typing, explaining that I'd lost my phone at some point in the night and that I'd call him later. I knew his schedule by heart, the result of struggling to find a spare five minutes to call between classes every day. He should be in class by now.

"Um, Isla?"

I looked up to find Sky frowning deeply. Her eyes fell to the corner of my floor, and I turned to find Lachie lying there, his hair messy and mouth wide open, completely knocked out.

"What did you do?" she asked.

"Nothing!" I said quickly. I winced, holding a hand up to my head. "I mean, I don't think..."

My hands quickly fell to my body, patting myself over to make sure I was still clad in Everett's hoodie and my shorts. When my fingers touched material, I sighed, my body sagging in relief.

"Oh, God," Sky said, although she was grinning widely. I rolled my eyes, practically rolling out of bed to kneel over Lachie. He was still clothed too. Thank God.

Sky shuffled into the room, standing over us.

"He's kind of hot," Sky muttered. I nudged her side roughly and her hands flew to her mouth, holding in a laugh.

"Lachie," I whispered, shaking his shoulder.

He didn't move.

Sky nudged his leg with her foot.

"Is he breathing?" she asked.

I groaned in frustration, shaking him harder. "Lachie, I swear, you better not be dead. I'm going to be really annoyed if you're dead."

He grunted and I exhaled sharply, grabbing his face, and turning him to me. His eyes narrowed at me.

"Isla?" he murmured before groaning again. "God, my head. I feel like shit. Where am I? What time is it?"

Sighing, I released him, and he fell back to the floor with a thump. I stood, walking right past Sky and into the kitchen. I needed some pain killers. Strong ones.

Sky followed me out, a sly grin tugging on her lips.

"So," she began slowly, "that was an exciting way to wake up, wasn't it?"

The night was coming back to me in snippets. Dancing on a table. Doing way too many shots. River definitely grinded his arse on me at one point. And then dragging a blacked-out Lachie to my bedroom floor so that no one would step on him while he slept.

"Look, I know what you're thinking, but nothing happened between—"

"It's none of my business," she cut off, still grinning. I groaned, turning to face her completely.

"Sky," I started, sharpening my voice. "Nothing happened. Got it?"

"Right," she said giggling. She clearly didn't believe me. "Nothing happened. Got it."

I sighed, giving up on her and turning back to the cabinets. I'd moved all of Everett's New York mugs to the front after I started missing him and I grabbed one of those to fill with water. I took a long swig, finishing the cup in one drink, and sighed at the instant relief.

I turned back to Sky who sat on one of the barstools and gazed amusedly around the ruined living room. Lamps had been knocked over, the couch had been flipped, and rubbish covered every surface. There were even a few people left, knocked out on the floor or against the couch.

I grimaced, hoping River wasn't expecting me to help clean.

Even the kitchen counter was still sticky and covered in plastic cups. I flicked one off the counter, watching it slide across before tumbling into a rubbish bag below.

"Lachie is one of my classmates," I explained as I moved around the kitchen. "I invited him to the party last night because I figured I wouldn't know anyone there anyway. Which, I'm glad I did, because it was honestly wild. River knows how to throw a chaotic party, that's for sure. I'm surprised none of the neighbours called the cops on us."

"Oh man, I haven't been to a party in so long. I'm jealous. You're going to have to tell me every detail so that I can live vicariously through you," Sky said, a sense of reminiscence to her voice. "I mean, remember the bonfire parties we'd have back in Shellside Bay? Those were the stuff of legends."

My mind drifted to Shellside Bay's bonfire parties, and then to River's last night. They had been polar opposites. Suddenly, a sense of longing filled me.

I had spent so long rushing to get out of Shellside Bay, I'd completely missed all the things that I wouldn't have here in Sydney. The bonfires, the beaches, our hidden lagoon in Isla, the Nauti Buoys and the Nauti Buoy boat itself—all of that had become a distant memory.

And I knew, no matter how often I visited, it would never be the same again.

We wouldn't be drunk seventeen-year-olds with nothing but tomorrow to look forward to, drinking by the fire, stumbling through the ocean with sand on our skin.

After I'd knocked back two pills and drained my mug of water another two times, I turned to Sky and rested my elbows on the kitchen counter.

"So, what are you doing here?" I asked, my voice still groggy with sleep.

"What, I can't just visit my best friend because I miss her?"

I lifted a brow at her. "Weren't you supposed to be in, like, Perth or something?"

She sighed, slumping onto the marble countertop. "Gap year's officially on pause. I am officially homebound and searching for a job."

"On pause?" I echoed. "What happened? Did something happen? Is everything okay?"

She waved a hand at me. "Oh, don't get me started. My cousin got pregnant."

I almost choked on my spit. "Pregnant?"

"Pregnant," Sky affirmed, nodding sagely.

"How—I mean, I know how, but I just..." I trailed off, shaking my head in disbelief. "How did she even get the chance? Aren't you guys sharing a van?"

"Well, remember Josh?"

"Oh no."

"Oh yes." She groaned, burying her face in her arms. "They're eloping this weekend. Her parents will be angry, but they'd be angrier about a child out of wedlock. And so, here I am. Gap year is officially on pause, and Josh is soon to be my cousin in law."

"Oh, Sky," I said. I moved to rest a hand on her shoulder when something occurred to me. I reeled back, wrinkling my nose at her. "You never..."

"No way!" she said, immediately catching my train of thought. "I mean, I thought about it, but never—I mean, thank goodness, right? Those would've been some interesting family reunions."

"That's one way to put it." I snorted. "He was cute though."

"He was," Sky whined, and we both sighed.

She had sent me photos of Josh right after she'd told me about him. He was something straight out of Love Island, with his jawline and those abs. It was rare that Sky and I ever had the same taste in guys, but Josh... he'd gained my stamp of approval immediately.

Not that it was worth anything, considering he was mid-elope with Sky's cousin. And with a child on the way.

It was weirdly comforting to hear that I wasn't the only one having a horrible start to the year.

"After they elope and all the family drama cools down, the rest of my cousins and I are going to continue our trip, but right now, my auntie has them on lockdown after what happened with their sister," Sky explained. "Give it a few weeks, though. I'm sure my auntie will be too distracted with all the baby arrangements to care about what my cousins get up to. She'll probably be relieved to get rid of us."

"So, what are you going to do until then?" I asked. "Back to Shellside Bay?"

Sky shrugged and smiled at me sheepishly. "Actually, I was hoping I could stay here for a few weeks until this whole thing blows over. I swear, if it's not over by next month, I'll move back home, but I don't really want my gap year to end on this note."

"Of course, you're welcome as long as you want!" I said, immediately grinning. Sky joining us would make that half the Nauti Buoys reunited in one place. I wanted her to stay forever, except—I winced. "Although, I guess that would really be up to River."

"Right," Sky said. She ran a hand over her face, then over her shaved head which had already begun to grow back, and I reached forward, grabbing her hand in mine.

"He'll definitely say yes, though," I reassured her. She nodded unsurely and I stepped back, shooting her a wide grin. "The Nauti Buoys reunion. I wish we could get the rest of the boys down here for a while. Have you spoken to them?"

She shrugged. The change in topic seemed to loosen her up a bit and she smiled down at her nails. "I've been texting them here and there, but they haven't really responded much. They've been busy with work, I think."

I nodded, knowing exactly what she meant. They had barely been talking with me too. I remembered the days I would text and call Austin daily. Some nights we'd fall asleep talking on the phone. Now, we were lucky to text once a week.

"It feels like the longer we stay apart, the further we drift," Sky said abruptly, her voice quiet.

I met her eyes and saw the uncertainty in them. I frowned. She'd said the words I'd been too scared to admit all term. I opened my mouth, searching for words to say, but I had nothing. She was right.

We were drifting.

Before I could think of how to respond, a door flew open, and a shirtless boy walked straight out of River's room.

He paused, his eyes widening when he saw me and Sky staring at him.

I narrowed my eyes at him. He looked familiar. He was that boy that River had been making out with last night. The quiet boy. What was his name again?

Now, in the light, I could see that he had brown hair, lighter than Everett's, and tanned skin. He was tall, but not quite as tall as Connor, although his eyes looked to be the same shade of blue.

"Alistair!" I said finally, the name resurfacing. His eyes snapped to mine, and he smiled coyly, lifting a hand in greeting.

"Alistair?" Sky echoed.

"Sky?" River stepped out from behind Alistair, and I gawked at him. Just like Alistair, he was shirtless, except he was covered in hickeys and bruises, all across his neck, collarbones and the rest of his torso.

My hand flew up to cover my mouth and I shared a look with Sky. Alistair had seemed shy, but I supposed he was much more assertive behind closed doors.

"River," Sky said after a pause, smirking at him. "Looks like you're still completely straight, huh?"

River rolled his eyes. While it had been somewhat of a secret back in Shellside Bay, River had done an awful job of keeping it one. All you had to do was get him in close proximity to Connor, and his entire façade would fall apart.

"What are you doing here?" he asked. "Who let you in?"

"I let myself in," she said, grinning. "Just smooth talked that fancy concierge downstairs into giving me access in the lifts. It didn't hurt that you left your front door unlocked. Seriously, River. Do you know how many murderers you cross paths with in your life?"

"You didn't answer my first question—"

"Thirty-six!" Sky exclaimed, ignoring him. "That's, like, sta tistically... a lot of murderers! You're lucky I was here to lock it for you."

"Thanks a lot, Sky," River said drily.

"Any time." She beamed.

"Now, back to my first question," River said. Alistair, discomfort written all over his face, ducked his head and slowly crept back into River's bedroom. "What are you doing here?"

"Cousin's preggo. Gap year's paused. Blah, blah. I need a place to stay for a few weeks," she said. "Is it cool if I crash here?"

River's eyes moved to mine, then to the closed bedroom door at the end of the hall—the one I'd never seen opened in the past two or so months I'd been staying here. I'd assumed it was his parents', although they were still yet to make an appearance.

River turned back to Sky. "Sure, but we don't have any bedrooms left. You can bunk with Isla."

"Oh, no, I could sleep on the couch," Sky started to say but I interrupted her.

"No way, you're sleeping in my room. I missed you so much, I'm going to have to get as much time with you as possible before you leave for the rest of your gap year," I said sternly. "I mean, seriously. Did you have to do a gap year? Why couldn't you just go straight to university here in Sydney?"

"I am beyond burnt out, Isla. I don't think my brain is ready to go back into exam season anytime soon. I mean, I asked to copy your assignments in high school," she replied, lifting a brow. "Think about that next time you feel lonely here in the big city, yeah?"

I laughed and River groaned, finally closing the space between us to join me in the kitchen.

"Is that Panadol?" he asked me. Before I could reply, he was in front of me, dry swallowing two pills.

Standing behind him now, I could see even more hickeys and bruises across his back. My eyes grew wide, and I met Sky's eye over his shoulder.

Kinky, I mouthed, and she fell into a fit of giggles.

As if sensing my words, River turned to shoot me a deep glare.

"Not a word," he said. I nodded quickly and he eyed me suspiciously for a moment before turning back to the counter. Over his shoulder, I rolled my eyes at Sky and stuck my tongue out, silently gagging, and she clapped her hands over her mouth, holding in her laughter.

Half of the Nauti Buoys were back together again, and it was already perfect.

CHAPTER 7

L ast Summer

I groaned, rolling over in my sleep, only for my hand to hit a shoulder. My eyes fluttered open, only to immediately shut with the bright influx of sunshine, straining my already bloodshot eyes.

This wasn't my bed. This was—

"Everett?" I muttered, my voice raspy. I eased my eyes open to see his face, just centimetres from mine. His brow furrowed and, without opening his eyes, he replied.

"What's wrong, babe?"

I couldn't help but warm at that. I leaned closer, tracing a hand across his jaw. His lips twitched and I traced a path higher, over his cheekbones until I reached his brow. I smoothed a hand over his forehead before wrenching his eyelids open.

"Wake up!"

He groaned, rolling away as I burst into laughter.

"You're evil, Isla!" he complained, rubbing his hands over his eyes.

"Hey, you're the one who said our time together is limited," I teased, sitting upright.

He turned slowly, glaring at me over his shoulder. We both paused, waiting for the other to make a move. And then, his lips pulled into a wide grin, and he leapt forward, grabbing me at the waist and tackling me into the mattress.

I giggled, wriggling out of his grip, but he was too strong—too big over me. He pinned me down at an awkward angle, leaning over me until his face hovered above mine.

"Am I still evil?" I asked, smirking.

"The most," he replied.

"Just because I woke you up?"

He laughed, leaning closer and closer until his lips brushed my jawline, and traced a line down my neck.

"For that," he hummed against my skin. "But mostly for making me fall so in love with you."

□□□□□□□□□□

Now

I rolled over in my bed, my hand smacking Sky in the stomach with a loud grunt.

"Move over," she groaned, shoving my hand off of her.

"You move over, this is my bed," I replied, my voice rough with sleep.

After Sky's sudden appearance, we spent the afternoon kicking out stragglers and cleaning the apartment. It was pointless, really, considering River had cleaners come in afterwards anyway, but it had felt like the old days for a moment.

It felt like Shellside Bay, with Sky nursing our hangovers and handling our drunken mistakes—and by our, I meant River's. His guests had destroyed half our furniture. The couch had a permanent tilt to it now.

Sky was moved in by sunset.

It hadn't taken long. All she had was a duffel bag of clothes, and then we were set. We were officially roommates—for the next few weeks. And then she'd be gone again.

I was going to make these few weeks stretch out for as long as possible.

She flipped over, her face burying in her pillow. Her words were muffled when she spoke. "Don't you have a class or something?"

I sighed, my eyes opening. I did, except I'd been planning on skipping it. It was a biology class—a class where I knew nobody and sat alone in the back, struggling to absorb any information while the professor read off a PowerPoint presentation.

"Why would I go to class while you're here?" I asked, teasingly.

She kicked me, her cold toes colliding against my thigh and I squealed, rolling to the edge of the bed.

"Education is important," Sky said sagely, as if she hadn't skipped school once a week back in high school. She had a talent for being 'sick'.

"I would just rather spend time with you," I replied. "Besides, I'm going to fail whether I go to class or not."

I was half-joking, but it made Sky sit up anyway. She leaned on her elbows, frowning at me, her hair thick and unruly from sleep. She poked me with a toe against my leg.

"What do you mean by that?" she asked carefully. "You always did good in high school. Do you miss Everett?"

I snorted, rolling over to bury my face into my pillow. That was an incredible understatement. To say I missed Everett was barely touching the very concept of missing him—of how I felt. Even thinking about him, hearing his name, brought a twinge in my chest.

Sky's toe poked me again and I reached down to pinch her calf. She squealed, pulling away and I flashed her a grin.

"I'm fine," I said, poking my tongue at her. "Keep your nasty toes away from me."

"Isla!" she said, her voice whining. She narrowed her eyes at me, and I narrowed mine back. "I can sense when you're lying, you know."

"No, you can't," I replied. "Because I'm not lying."

"Yes, I can. Your nose twitches." My hands flew up to my nose and she smirked, lifting a brow. "See? Now tell me for real—what's up?"

"You're sneaky," I scowled, but I hoisted myself onto my elbows anyway, meeting her eye properly. "I just—I don't know. It's kind of everything, you know? Everett's gone. Austin and Connor are gone. You'll be gone again soon. And uni is hard. Like, so much harder than I expected. I don't know. I just... I never thought I'd say this, but I miss Shellside Bay. I miss summer."

It was true, and when I said it out loud, it suddenly felt very real. I hadn't realised how much I missed Shellside Bay until I said it.

I missed the beaches and bonfires. I missed Austin, throwing me into the lagoon at Isla, I missed River's terrible steering on the Nauti Buoy boat each evening, I missed Connor skinny dipping while half drunk on sticky summer nights. I missed my mum, hugging me. Kissing my forehead. I even missed my boss, Tom, and working at the Shack every summer.

Most of all, I missed having Everett beside me. I missed being able to kiss him and touch him whenever I felt like it. I missed his arms around me, and his hands in my hair. I missed every part of him.

Sky shuffled closer until she could reach me. She took my head into her hands and pulled me into a hug, burying my face in her neck, and her fingers untangling my bed hair as she massaged my scalp. It felt like I was hugging my mother for a moment, and I melted into her touch.

"Things are different," she said slowly. "It'll probably never be the same, but different isn't necessarily bad. I mean, yeah, things are tough right now. You're at uni, my cousin's pregnant. It's tough."

I laughed and she chuckled quietly before continuing.

"But it'll be fine. I mean—" she shifted so that she could look at me properly— "you're Isla Monroe. When have you ever given up when things got tough, huh? When Austin would destroy you in every surfing competition and race, you trained before sunrise every morning. When you decided you wanted to move to Sydney, you worked every summer for years. And when River offered you this place, you studied like crazy for the rest of Year 12. You'll get through this. I know it."

I smiled at her, my eyelids beginning to burn with the promise of tears. My lips wavered and I leaned forward, pulling her into a fierce hug.

"What did I ever do to deserve you?" I teased.

Her voice came out strained from how tight I was hugging her. "Oh, so now my toes aren't nasty, huh?"

I laughed.

□□□□□□□□□□

Sky had motivated me like crazy and by noon, Lachie had joined me on the kitchen counter where we tackled the monster that was our biomolecular lab manual. We'd made it a habit to study together, and ever since the party, some of our study sessions had moved to River's kitchen counter.

I couldn't blame him. River's place was like a hotel.

Lachie sat beside me, flicking through his lab manual with a furrowed brow and twisted lips.

"I just don't understand how I left so many pages blank," he said, his page-turning growing rough with frustration. The pages almost ripped as he aggressively flipped through them. "I mean, I attended these labs, didn't I? What was I doing the whole time?"

"Annoying me," I said, shooting him a mock glare.

He rolled his eyes, sliding the manual towards me and collapsing against the table. "I'm not cut out for this degree."

Laughing, I picked his lab manual up and flipped the workbook to the same page I'd been looking at.

"On the bright side," I began brightly, "it looks like the questions you missed, I filled out and vice versa." I flipped to the next week's practical activity and frowned. "At least for last week. You really don't have any other friends in the lab?"

"No!" he groaned, dragging his hands over his face.

"But you know, like, half the uni."

"I'm only friends with idiots!"

"Great," I replied, settling him with a deadpan stare. "So am I."

"That's harsh, Isla." He pouted and held a hand to his heart. "I'm going to have to go cry that off. You got a bathroom?"

"No, we use buckets like in Medieval England."

He glared at me and I rolled my eyes, jabbing my thumb over my shoulder.

"Second door on the left," I said.

I'd thought about sending him to River's room as a joke for a second, but he'd probably murder the poor guy.

Besides, I was pretty sure that Alistair was still camping out in there. He was beginning to look like he'd be a regular around here, and I wasn't sure if I'd come to terms with it yet.

It had always been River and Connor—not River and Alistair. It didn't even sound right.

Lachie bowed his head to me, a teasing smirk on his lips, before he spun and left down the hall. I sighed, turning back to the lab manuals spread on the table, sticky notes and calculators scattered over the pages.

Most of my notes were scribbled nonsense, while most of Lachie's were smiley faces and bad renditions of the animals we examined in class. I traced a finger over one margin where a rat played leapfrog with a cane toad.

Lachie reminded me of Connor. I knew they'd get along if they ever met. Maybe Lachie was Connor in an alternate universe where he grew up in Sydney and decided to go to university. The thought of that seemed to comfort me. I missed having all my Nauti Buoys around.

As I was flipping to the next page, my phone buzzed on the counter and I turned to see Everett's name flashing across the screen.

I didn't have to think twice. I scooped it into my hands, answering the video call with a wide smile.

"Ev!" I smiled in way of greeting.

He grinned back at me, his eyes softening as the screen lit up his face. His hair was messy, and his shoulders were bare. It looked like he was lying in bed.

"Hey," he murmured, his smile still wide on his lips. "I miss you."

"I miss you more," I replied, shifting to lean my hand on the counter. "What time is it there?"

"Eleven." That explained why he was in bed. I opened my mouth to tell him the time in Sydney, but his eyes twinkled, and he said, "It's one over there, right? What are you up to?"

I groaned, tilting the phone down to show him the lab manuals spread out on the counter. "Studying. Please save me."

"Huh," he said simply, his brow furrowing. "Alone?"

"No, actually. Guess what?" Before he could reply, I quickly added, "I made a friend! We're in the same lab and everything. I mean, I'm really starting to think that this isn't so bad. I think I'll actually do pretty good in my next exam."

Everett's smile seemed to soften on his face. He watched me through the phone, eyes half-lidded, and my pulse quickened, looking at him.

It struck me suddenly how much he'd managed to change in the time since we'd last video called. His hair had gotten slightly longer. His smile—when was the last time I'd seen him smile at me like that? Too long.

His eyes seemed darker, with bags lining the skin beneath them. He'd even grown a stubble. He looked tired. It had only been days, weeks, and Everett was changing, growing, without me.

"What's wrong?" he asked, sensing my sadness.

I shrugged, shaking my head. I wouldn't ruin our call. Not when we barely had any time together. Not now.

"I just miss you," I replied. "I don't know how we survived last year."

"It was easier when we both weren't busy with college all the time."

"Uni."

"Whatever," he groaned, though he grinned wildly at me. "It'll be over before we know it."

I nodded firmly. Three years would be nothing. And I'd have him for summers. We'd be fine.

Suddenly, his eyes flickered, and footsteps came from behind me. I turned to see Lachie pausing at the edge of the living room.

"Oh," he said, rubbing the back of his neck. "Am I interrupting?"

"Who's that?" Everett asked. His smile had vanished, and he frowned at the screen. "Is that River?"

I snorted. "Yeah, River grew blond hair and blue eyes in three months," I teased. "No, this is Lachie, the friend I was telling you about. Lachie, this is Everett."

"Her boyfriend," Everett added curtly.

"Ah, the boyfriend," Lachie said. He flashed a smile, stepping closer to wave at Everett through the camera. "Nice to meet you."

"Nice to meet you too."

"Woah!" Lachie exclaimed. His eyes grew wide, and his grin split across his face. "You're, like, proper American! I thought you were just in New York on exchange or something. You live there?"

"Uh, yeah," Everett said. His eyes moved and I knew he was watching me.

"We're studying together," I said quickly. "We're in the same lab."

I knew I'd said it already, but I felt compelled to explain again. When Everett didn't reply, the silence seemed to stretch for too long. I cleared my throat and added, "River's here too."

"Oh," Everett said. He wasn't exactly best friends with River, but the affection was obvious. They had similar senses of humour, anyway. His smile grew slightly, his eyes lighting up. "Where is he? Haven't spoken to him in ages."

I pursed my lips. "Well, he's actually in his room, but..."

"Oh," he repeated, the disappointment clear in his voice and expression.

Another silence drifted over us. Lachie had taken his seat beside us and was beginning to flip through the lab manuals again, the pages turning loudly.

"Well, I don't want to interrupt you two," Everett said eventually. I frowned. Was that bitterness in his voice?

"You're not interrupting," I said, my brow furrowing.

"No, no. You should get back to studying. I need to sleep anyway. Talk tomorrow?"

He was speaking so quick; I could barely process his words. I shook my head, blinking.

"Right. Okay. I miss you a lot," I said. I glanced at Lachie, suddenly feeling awkward with him listening to the conversation. He stared intently down at our workbooks. "Love you, Ev."

"Love you more," he replied. He smiled at me, but it didn't quite reach his eyes before he hung up.

My heart wavered. There had been so many things I wanted to ask him about—his classes, his friends, his family. And I had so much I needed to tell him. I sighed, putting my phone down. I'd just have to find another time. Always another time.

"So," Lachie said. I turned to find him smiling gently at me, sympathy wrought on his face. "Where should we start?"

CHAPTER 8

I first met Sky when I was twelve.

Back then, the Nauti Buoys only consisted of Austin, Connor, and me. Really, we weren't even the Nauti Buoys yet because River hadn't joined us yet and we hadn't given his dad's boat its legendary name.

River came that summer, but Sky came first.

She arrived in Shellside Bay two weeks before school started, and everyone knew about her arrival within two hours. She was the talk of the town. Everyone was whispering about the moving truck that had parked outside the little blue house that had been empty for the past six months.

We weren't friends right away, but when she joined the group, it was like she was always meant to be one of us.

The day we met, she was standing outside of her new house, helping her parents unpack the moving truck. I had been riding past on my bike with Austin and Connor and stopped in front of her driveway.

We stared at each other for a moment. She was paler back then, untouched by the glaring sun of Shellside Bay's summers. She was coming from a town closer to the city, but further from the beach. Back then, she hadn't even touched a surfboard yet.

Her hair, though, was just the same. It was unruly and wild but, back then, cropped to her shoulders—just like mine was.

She touched the ends of her hair as she stared at me, then flashed me a smile.

"Looks better on me," she said.

I gaped at her in disbelief that she'd said that to me, that those had been the first words out of her mouth—and then I started to laugh.

□□□□□□□□□□

Sky was gone as quick as she'd appeared.

Her cousin had broken the news to the family and chaos had broken loose. The marriage certificates were already signed, and the baby was already brewing in her womb, but Sky's family would be damned if there was no real wedding ceremony.

And so, Sky had been summoned back to her cousin's hometown to plan a wedding in less than a month. A wedding that would hopefully distract from the fact that her cousin's baby would be born two months 'early', when the time came.

My room seemed ten times larger without her clothes strewn on the floor, or her duffle bag tucked in the corner. I even missed her cold toes against my legs in the middle of the night.

I sat on my bed, lying on my stomach as I revised a lecture on statistics. We had a test coming up and I still couldn't wrap my head around the concept of a null hypothesis. And there were so many Greek letters. I groaned, pressing my hands against my face. This was maths, why were there so many Greek letters?

I knew I would regret dropping out of the higher maths class in high school. I hadn't expected to go to university—and I definitely hadn't expected to need to do maths for a degree in marine biology.

I used to be good at this stuff. Now, it seemed the letters floated meaninglessly on the page, only there to make my life harder.

Outside, music was pounding. I could hear the quiet clink of drinks and chatter beneath the pounding bass of River's speakers.

He was throwing another party and, while it was less chaotic than the previous one, I'd had my fill of parties for the term. I was preoccupied. Not only did I have a statistics exam soon, but I also had a practical exam for my biomolecular science lab, and then an essay due for my biology class. It was piling up.

I wanted to tear my hair out.

I glared down at my blank paper, my pen hovering over the page. I'd listened to the lecture twice now and I had nothing to add to my original notes. It hadn't helped at all.

I groaned, dropping the pen, and rolling onto my back.

It was a shame that Lachie wasn't in any of my other class-es. I had no other friends, no one to call, no one to ask for help from.

It seemed like most of my classmates were friends with people from their high schools. My high school friends were back in Shellside Bay, working full time, barely responding to my texts. And even then, they probably wouldn't know much about my statistics exam.

I sighed, tapping on the one contact I needed to speak to right now—needed to see.

Everett answered almost immediately.

He lifted the shaking camera to his face and flashed me a smile. I frowned at him.

"Ev," I said, blinking at his video. "Where are you?"

"Subway," he replied, right as the camera shook again. He flipped the camera momentarily, showing me the stained seats and crowded carriage before turning it back to him-self. "Like, the train subway, not the fast-food restaurant. Although I could go for a meatball sub. What's up?"

"I'm studying," I said with a pout. "Please save me."

"I'm on my way right now," he teased. After a pause, he added, "Lucky's not there to help you today?"

"It's Lachie," I corrected before rolling my eyes with a smile. "And no. He's not in my statistics course. You're not jealous, are you?"

His brow furrowed. "Me? Jealous?"

"Yes, you. Jealous."

"Of course, I'm jealous," he said immediately. "I mean, he can pull up whenever he wants. He can see you in person every day, hear your voice live. I'm incredibly jealous. I'd kill just to hold your hand right now."

My smile wavered. I'd only been teasing him but now that he'd said it, I was missing him all over again.

"You know I love you, right?" I asked.

He cracked a smile at the camera. "I don't know, you never really mentioned it."

"Well, I do. Like a lot. And I miss you way more than I thought was possible."

He smiled at me, his mouth opening, then closing. He frowned.

"What's that sound?" he asked, pressing his earphones further into his ears.

"Oh, River's having a party, of course," I said, glancing over my shoulder to my bedroom door. Colourful lights flashed beneath them with shadows passing by a sign of the strangers dancing in the hallway.

"Why aren't you out there?" Everett asked, wiggling his brows. "I thought you were a party girl. Don't get too drunk, though. Not unless I'm there."

My lips twitched and I remembered him calling me a cuddly drunk. I thought of the morning I'd woken up pressed against him in his bed after I'd been so drunk that I held him until he fell asleep beside me.

"You thought wrong," I said, holding up my statistics notes. "I'm actually a massive nerd."

"It's why I love you," he teased.

"That's the reason?"

"Well, that and your massive—"

"Everett!"

"—heart. What? What did you think I was going to say?"

"Ah, because it was my heart that you were staring at the day we met," I shot back, raising a brow at him.

His cheeks turned pink, and he looked away for a second, as if just remembering he was sitting in a subway surrounded by people.

"I was staring near your heart. Admiring your beauty," he said simply.

"I seem to remember you having some choice words too. What was it you called me?"

"A gorgeous beauty?" he asked.

"Not quite. Try again."

"Most wonderful woman in the world?"

I laughed. "Yeah, it was definitely along those lines."

He smiled at me, and a speaker muffled some words in the background. The camera shook as he stood and suddenly his face was right against the screen.

"I'm getting off the subway," he said. "Give me a minute."

I nodded and watched in silence as he walked, the phone occasionally pressing up against his chest or turning upside down.

This was what our relationship had become. Stolen moments. Muttered conversations on subways and light rails. The two of us, thousands of miles apart.

And so, I smiled, watching as he made his way through the subway station, and pretended that I was there beside him. I pretended that I wasn't watching through a low-quality screen. No, I was there beside him. I was holding his hand

and bumping shoulders with him—two university students walking through New York City together.

Together.

The camera shifted again, and his face was back in view from a low angle. He smiled at me, the sky clear in his background, which was indication enough that he was halfway around the world. It was almost summer in his universe, almost winter in mine.

"I'm back," he said through a grin and I felt my lips twitching to reflect his smile.

"Where are you going?" I asked, leaning my cheek against my palm as I watched him walk. The wind pushed his hair back so that it looked almost like he was sprinting. I wondered how it would feel beneath my fingers at that length.

He took a moment to answer.

"Class," he said.

I frowned, my eyes darting to the date in the corner of my screen. It was May. I knew his schedule. Or—I thought I did. He should have finished his final exams by now. What class was he going to?

"I didn't know you had a class at that time," I started slowly, watching his expression carefully.

"Oh, you know, sometimes they change the times around," he said nonchalantly before quickly adding, "And then I'm thinking of going out for ice cream. The weather's getting hotter, it reminds me of Shellside Bay. Remember that ice cream truck that was always on the edge of the beach?"

He was definitely trying to change the subject.

"That sounds fun," I said before shifting the conversation back. "What class is it?"

"It's a finance class. Really boring," he replied. "What was the name of the chocolate they used to put on the soft serve again?"

"Flake," I said, my voice curt. He was changing the subject. I lifted a brow at him. "I thought you weren't taking any finance classes this semester."

He blinked, glancing down at his phone—at me—before looking away, continuing on his walk.

"Ah, did I say that? Turns out I had to take one course after all," he said. He cleared his throat, glancing at the screen again. "I'm actually almost there. Can we talk later?"

I pursed my lips staring at him through the camera. He didn't look back, only continued walking, his eyes straight ahead. With a sigh, I nodded, although he didn't see it.

"I'll call you when I wake up," I said.

His eyes flickered back, and he shot me a smile. "Love you."

"Love you more."

I hung up before he could sense my disappointment. I dropped the phone onto the mattress, watching dully as it bounced and bounced until it fell still.

He was hiding something from me.

Everett was half-way across the world, sprinting some-where. Somewhere important. Somewhere he didn't want to tell me about.

And I was here sitting on my bed, studying statistics. What was I doing? This wasn't how it was all supposed to go.

I groaned, slamming my workbook shut and rolling onto my back, covering my face with my hands. Outside my door, the music only grew louder, pounding over the murmur of voices beneath, occasionally interrupted by a shout or a bang of furniture hitting the ground.

This wasn't right. None of this was right. I wasn't supposed to miss Shellside Bay. None of it made sense.

I was supposed to love Sydney. I was supposed to do well in university, and make new friends, and call the Nauti Buoys every morning, and video chat with Everett every night. He was supposed to visit me. I was supposed to visit him.

We weren't supposed to be keeping secrets from each other. We weren't supposed to be ending our calls with hurried goodbyes and shoving our feelings into scattered texts.

My stomach twisted and I was suddenly hit with the fact that I was lonely.

For the first time since my dad's funeral, I felt completely alone.

I didn't have Austin here, holding my hand anymore. I didn't have any of the Nauti Buoys, except River who practically hibernated in his room all day only to get plastered at night.

I didn't even have my mum anymore. She was hours away, probably asleep by now, resting for a morning on the beach before her next shift.

Anyway, it wasn't like she'd understand.

My mum was nothing like my father. Where my dad was warmth and dreams bundled into an ear-splitting smile, with books stacked on his desk about passions he'd never reach, my mum was all about the familiar sands of Shellside Bay.

Shellside Bay was her home. She never dreamed of leaving. Shellside Bay held her childhood memories, her family home, her closest friends, the people she grew up with. Her Everett had died, years ago, and their memories together lay in Shellside Bay. She had her own Austin and Connor waiting for her, and for her, that was enough.

I was beginning to understand her now.

What wouldn't I give to be back in Shellside Bay, surrounding by my friends, Everett by my side for the summer? To visit Isla and lay on the sands until the sun turned our skin hot and faded into hues of orange and purple beyond the horizon.

Hell, even for Mia to steal my surfboard again, calling me names and sending me smirks.

I missed it all.

My hands slid off my face and I turned onto my side, frowning at my stack of pencils and papers at the edge of the mattress.

Groaning, I sat up, sweeping a hand against the bed to toss all my statistics work onto the floor in a heap. I stood, crossing the room to tug a sweater over my head before making for the door.

Maybe I was alone. Maybe Everett was halfway across the world, having fun without me. Maybe Sydney was nothing I'd hoped it to be. But that didn't mean I had to sit here moping.

I tugged the door open and stepped into the hallway.

Into the party.

CHAPTER 9

Content warning: light smut in this chapter. stop reading after Isla takes her pills if you're not into that <3

The next day, I woke up to a loud knocking on the door. I turned on my stomach, pulling my pillow up around my ears. My alarm hadn't even gone off yet. The sun wasn't even up yet.

Knock, knock, knock.

It wouldn't stop. I groaned, squeezing my hands tighter around my head. I wasn't expecting anyone. It must have been someone from River's party last night—if it had even ended.

My head was already pounding with a hangover and this relentless knocking wasn't helping at all.

"River!" I shouted weakly, my throat sore from sleep and my voice muffled by my pillow.

Knock, knock, knock.

"River!"

There was a creak of the door beside my room and the quiet thudding of steps in the hallway, passing my door and moving to the living room.

I closed my eyes, letting myself drift back to sleep.

"Who the f—"

My eyes flew open. That sounded like—

"What are you—"

There was a loud thud, and I was out of my bed. I tripped over my blankets and bedsheets, stumbling across my room and to the door. I ripped my bedroom door open, slipping down the hallway until the front door came into view.

"Everett?" I mumbled.

His eyes snapped to me. His expression was angry, his eyes narrowed, and lips puckered in a sneer. And against the wall—his arm was pushed against Alistair's chest, his other hand hovering dangerously above his face. He had Alistair pinned.

Worse, Alistair was half-naked.

"Oh, my God," I muttered.

"Isla, who the hell is this?" Everett asked, shoving Alistair more firmly against the wall.

"Who the hell are you?" Alistair shot back.

Everett's eyes snapped to his and Alistair shrunk back, his mouth slamming shut. Behind me, a door creaked open, and I spun to find River walking out of his room, tugging a shirt on.

He rubbed his eyes, half-yawning as he asked, "What the hell is going on?"

"Yeah, River, what the hell is going on?" I echoed, lifting a brow at him. I was steaming. My head was pounding, and blood was rushing through my body and he had the nerve to yawn?

Everett was here. Here, in the flesh, standing right in front of me. Except, instead of running to hug me, he was pinning River's fling against a wall, threatening to punch him through it.

This was all River's fault.

He froze, his hand dropping to his side and eyes settling on the scene before us. Everett glared at him, his arm still pressing Alistair up against the wall. Alistair looked like he was deciding between crying and laughing, his eyes wide and lips twitching in an uncertain smile.

"Oh, this is great," River said. He'd decided—his lips were wide, and he was chuckling lowly. He stepped closer, throwing an arm around my shoulders, and watching on cheerfully. "Please, continue. Pretend we're not here."

"River," I groaned, nudging him hard in the ribs with my elbow.

He winced but kept his arm firm around me. He flashed a smile at me. "Come on, Isla. This is the most entertainment I've had all week."

"You had a party last night."

"And me," Alistair chimed in.

River hummed. "Close second, I guess."

"Does anyone want to explain what the hell is happening here?" Everett shouted. He lifted his fist higher, ready to drive it into Alistair's cheek.

I leapt forward, grabbing Everett's arm. For a moment, all I could think was he's here. He's really here. I could hold him. I could grab him.

His secret—I'd been worried for nothing. Everett had always been mine.

But then, I saw the anger in his eyes and snapped back to the present.

"This is Alistair," I said, slowly pulling his arm to lower it. "He's here with River, not me. Right, River?"

We both turned to look at him and he shrugged.

"No comment," River said, a shit-eating grin on his face.

I rolled my eyes, tightening my hold around Everett's arm. "He's with River. Not me. River."

"River?" Everett echoed. He turned, his eyes roaming over Alistair's bare chest, the hickeys that covered his neck and collarbones, then River's bruised skin. He blinked hard.

He turned to me, eyes falling over my neck, my jaw, taking in the unscathed skin. I smiled gently, nodding and he loosened a hard breath.

His grip must have loosened on Alistair because he scuttered out from beneath his arm and practically sprinted to River's side.

"River," Alistair confirmed.

Everett blinked again, his arms falling. Then, he shook his head and released a dry laugh.

"I totally misread you, man," he said. He rubbed a hand over his face. "I thought—I mean, I was jealous when Isla said she was moving in with you."

River shrugged. "I get it. I'm irresistible."

"Oh, shut up, River," I said, waving a hand at him before turning towards Everett. My hands moved to his shoulders, then his arms, his chest, his jaw. I shook my head, feeling tears burn behind my eyes.

"What are you doing here?" I asked.

Behind me, I could hear River's footsteps and the creak of his door, signalling that he'd left. Everett's eyes flickered, waiting for them to retreat before replying.

"I'm on break, remember?" he answered, turning completely to me. His hands clasped over my own before sliding down my arms to my waist. He lifted me, pushing me against the wall, lips splitting in a grin. "You sounded stressed from college. I thought I'd surprise you. Wasn't expecting... all that."

I laughed, tears finally slipping from my eyes. He wiped at my cheek.

"Why are you crying?" he asked.

"I just missed you so much." My hands moved from the back of his neck to his hair, my fingers pulling at the strands before drifting over his jaw and his cheeks. I traced the freckled skin of his nose. "I need to take all of this in. I just—You wouldn't tell me what was happening, and I knew you were lying about that stupid finance class, and—"

The words died in my throat, and I shook my head.

"You're actually here," I added finally.

His hair had darkened back to its natural dark brown without the harsh Australian sun to lighten it, but his freckles remained. They were faded, and there were less than usual, but they reminded me of the Everett I knew—the Everett who belonged here, with me.

I leaned forward, kissing a freckle beneath his eye and his smile softened. He leaned closer, his lips hovering over mine before I turned my head, his lips colliding against my cheek.

"What's wrong?" he asked, frowning.

I wrinkled my nose. "As much as I want to kiss you Ev, I'm hungover and probably have some killer morning breath right now."

Everett lifted a brow at me. "Hungover? I thought you were studying last night."

"I was, until you decided to hop on a plane without telling me. You're a bad liar, Ev. I was worried all night for nothing," I chided.

He laughed, his face reddening in the way that I loved. "No more bad lies and surprises. We both saw how well that one went."

I snorted, remembering the sheer fear that had taken over Alistair's usually timid face.

"Don't let that stop you from visiting as often as possible, though," I added.

"Never."

He leaned in again and I turned my head, letting his lips hit my cheek. He turned back to me with a pout, and I lifted a mocking brow.

"You're not going to trick me that easily."

"Well, I've been on a plane for about twenty-three hours, so—" he leaned forward, pressing a quick peck to my lips before smiling cheekily at me—"I guess we could both use some freshening up."

"Let's go to my room," I said. "It's a mess out here, and you have to tell me everything about New York."

He looked around the destroyed living room. It was still a mess after River's party, with furniture flipped and trash scattered around the floor, but at least there were no stragglers sleeping against walls this time.

The counter was covered in empty glass bottles and knocked over plastic cups. I grimaced, the memory of the taste of alcohol still fresh in my mind from last night. It had turned out to be as miserable as if I'd just continued with my statistics studies.

River was preoccupied all night and I didn't know anyone else at the party, so I'd spent most of the time drinking in the corner, my mind wandering to all the things Everett could've been doing that required him to lie to my face.

Him boarding a plane to Sydney was the last thing I would've thought of.

Everett nodded and slowly dropped my legs back to the floor. He reached down, throwing his duffel bag over his shoulder. I hadn't even realised it was there. I was too preoccupied with Everett, Everett, Everett.

Grabbing his hand, I led him to my room. I was suddenly grateful that I'd left some painkillers and a water bottle on my bedside table. Drunk Isla was kind to sober Isla. Besides, I didn't want to let Everett go for one moment in fear of him vanishing again. Leaving me.

My mind was already beginning to race with the things we could do now that he was here in person. Maybe I could give him a tour of my university. I'd always been jealous of the couples that passed, holding hands on their way to lectures. Maybe we could pretend. Just for a few weeks.

By the time we'd both freshened up and I'd popped two pills in my mouth, draining a whole water bottle to wash it down, the tension between us had grown palpable. I thought I might die if I didn't kiss him soon—or at least feel his arms around me.

Closing the door behind him, Everett emerged from the ensuite looking a lot more awake than he did before. We sat on my bed, him with his legs dangling off the edge, and me cross-legged beside him.

He stared at me as I settled on the edge of the mattress and I laughed, pushing my hair back self-consciously.

"What?" I asked.

He smiled gently, reaching out to take my face in his hands. "Nothing. I just want to keep staring at you."

I smiled back, leaning my face against his palms. He moved them forward, pushing my hair back.

"It's longer," he said simply. He took a curl between two fingers and tugged on it, watching as it sprung back up. "Still as wild."

I laughed, crawling towards him until I was straddling his lap. I buried my face in his neck and his arms came to wrap around my waist, tugging me closer and closer until his chin rested on my shoulder. Our chests pressed against each other, and I breathed him in.

This was my Everett. He'd finally come back to me.

"How long are you staying?" I asked. Before he could answer, another dozen questions popped into my brain. "Are you going to stay here? How were your final exams? Did you pass them all? What subjects are you taking next—"

"Isla," he said. "One at a time. And then it's my turn to ask."

I pulled back, smiling coyly at him. "Sorry. I'm just so excited."

"I am too," he said. His voice had turned low, quiet—almost husky. "I haven't seen you in so long. There are so many things I want to do."

"Oh?" I lifted a brow at him, my lips twitching. "Like what?"

"Like..." His hands slipped lower until they grabbed my bum. He pulled me higher on his lap. He wore sweatpants beneath me, and I inhaled sharply at the feeling of him under me. "This."

And midway through my gasp, he kissed me.

He kissed me hard, pulling me tight against him. My mouth was partially open, and he slipped his tongue inside, his hands gripping frantically at me. I arched into him, my hands moving into his hair and tugging, pulling.

And then he was moving down my jaw and across my neck, leaving kisses as he swept towards my collarbone.

"You taste the same," he muttered against my skin, teeth grazing the spot his lips had claimed.

I released a breathy laugh. "What did you expect?"

He paused, moving back to meet my eye. His gaze had darkened, his pupils blowing wide as he looked at me, his jaw setting. Suddenly, he flipped us, pushing me into the mattress and hovering over me. His legs pinned me on either side of my hips, my hands dipping into the mattress beside my head.

"What were we talking about a minute ago?" he asked.

I blinked, not expecting that question. My mind drew up blank. All I could think of was Everett's body over mine, his lips just centimetres away.

"I don't remember," I said.

He dipped his head lower, his mouth hovering over my neck, his breath hot against my skin. "Yes, you do. What was it, Isla?"

My head spun. All I could think was Everett, Everett, Everett.

"I..." my voice died in my throat. I blinked hard and tried again. "What we want to do while you're here?"

"Good girl," he murmured, his lips finally pressing against my neck.

His hands moved to grip the hem of my shirt, his fingers grazing the skin of my waist. "Tell me, what do you want us to do together?"

I hummed teasingly, as if my heart was not pounding out of my chest and my breathing had grown ten times heavier. "I don't know. See the Harbour Bridge?"

He smiled against my skin, his hands beginning to travel higher. My shirt rode up as he hands drifted over my stomach, leaving butterflies and a trail of heat where he touched. His fingers reached just beneath my breasts, and he flattened his hands there, waiting.

"What else?" he asked, playing along.

"I don't know, maybe the Opera House too?" I said, attempting to keep my voice steady. His fingers crept higher. "We could go to the zoo."

He hummed, the sound causing his lips to vibrate against my skin. His hands had covered my breasts now and his lips worked their way up to my jawline. My chest rose and fell heavily, the feeling of his calloused fingers over my skin causing my stomach to stir—releasing a fire in my veins.

"Everett," I whispered. My hands drifted to the band of his pants. He released me with one hand, moving to grab my wrists and stop me.

Pulling away for a moment, he held both my wrists with one hand and pinned them above my head. He looked down at me, lifting a brow.

"Not so fast," he said, smirking. "I haven't seen you in months. I'm going to savour this."

"Ev," I muttered again. I arched towards him, and he breathed sharply.

"What is it?" he asked. "Tell me what you want."

I rolled my eyes. "You know what I want."

His lips twitched. "All you've mentioned is the Harbour Bridge, the Opera House, the—"

"Ev!" I hissed. "Just—I just—Please."

He stared at me for a moment, satisfied with my answer, before his eyes began to slowly drift down, over my body.

With one hand, he tugged my shirt up, revealing my entire chest. I'd been sleeping before he arrived and hadn't worn a bra. My face felt hot, and I turned away, embarrassed to see his reaction, but he didn't notice.

His head bowed and he began tracing a hot trail with his mouth over my breast, then down, down, over my stomach, before pausing at the band of my shorts. He pressed a kiss there.

"I'm going to murder you," I said simply.

"That's not very polite, Isla," he replied. He tugged at the waistband, and I arched into his touch.

Immediately, he pulled away.

"Patience is a virtue."

I scowled. "I've been patient for months."

"So, what's five more minutes?"

"Minutes?"

He laughed, his fingers slipping beneath the waistband and sliding across my stomach, from one hip to another. I groaned, turning my head.

"Everett," I whined.

"Hush," he said. "Or River will hear us. Unless you're into that."

"Oh, shut up."

"If you insist," he said, and planted his lips back onto my skin. He kissed his way downward, tugging the waistband as he moved before slipping my shorts and underwear off completely.

His fingers continued to drift when I finally found my voice and muttered, "Wait."

He paused immediately, his hands leaving me and eyes finding my own. For all his arrogance, his face had turned pink too, and now that I'd told him to wait, he looked entirely flustered.

"What's wrong?" he asked.

I leaned up, tugging on the collar of his t-shirt. "You're too dressed."

He cracked a slanted smile at me before reaching over his neck and pulling it off in one go. I traced my hands down his chest. He'd gotten more fit since I'd last seen him, but he was paler too.

He was different.

Somewhere between summer and now, he'd changed without me. If this was just his appearance, how much of him had really changed? I paused at his hips and looked up to meet his eyes.

He smiled at me—his usual Everett smile—and my heart melted. It couldn't have been that much. We were still Isla and Everett, Everett and Isla. This was where we were meant to be. Not Shellside Bay—not even Sydney or New York—but together.

And now we finally were.

For a limited time.

I pulled at his waistband, and he shifted, kicking his pants and underwear off. My hands drifted lower, fingers hovering teasingly, and Everett groaned.

I grinned, mocking him. "Tell me what you want."

His eyes snapped open.

"All I want is you," he murmured.

He leaned forward, pulling me into a kiss, skin against skin, body against body on the mattress of my bed. His hand moved between my legs, and I moaned into the kiss, all the oxygen in my body, all my thoughts, all my everything vanished—and it was just Everett.

His thumb found the spot I needed him most and with a flick, I was practically undone. He was moving slowly, teasing me, savouring as he'd said he would. And I was bursting at the seams, falling apart with every touch, kiss, sigh, breath—with all of him.

I bucked my hips towards him, and he laughed, pressing light kisses to my jaw. "Patience."

"Fuck patience," I groaned, my voice faltering with every stroke. My eyes squinted open, and he looked down on me, one hand on himself, the other on me. I whimpered, grabbing his hand and tugging him closer. "Please."

"Please, what?"

"Please, before I murder you," I managed between clenched teeth.

He laughed but complied anyway. His fingers ventured lower over my core, and with a sharp inhale, he slid them into me. I groaned again, louder this time, and he swallowed it with a hard kiss.

"River will hear you," he murmured against my mouth.

"I don't care," I said.

"You will when he evicts you."

I slammed a hand against my mouth, muffling another groan as Everett began to pick up speed. My head lolled back, and I arched my chest towards him.

"I didn't even ask how you are," I muttered, my voice sounding distant and faraway to my own ears.

"Plenty of time for that later," he replied with a strained chuckle. His fingers left me, his hands planting on my hips as he dragged me closer. "After the Harbour Bridge, the Opera House, the zoo..."

"Oh, shut up and kiss me."

He did.

And we swallowed each other into the night, skin on skin, lips on lips, until I had come completely undone, until I was bursting at the seams, and until our limited time together was nothing but a distant memory.

CHAPTER 10

Last Summer

I sat on the floor between Everett's legs, my back against his chest as he took a towel through my dripping hair. He tugged and I winced, grabbing his hand with a laugh.

"Not like that," I said. I took his hand in mine, pushing his hand upwards towards my hair in a scrunching motion. "Like this. You'll pull my hair out and destroy my curls if you keep that up."

He laughed, continuing the scrunching motion with the towel.

"You know, the last time I went to a beach before I met you was when I was, like, five years old?" he asked suddenly. I blinked, shifting to look at him with wide eyes. He nodded. "Yeah, it was with my mom. Now it's like I'm there every day."

"Do you like it?" I asked.

His grin widened. "I love it."

I smiled, satisfied with his answer, and leaned back against his chest. It felt nice knowing I'd changed a part of him, that he'd leave Shellside Bay, but it would never leave him. Not anymore. No matter how far he went, he'd always have a piece of Isla with him. And me. He was stuck with me now.

He continued drying my hair for a moment before leaning forward, pressing a kiss to my cheek. I warmed, turning my head to face him with a coy smile.

"What was that for?" I asked.

He shrugged. "I just wanted to kiss you."

"Oh?" I lifted a brow, slowly leaning towards him. "Then kiss me."

And he did.

□□□□□□□□□□□

I woke up with the sheets bunched around my thighs and Everett sleeping half-naked beside me.

My first thought when I opened my eyes was to reach for my phone and text him good morning, until I stilled and realised his warm body was beside me, dipping the mattress sideways. I shifted onto my side and there he was. It hadn't been a dream.

A soft breath left my lips and I stared at him, silent. When was the last time I'd woken up beside him? How long would this moment last?

I wanted it to last forever.

I reached up, my fingers reaching for his hair. Looking at him this closely, I could see how long it had really grown, how dark it had turned. I could almost remember how light it was during the summer. I wondered if I could change it in the few weeks he'd be staying here—lighten it back to that almost toffee colour. Bring the freckles back to his cheeks.

No, we'd have to go to Isla for that.

Isla was where it had all began—where I'd first seen the lightness of his eyes, the curve of his smile. Sydney was hopes, and bustle, and food other than the one McDonald's and Boost Juice of Shellside Bay, but Isla—Isla was sunshine, crystal water, hot sand and sea foam that kissed your ankles.

Isla was an escape. It was what I was used to, where I'd grown up. On Isla, Everett and I were splashes in the lagoon and late walks on the shore. We were tumbles in the sand and sea salt kisses on his bed.

Sydney was the complete opposite. What would we be here? Coffee runs? Café dates? Train rides and fancy restaurants? I didn't know what to expect.

"Are you checking me out?"

Everett's eyes blinked open, his voice coming out thick and raspy with sleep. I laughed, pushing my fingers through his hair. He caught my wrist, pulling my knuckles to his lips.

"I missed waking up next to you," he muttered. "And these hot pink sheets."

I rolled my eyes, shoving his shoulder hard. "You're such a bully."

"Hey, it was a compliment," he shot back. "I don't know how I'll ever sleep again without them. Without you."

"It's simple," I said, shifting to move closer until our chests were pressed together and my arm was tight around his waist. "Just never leave me again."

He laughed lowly, the sound rumbling through his chest. "If it were up to me..."

His arm wrapped around me, and I let him hold me until a few minutes passed and I had to pull back.

"I'm going to shower," I said, standing from the bed. His eyes roamed over me briefly, skimming past my crumpled t-shirt and my shorts which had ridden up.

"Shower?" he echoed. "Where are you going?"

"Nowhere," I replied. I turned, pulling some clothes out of my wardrobe. "I just need to study. I have midterms soon." I paused, spinning to face him. "But after my shower, you can tell me all about New York, yeah?"

He grinned at me. "Of course. And then we can do something."

"Do something?" I lifted a brow, glancing deliberately towards the mattress. He laughed, rolling his eyes, and falling back against his pillow with a groan.

"Something outside of here, far away from River and his... friend." He nodded towards the wall that separated River's room and mine. If we were both quiet, we could hear someone snoring. Whether it was River or Alistair was hard to tell, considering how often Alistair seemed to stick around these days.

I missed the River that would pine over Connor, panicking with every glance and brush of skin. Where had Alistair appeared from all of a sudden? Where had the River I was used to gone? I had never known a River outside of Shellside Bay, but now that I did, I wasn't sure how much I liked him. He seemed distant. Sadder. Like Sydney was a drain on his energy, and the sands of Shellside Bay was how he recharged.

"How about this," Everett started. He lifted himself onto his elbows and grabbed at the hem of my shirt, tugging me closer. "You go shower, and we get breakfast somewhere nice? To make up for all the breakfasts I've missed in New York. You know, energise you for studying all day."

I smiled, my chest filing with warmth, and leaned down to peck his lips.

"I'll be quick," I said and left for my ensuite.

By the time I had showered, Everett was fast asleep again. I snorted, throwing my hair into a cotton t-shirt, and securing it around my head before grabbing my laptop and sitting on the bed beside him. I nudged him with my toe.

"Ev," I whispered.

He didn't even stir.

"Wake up," I said, louder this time.

He lay there like the dead—unmoving, unflinching. In fact, I'd think he was dead if it weren't for the occasional grunt that slipped from his lips. I sighed, moving to sit on the edge of the mattress.

He was completely out.

He seemed tired. His face was peaceful in his sleep. He looked the same as he did over the summer when we'd crash in a pile of sunburnt limbs on his bed at Clemente House every night—and yet so different all at once.

I lifted my hand, tracing a finger over his brow and down his cheek. His skin had turned paler. His freckles had faded. I wanted to drag him back to Shellside Bay and breathe life back into his body.

Instead, I sighed and stood again.

He was jet-lagged. The time difference between here and New York was fifteen hours. I had memorised those fifteen hours over the past year. Even when he was in Australia, those fifteen hours could still rob us of our time together.

It looked like breakfast and adventures in Sydney would have to wait.

Turning, I grabbed my books, gathering them into a pile against my chest, and sat beside him on the mattress. With his heavy breathing in the background, and his bare shoulder pressing hot against my knee, I began to study.

□□□□□□□□□□

Lips pressed against my leg and my heart flipped. I turned away from my laptop to Everett who had been sleeping soundly beside me just moments ago.

He looked up at me, his eyes narrowed and hair messy from sleep. He kissed my knee again before sending me a groggy smile.

"What time is it?" he asked. "Did I miss breakfast?"

"Breakfast, lunch, and everything in between," I teased. "It's already three."

He blinked, then blinked again, shooting up onto his elbow. The blanket slipped to his waist, revealing his bare chest.

"Three?" he echoed. He groaned, running a hand over his face before shoving his hair back. "I'm sorry. I really messed up."

"It's no big deal," I said. I shifted, placing my laptop on the bedside table to give him my full attention. "We still have time. How long are you staying?"

I'd asked him that question this morning, but then we'd gotten distracted with... other things. My face warmed at the memory and, judging by the tilt of his lips, Everett was remembering the same thing too.

"Two weeks," he replied. Two weeks seemed like no time at all, after months apart from each other. "My return flight is the Sunday two weeks from now so I'm back in time for my first Monday classes of the semester."

"Sunday? Won't you be too jetlagged for class on Monday morning?"

He shrugged. "I wanted the full too weeks."

"Two weeks," I repeated, testing the words on my tongue.

Everett's arms snaked around my waist, and I turned towards him. He smiled at me, stroking my skin. "I know, it's not long. But remember what I said a year ago? When I had to leave you the first time?"

My lips twitched. I remembered. I had it memorised, the words like ghosts, permanently etched into my skin, whispered on my breath even as I slept. I could quote it word for word. But I wanted to hear him say it.

"You might have to remind me," I said coyly.

He raised his brows knowingly but pulled my closer anyway.

"I'll take you anyway I can get you," he started. I loved the next part. "For a minute. For a day. For a week. I want you."

He ended his sentence by leaning down and peppering light kisses along my jaw, travelling down my neck, towards my collarbone. I giggled, wriggling out of his grip.

He pouted, his arm reaching out and dropping to the mattress.

"I need to study," I chided.

He groaned. "Your colleges here are all twisted. It's spring break, how do you have midterms coming up?"

"You're the twisted ones, starting uni in the middle of the year," I replied easily, turning to grab my laptop. I sat back on the edge of the bed, pulling my laptop with me. "Now, unless you can recite to me every part of the cell and its function, I need to get back to studying."

I had just turned my laptop back on and opened my notes, when Everett was sliding closer, his fingers tracing up my thigh.

"I'm sure I could figure it out."

I lifted a brow, not looking away from the screen. His fingers reached the hem of my shorts and, after tugging a string, slipped beneath, fanning out across my skin. I kept my stare sharp, pretending my heart hadn't flipped into my stomach and my blood wasn't pumping hot through my veins.

"Mitochondria," he began. I glanced at him, and he raised a snarky brow at me. "Powerhouse of the cell."

"Do you even know what that means?"

"That it powers the cell," he shot back. "Duh."

I rolled my eyes and he grinned back, mischief glinting in his eyes. His fingers crept higher.

"Well, now that that's out of the way..." he trailed off.

I laughed.

"I suppose I could spare five minutes."

"Perfect."

CHAPTER 11

"I sla."

"Wake up."

"Isla."

I groaned, rubbing a hand over my eye. The room was too bright. Had I left my blinds open last night?

"Good morning, sleepyhead."

I opened my eyes only to immediately squeeze them shut again.

"Everett?" I murmured, my voice thick with sleep. I had forgotten he was here. It all felt like a dream. Except, he was here. He was really here, with his fingers in my hair and his leg pressed up against mine. I shifted onto my side to find him sitting up beside me. "What time is it?"

"Time for you to get up," he replied. "There's a lot we need to get done today. I owe you breakfast, you know?"

I shoved my face into my pillow. "Five more minutes?"

"That's five less minutes we have together."

I looked up, narrowing my eyes into a glare. "Are you trying to guilt trip me?"

"Is it working?"

I paused. He batted his lashes at me, smiling innocently, and I rolled my eyes. "Yes. Let me go brush my teeth."

He bolted out of bed, a wide grin on his face. "Yes! Great. So, I heard of this café a few minutes away, I was thinking we could—"

"Oh, shit." I paused, my phone gripped in my hand.

Everett's mouth snapped shut as he turned to me. I sat at the edge of the bed, my legs swinging off, feet brushing the floor as I unlocked my phone. I stared at the time, the date glinting at me beneath it, along with a reminder I'd set weeks ago. 3 days to midterms.

"I completely forgot," I continued, pressing a hand to my face. "I have, like, three days left until my midterms start. I'm sorry, Ev. I really need to study today."

"Oh." I didn't have to look at him to know his smile had fallen, but I did anyway. A whisper of a frown grazed his lips before they were tugging into a small smile again. "It's okay. We can postpone it, yeah?"

I nodded, shooting to my feet, and rounding the bed to face him. "We can get breakfast every day. And—And I mean, summer's not far away, right? Or—I mean, your summer. We can spend every day of every week together. I've still got some savings. Maybe I could go visit you in New York?"

His smile grew, but it was still a shadow of the grin he'd had earlier. I hadn't visited him in New York yet.

While I was in school and he was starting college, our holidays never seemed to line up—not until Christmas, and Christmas in Shellside Bay seemed to outrank Christmas in New York. At least, that was the case for Everett.

Christmas in New York meant family bonding with his dad and new stepmother. It meant cold weather and slippery roads. Shellside Bay was hot sand, surfing, and a few weeks with his grandmother.

So, I hadn't visited New York yet. Sometimes I wondered if he even wanted me to visit. It wasn't like he ever brought it up.

"Alright," Everett said eventually. He leaned closer, pulling me into his arms and squeezing me in a brief hug. "You start studying. Maybe you'll finish early, and we can watch a movie or something."

I smiled, leaning up to press a quick kiss to his lips. "Did I ever mention you're the best?"

"Not as often as you should," he teased.

By the time I got out of the bathroom, Everett had vanished. Frowning, I grabbed my laptop and stalked out of my room. As expected, he was sitting in the kitchen, River standing behind the counter.

"Look at you two bonding," I teased, taking a seat beside Everett.

"Yeah, we've had a lot to catch up on," he said, throwing a look at River.

River snorted. "By that he means he just realised I'm gay." He spun suddenly, glancing between us with a growing smirk. "Hold up. I know you said you were jealous of Isla moving in with me, but does that mean you were jealous that whole summer?"

Everett's eyes grew wide, his ears tingeing pink. "No."

"Oh, shit, you were!" River's smile stretched across his lips, and he pushed away from the counter, throwing an arm around me, and tugging me towards his chest. His eyes flashed at Everett. "Jealous?"

I rolled my eyes, throwing River's arm off of me and taking my place beside Everett. I set up my laptop and books, deliberately letting my arm brush his with each movement, a small reminder that he was there—That this was real.

"So, I've only got two more subjects to revise," I started. "I could probably get it done by dinner?"

"Don't push yourself," Everett replied. His fingers grazed my elbow and I leaned towards him, turning to throw him a reassuring grin.

"It's fine, this is a first-year subject. How bad can the exam be?"

Everett's smile wavered and he glanced away, pushing off from the counter. "Well, either way, just don't push yourself too much. I know how overboard you can go with things sometimes."

He rubbed his jaw knowingly and I rolled my eyes, shoving him. He staggered to the side with a laugh.

"I don't go overboard. I give the appropriate response to the appropriate annoyances."

Everett waved a hand.

"Whatever you say," he replied, though the smirk on his face clearly didn't agree. "I'm going to shower and try dig out some fresh clothes from my bag."

He was behind me now, leaning forward to press a soft kiss to my head. His hand smoothed my hair down before squeezing my shoulder reassuringly.

"You've got this," he said.

I nodded, turning back to my laptop.

I had this.

I had this.

I had spent hours studying and writing notes. I hadn't missed any lectures. This should be easy to review. I pulled up my syllabus, silently reading the first learning outcome.

My smile fell.

I didn't have this.

The first learning outcome—a week one concept, the easiest of them all—and I already couldn't remember learning it. I mean, I could remember learning it. I remembered sitting in the lecture hall, excited to be attending my first lecture, nervously sitting alone while the other first-years seemed to be chatting in groups already. I remembered my professor and sending a sneaky photo to Everett—but I didn't remember what was on the slides that week. What had we done in the lab?

I exhaled, scrolling further down. It was fine. That was weeks ago. Surely something more recent... My eyes landed on the next outcome. Then the next.

Oh God, I really didn't have this.

My head fell into my hands. In the distance, I could hear the shower turn on, Everett preparing for a day that was supposed to be spent with me, pretending through the streets of Sydney.

"Bet you wish you did business now, huh?"

I spun to find River standing behind me, his phone in one hand and a half-eaten muesli bar in the other. He took another bite, smiling at me teasingly with a mouth covered in oats.

I groaned, rolling my eyes, and turning back to my laptop.

"I've got this, River," I said. My voice sounded so confident, I started to believe myself.

It would be fine. I had already finished my biology revision last week, so I only had this subject and statistics to revise before my exams. That was plenty of time.

I sucked in a sharp breath, straightening my back, and beginning to open my old notes and practice quizzes.

It'd be fine.

Behind me, River took another loud bite from his muesli bar. I squeezed my eyes shut, grimacing at his loud chewing, chewing, chewing, then another bite. River was never a loud eater. In fact, he'd definitely elbowed Connor before for chewing with his mouth open.

He was intentionally trying to annoy me.

Huffing, I grabbed the nearest object—a banana—and whirled, tossing it directly at him.

I was slow enough that he had time to lift his hand, the banana knocking his elbow rather than his face and falling to the floor.

"Take your muesli bar elsewhere, River," I seethed.

He smiled, slowly reaching the bar up to his open mouth and my hand reached for another banana. He stopped, laughing, and holding his hands up in defence.

"Alright, alright," he said. He leaned down, swiping the banana and holding it up at me. "Thanks for the banana then, roomie."

I narrowed my eyes into a glare, watching as he made his arrogant way back to his room. Turning back to my laptop, I sighed.

Now I could focus.

I had this.

□□□□□□□□□□

Clink.

I blinked. A coffee cup had appeared beside my laptop. Spinning, I found Everett smiling back at me. He lifted his hand to show a brown paper bag. "Hungry?"

As soon as he asked, I realised just how hungry I was.

I nodded eagerly as he took his seat before frowning. He'd changed out of his pyjamas. When had he finished his shower? When had he left?

"What time is it?" I asked.

"Two-ish," he replied, and my heart sunk.

"Oh, God," I muttered. My eyes shot up to Everett's. "I'm so sorry. I just wasted the whole day, didn't I? I didn't realise how quickly time went, and there was just so much I didn't know, and I haven't even started on statistics yet—"

"Isla," he interrupted, setting the paper bag beside the coffee cup. "It's fine. I want you to do well in college. Besides, we'll have plenty of time to hang out later. Weather's pretty shit anyway."

I laughed lightly, deciding not to correct him on "college". Instead, I leaned forward to peek into the bag, finding a toasted sandwich and a cookie. As if on cue, my stomach growled loudly.

I warmed, turning to grin at Everett. "You have no idea how hungry I am."

"Well, my plan was to grab you lunch, but you know that café I mentioned? Turns out it's an hour away. And I got lost. It wasn't even that good. I bought this at some stall down the road."

My hand flew to my mouth, stifling a laugh and he rolled his eyes, slumping into a seat beside me.

"Go ahead and laugh. Your city is more confusing than mine," he muttered.

I chuckled, pulling the sandwich out and taking a large bite. God, that tasted good. Everett smiled at my reaction, raising a brow.

"Good?"

I nodded eagerly, shoving another bite into my mouth before I could even swallow the first.

His smile grew. "I'm glad it was worth the two-hour train ride."

"So worth it," I agreed through a mouthful of food. Behind him, I noticed River kicking his shoes off, a coffee cup in his hand too. My eyes widened. "Did River go with you?"

Everett nodded.

River craned his neck from afar, quickly tuning into the conversation. "We had a boys' bonding trip."

"He slept the whole train ride, and he's the reason we got lost," Everett dead panned.

"Great bonding, though," River added.

"I'm sure." I grinned.

Before I could move onto my cookie, there was knocking at the door. I paused, meeting Everett's eye, then River's.

"Are you expecting someone?" I asked, expecting Alistair to appear before us. He seemed to have become our third roommate recently.

When he shook his head, I frowned, dropping the paper bag onto the counter, and moving to open the door. Instead of Alistair as I expected, Lachlan stood at the threshold.

"Lachie!" I exclaimed, blinking.

"Hey, Isla." He grinned, lifting his arm which clutched a laptop and booklet to his chest. "You up for a study date?"

I lifted my brows. I was always ready to study together rather than stressing out by myself, but today—

"Study date?"

I spun, finding Everett standing behind me, arms folded as he watched Lachie. Lachie didn't even hesitate.

"Everett!" he exclaimed, as if they were reunited best friends. "You're Isla's boyfriend, right? I'm Lachie."

Everett didn't respond. His eyes stuck onto Lachie, unwavering as he stared him down in silence. I cleared my throat, stepping back and gesturing towards the kitchen.

"I'm already set up on the counter, Lachie," I said.

He nodded, grinning, and waltzed right past me to set his own things down. As I closed the door behind him, I turned, nudging Everett in the stomach.

"What are you doing?" I whispered, frowning at him.

"Me?" he echoed quietly. His eyes darted towards Lachie, then back to me. "What are you doing?"

"Aren't you the one who told me to make friends?"

"Well, yeah, but..." He caught my pointed look and sighed. "I don't like that he gets to stay here when I leave."

Smiling, I stepped closer to him, throwing my arms around his neck.

"Yeah, well, I chose you, didn't I?" I asked, before standing onto my toes and pressing a quick kiss to his lips. He leaned closer but I stepped back, trailing a finger along his chest and turning towards the kitchen. "Let's go study, lover boy."

"Great," Everett muttered. "Exactly what I wanted to be doing during my spring break."

"Maybe if we get this done quickly," I began, throwing him a grin over my shoulder and lowering my voice to a whisper, "We can do some other fun things later?"

Everett glowered, but his mouth snapped shut as he followed me back to the kitchen.

It seemed River had retreated to his room, leaving Lachie sitting at the counter with his study material laid out in front of him. He turned to me as I retook my seat beside him, pushing my paper bag away. The cookie would have to wait for later.

"The library was so full today. The only seat I could find was next to this girl eating hard shell tacos, literally crunching it all over her textbooks," Lachie explained with a grimace. "I guess everyone's cramming for mid-terms."

"Glad I'm not the only one," I said. "I've been working on this all day. I didn't realise how little I knew, and we're only half-way through the term."

"At least these mid-terms are worth a lot."

"How is that a good thing?" I sputtered.

"If you do well in these, it's easy-going for the rest of the term." He shrugged, leaning towards my laptop. "You're up to week five?"

I nodded, subconsciously leaning further away. I could practically feel Everett right behind me, glaring daggers into Lachie's head.

"I'm pretty much done with this. I just have statistics left now, and then all those practice exams to go through," I said.

"Lucky for you, I'm a master of statistics," Lachie said.

"I did statistics too," Everett chimed in. We both turned to him, and he pursed his lips. "I mean, I took a course on it. Last year."

The silence turned heavy, and I cleared my throat, attempting a cheerful voice to break the tension. "Great! I've got two statistics tutors all to myself. I'm basically set to ace it at this point, right?"

"Well, where are you up to?" Lachie asked, sliding my statistics book closer.

"Can we just start from the beginning?" I chuckled, tugging on the hem of my sweater. "I'm kind of a dunce with this subject."

"Of course," Lachie said, smiling. "It's a tough subject. Let's begin with standard deviation and z-scores. The basics of the basics."

I nodded, leaning over the book to flip to the page where I'd scribbled definitions—definitions that were no help, considering how I didn't even understand those.

"Right, the basics," I echoed, frowning at the page. It felt like gibberish to me. "Standard deviation, that was..."

"This formula," Lachie said, leaning towards me. He pointed at a spot on the page filled with scribbled numbers and Greek letters that I hadn't labelled. I blinked, vaguely recognising it.

"Right, and the N stands for number?" I asked.

He hummed in confirmation, leaning closer to add a label to the page. "Number. Size of population. Whatever you want to call it."

"Oh, right!" I exclaimed, the formula starting to come back to me. "And this letter, that's for the mean of the population, isn't it?"

"Yep!" He added another label before turning to grin at me. "Good work, Isla."

Suddenly realising how close we'd moved towards each other, my smile wavered.

"Thanks," I muttered.

"You know, you're much smarter than you give yourself credit for," he continued, smiling. "You shouldn't doubt yourself so much."

"Thanks," I repeated. Why did I feel so embarrassed? My face warmed and I inched away.

Lachie's smile didn't falter. His lips parted to speak again—

"Luke," Everett's voice cut in. He leaned closer, his hand slamming onto the counter between us, causing us to jump further apart. "Did you say you have a girlfriend?"

Lachie blinked, though his smile still refused to slip. "I didn't say, but no. No girlfriend here, mate."

"Interesting," Everett replied. His smile seemed more like a snarl to me, but Lachie didn't seem to notice.

"It's Lachie, by the way," he added.

Everett's smile turned innocent. "Sorry?"

"My name. It's Lachie. Short for Lachlan."

"Isn't that what I said?"

"You said Luke." He shrugged, waving a hand. "It's fine. Guessing you Americans don't meet many 'Lachie's, hey?"

Everett blinked, his expression morphing into a grimace, and he turned away, pushing off the counter. "Guess not."

"Maybe Isla will rub off on you if you guys date long enough," Lachie added.

Frowning, Everett turned back. "We've been dating for over a year, you know."

"Over a year?" His brows shot up. "Isla never mentioned it."

Everett glanced at me, and I warmed. It had never really come up in conversation. Everett turned back to Lachie, his back straightening.

"Well, it's true. I visit pretty often too, you know. I've known Isla since we were both in high school," Everett continued. "She used to live in Shellside Bay, and we spent two summers there together."

I rolled my eyes. He was really starting to layer it on thick now.

"That's good," Lachie said, smiling. "I've heard long distance can be hard."

"Not for us," Everett said quickly. "We're doing great. Really great, actually. I mean, I'm here for another week and a bit, and then my summer break's coming up soon."

"You really visit every break you get? Isn't that expensive?"

Only then did Everett waver. It was only a second, a glimpse of a frown, but it was quickly replaced with indignation. "No. We're doing great, Luke. You just don't know Isla like I do—"

"Everett," I cut in. He looked at me and I sent him a stern frown, hoping he'd get the message.

He clearly didn't.

"Isla—"

"No. This is—" I let out a long breath before turning to Lachie with a weary look. "Lachie, can you excuse us for a second?"

"Nah, yeah, go for it," he said, waving a hand. He gestured vaguely to his books. "I'll just look for my stats notes and get started."

I smiled a thanks before narrowing my eyes at Everett and leading the way to my room. Once we were safely behind a closed door, I spun to face him.

"What was that whole dick measuring contest about?" I asked, frowning.

"What do you mean?"

I scoffed.

"Bragging about how long we've known each other? How long we've been dating? Calling Lachie the wrong name?" I listed. "It's like you're trying to make it clear I'm your—your possession or something."

"No!" Everett breathed. He stepped closer, his hands flying to my waist. "No, Isla, that's not how it was at all. I didn't mean—"

"What did you mean then?" I asked. "Do you not trust me or something? I told Lachie that I had a boyfriend the day we met, Everett. I'm not stupid, and I'm not unfaithful either."

"No, God." He sighed running a hand over his face before frowning at me. He lifted a hand to hold my face, keeping his eyes on mine. "I didn't mean it that way. I trust you. It's just—I don't know. Seeing him close to you, seeing him compliment you and talk about stuff that I just don't get, and don't get to do while I'm in America."

He sighed again, his eyes finally dropping.

"I got jealous," he admitted. "I got jealous that he gets to see you whenever he wants. He can text you without calculating time zones, he can help you with college classes and go to lectures with you. I just—I wish that was me."

My heart shattered, the pieces sinking into my stomach and stabbing the flesh there. It was my turn to take his face into my hands.

"Oh, Everett," I mumbled. "I don't care about the distance. I'd choose you every time. You know that."

"I know, I know," he said. "I just wish we could be like a regular couple. I wish I could give you that life you deserve."

"You're making it sound like it's a chore to date you," I said pointedly.

He chuckled, lifting a brow. "Isn't it?"

"Oh, it is. Especially when I have to lecture my boyfriend for fighting with my literal only friend at university," I teased. He smiled and I leaned closer, pressing a quick peck to his lips. "But I love every second of it. Of course, I wish I could have you here all the time, but I'd rather have you long distance than not at all."

He frowned at me, unsure. "Really?"

"Of course," I replied.

"Good," he said, leaning in until his lips brushed mine and his breath fanned over my face with each word. "Because you're stuck with me, you know?"

I smiled back. "Wouldn't have it any other way."

I lifted onto my toes and connected our lips. He smiled into the kiss, his arms wrapping tightly around my waist as he pulled me forward until his back hit the wall. In one swift move, we were flipped, and his hands were on my hips, my thighs, lifting me until I was sliding up the walls with my legs wrapped around him.

His tongue slid over my lips and into my mouth and I sighed at the taste of him, at the feeling of him. I grabbed his shirt, pulling him closer, closer, as if possible.

He was here, and this was real—at least for another week or so.

I had my Everett back.

His lips moved from mine, tracing a path over my jaw to the skin of my neck. His teeth scraped against a spot beneath my ear, and I released a breath, squeezing his shirt in my fist.

"Everett," I whispered, my head craning back, my chest moving up towards his.

Outside, a door slammed, and we both froze, our minds ripping back to the present. Quiet footsteps echoed, and then River's voice, to who I could only imagine was Lachie.

"You're still here?" River asked.

Everett met my eyes, our grins matching each other's.

"We'd better get back out there before River scares off my only friend."

And we went back out, together.

CHAPTER 12

L ast Summer

"Get in the car, we're going on a road trip."

I stopped in my tracks, halfway through closing the front gate to my house. Everett was in front of me—or more accurately, Everett sat in the driver's seat of a car in front of me. A fancy car. I blinked.

"Everett did you steal a car?"

"Depends on your definition of steal."

"Take without asking."

He hummed. "No. No, I definitely asked."

I rolled my eyes striding up to the driver's window to frown at him. "Whose car is this?"

"My grandma's," he replied easily.

"This?" I gazed over the red, soft-top Porsche and frowned. I couldn't imagine Mrs Clemente cruising down the highway in this car, the wind blowing her glasses and dentures askew. And even more—I knew Everett's family was well off, but a Porsche? Even my old, beat-up car had been a 1997

Mitsubishi that had cost me a few thousand from my old neighbour. Compared to that, this car could've been a Ferrari, worth millions, and I would've had the same reaction.

"Are you getting in or what?"

He didn't have to ask me twice. By the time I reached the passenger's side, Everett had leaned over to push open the door for me. I slid into the cool leather seat and looked around in wonder. This car was probably worth more than my house.

"So, where are we going?" I asked, buckling my seatbelt.

He grinned at me. "It's a surprise."

I quirked a brow, suddenly unsure. "Should I bring, like, an overnight bag or something?"

"We'll be back by then." He turned the key and the engine roared to life. I startled, facing him uneasily as he flicked through the buttons on the console. My frown only deepened.

"Are you sure you can drive in this country?"

He glanced at me, a wide grin on his face. "How hard can it be? It's just all... reversed. Right?"

"Not exactly."

"We'll be fine." His left hand left the wheel and wound our fingers together. "Ready to head to Sydney?"

I snorted. "I thought it was meant to be a surprise."

"Shit," he muttered. He shook his head, frowning. "Can you pretend you never heard that?"

"Heard what?"

Everett chose the worst possible time for a spontaneous visit because my midterms didn't finish until Everett's last day in Sydney.

Our week together was filled with stolen moments between studying, assignments, and Everett's stubborn jetlag. They were kisses between study breaks, lazy cuddles in the mornings we were too tired to get up, and... slightly more than cuddles in the nights we couldn't sleep—him because of his perpetual jetlag, and me because my mind was filled to the brim with formulas and definitions.

It seemed every time I shut my eyes, a number or a biological structure floated beneath my eyelids.

It didn't matter, though. Exams were over, and I'd done the best I could. Everett was back in America. And I still had a few days before my first class back at uni.

I rolled over in my bed, groaning into my pillow. Why did he have to leave right when my schedule freed up? We'd barely done all the things we'd had planned.

Really, I just wanted him here to hold, to talk to, to complain to—just here with me.

Before I could turn over and wallow in my own self-pity further, my door was thrown open.

I sat up on my bed, eyes wide to find River standing there, his head freshly shaved in the choppiest haircut I'd ever seen and a fire in his eyes.

"River?" I sputtered.

He marched into my room, tossing a duffel bag onto my bed.

"What are you doing? I could've been naked or something!" I screeched.

"Get packed," he said simply. "We're going to Shellside Bay for the weekend."

"What?" I blinked, hard. Was I dreaming? Had I slipped into a coma somewhere along the night? I reached for my phone, squinting at the time. "It's three in the morning, River. Why are you awake? What happened to your hair?"

"Why are you awake?" he shot back, narrowing his eyes.

I glared back. "Touché."

"And I shaved it," he said, answering my second question.

I snorted, stepping out of my bed to cross the room, and run a hand over his choppy hair. "I can see that. Looks like you shaved it with a chainsaw. Why?"

His mouth opened, then he hesitated. He turned away with a shrug. "Get dressed and get packed. We leave in fifteen minutes."

He left my room without a look back, leaving me with a sagging duffel bag and confusion. Stunned, I stood and began to pack, tossing random clothes into the bag—whatever was clean—without any thought.

Why did River suddenly want to go to Shellside Bay? And at three in the morning?

I snorted at the idea. In a way, it was like the old River had come back, the Summer River, the River who loved spontaneity and stupid ideas, because that was what our summers had been crafted of after all.

Ever since we'd arrived in Sydney, he'd morphed into this River I'd never seen before. He was still River, but he had lost that spark that he seemed to carry on his shoulders and in his smirk back at Shellside Bay.

River in Sydney was all about moping and sleeping in, parties with no meaning to them, daily hook-ups with Alistair who seemed to be a bad replacement of Connor—and between all that, I'd barely had a moment with him.

Maybe he needed Shellside Bay as much as I did in that moment.

Fifteen minutes later, true to his word, River reappeared at my door, a bag slung over his shoulder and a hood pulled over his shaved head.

"Ready?" he asked.

I nodded. He turned, and I followed him as we left.

"We swapped!" Sky exclaimed, grinning, and pointing between her head and River's.

Her hair had grown a few inches since I'd last seen her in person and it seemed to jut out at all angles, brushing the tips of her ears. She leaned forward in the backseat, grabbing River's hood, and tugging it completely off his head.

Her lips twisted in a grimace. "My shaved head looked way better than that, though."

River frowned, pulling the hoodie back over his head. "Why did I decide to pick you up on the way?"

"Oh, come on River," she teased. "You know Shellside bay isn't the same without all the Nauti Buoys."

"It's also not the same when summer's over," I said, lifting a brow. It was true—we were all dressed in hoodies and sweatpants. Summer had ended. This was Shellside Bay in autumn mode.

"Shellside Bay in autumn is better than no Shellside Bay at all," Sky added wisely. She leaned forward again, her seatbelt pressing against her chest. "So, what's the plan, Riv?"

"Riv?" I echoed.

"Bad nickname?"

"Horrible," River replied with a glare. He shot us a half-shrug; his eyes focused on the road as he drove. "I was thinking go for a surf, take the Nauti Buoy for a spin, and then wrap it up with a classic bonfire tonight."

"A bonfire party in autumn?" I frowned. While bonfires were a summer staple in Shellside Bay, they definitely weren't as much of a thing in autumn.

In autumn, the sun set earlier, and the heat of the sand faded quickly, the sun ducking behind clouds pushed by wind. It wasn't the same.

"Well, I think a bonfire party sounds great," Sky said, grinning.

"You think any party is great," I said.

She shrugged, her grin growing larger.

"That's my kind of attitude," River said, reaching a hand out. Sky slapped it in a high-five, and I rolled my eyes, leaning back into my seat.

"Did you tell Austin and Connor about these plans?" I asked.

River's smile wavered. "It'll be a surprise for them."

I blinked, exchanging a look with Sky before turning towards him. "You didn't even text them?"

River shrugged. "They'll find out soon enough. We're thirty minutes away."

"Besides, they probably won't even check their phones," Sky chimed in.

I released a breath, sinking into myself. She was right. A few months away from the Nauti Buoys and we'd managed to fade into monthly texts and clipped conversations. The most depth I'd had in a conversation with Connor since I'd moved to Sydney was a reply to an Instagram story.

"They're busy working," I muttered because it was true. Not that it made it hurt less.

"Exactly," River affirmed. "Which is why I didn't bother texting them. It's more fun as a surprise anyway."

"Is it though?" I asked, tilting my head.

River scoffed. "Just because you didn't like your surprise doesn't mean you need to shoot it down, Isla. They'll love it."

"Whatever you say, River," I replied. "So, who are we surprising first?"

His face fell, his brows scrunching and lips parting before he shook his head and tapped his fingers against the steering wheel.

"Austin," he said with a nod. "We'll surprise Austin first."

Austin wasn't home.

Austin wasn't home, or at work, or at Connor's, or at the beach. Neither was Connor. No, both had vanished into the mysterious world of construction sites, hours away from Shellside Bay.

I frowned, digging my toes further into the sand.

After the surprise was a bust, we'd parked by the beach. The beach that I'd grown up on. Had it always been that small? That empty? Was the sand always that brown? I remembered it whiter.

I walked up to Clemente House to see Everett's grandmother, Mrs Clemente, and visit my mum for her lunch break at the café near there.

Even my mum seemed to have changed in the time that I'd been gone. Her skin had turned paler, her hair chopped short. It looked longer on camera, in our video calls. Her voice was the same though. Her smile, her hugs.

I'd needed one of her hugs.

A thirty-minute lunch break wasn't enough to even touch on the existential crisis that university had brought on.

When I got back to the beach, River was standing at the shore, the water up to his knees where he'd rolled his track pants up. Sky was watching from the sand, her feet buried in the sand, and I joined her.

Minutes of silence ticked past us.

I leaned towards her, knocking her shoulder with mine.

"How long has he been standing there?" I asked.

She sighed, shaking her head. "Since you left."

"And he's just been standing there?"

We both turned to look at him, watching as he kicked at the water, took two steps forward, then stilled.

"I think he really needed that surprise," Sky muttered. She lifted her knees to her chin. "He needed something to go right."

"What he needed was a reminder of summer," I said.

As much as he tried to avoid saying it aloud, it was obvious to me. He needed the Nauti Buoys together and his shaved head. A surfboard over the waves and his boat, speeding towards Isla in forty-degree heat.

He didn't need to say it to me. I knew because I needed it too.

"Except summer's over," I continued, pulling myself to stand. I dusted the sand off my clothes. "Austin and Connor are working, the sun disappeared hours ago. Even the Shack is closed."

"You want to tell River that, or should I?" Sky teased.

I shook my head, beginning to trace my path across the sands. River heard me before he saw me, my feet splashing wet sand and sea foam behind him. I came to a stop beside him, tilting my head until I was looking at him directly, as much as he refused to turn to me.

"What are you doing?" I asked.

He kicked at the water, finally looking at me. "Water's shit. No waves. Bad surf."

"Well, maybe tomorrow—"

"Doesn't matter," he cut in, turning, and beginning to walk back to the sands. "It's getting dark anyway. People will be here soon."

I frowned, trailing after him. "I texted Austin and Connor. I know they have work tomorrow, but I'm sure they'll come, at least for a bit."

"They will come," River said. He didn't turn to look at me, only continuing to wade through the water towards Sky on the sands.

"Of course, they will," I replied.

It wasn't until the sky had turned completely dark, the sun disappearing over the horizon and the shore creeping higher up the sand, that the boys turned up.

I stood beside Sky, holding a beer to my lips as we stood at the edge of the party. The bonfire was burning hot, the music was loud—everything was just how it was in summer, and yet nothing was the same.

Half of our graduating class had vanished. They had either moved out of Shellside Bay or, like Austin and Connor, were stuck working. We were all adults now, after all. Not everyone had time to drink on the beach at a bonfire, as if tomorrow wasn't a promise.

"Do you have any idea who these people are?" Sky muttered to me; her voice low beneath the music.

I shrugged, taking a swig of my drink. "I think they're the grade below us from high school?"

"Ah," she murmured. "Children. Enjoying life. Not thinking about their chemistry group project due in two weeks which, if they fail will delay their graduation by at least another semester. They don't know how good they have it."

I snorted, elbowing her in the ribs. "You're talking like you're about fifty years older than you are."

"I feel fifty years older after these past few months."

"You can say that again."

I held my bottle out to hers and we clinked them together in a cheer before lifting them to our mouths simultaneously.

Suddenly, an arm was slung around my shoulders. I turned, half-way through shoving it off of me, only to find Connor's grinning face. Behind him, Austin stood with a matching smile.

My eyes widened, a sound that was a mix of a gasp and a squeal spluttering from my lips, and I jumped forward, pulling Connor into a tight hug.

"Oh, my God!" I shouted.

I threw my arms around his neck, squeezing him, before pulling back, my eyes darting all over him. His face, his hair, his clothes. He still wore his work clothes, and I felt a strange sense of not belonging. When had he become those tradies that I used to see on the bus? When had he become a man?

I shook my head, smiling at him. "Look at you! Your hair is longer!"

He shrugged, pushing a hand through his hair. "D'you like it?"

"Like it? You look like a proper surfer boy now," I teased. I grabbed his face in my hands, forcing him to look at me properly. "And you're so tan! You have freckles! It's, like, basically winter. How the hell did that happen?"

He shrugged again, chuckling, and wriggling out of my grip. "I work outside every day."

"I hope you've been wearing sunscreen."

He rolled his eyes. "All this about me, look at you."

"Me? Nothing's different about me!"

He shook his head, gesturing towards me. "Your hair is longer and darker—did you dye it or something?"

I frowned, subconsciously pulling at a curl. "No, I—"

Before I could finish speaking, Sky flung forward, pulling Connor into a hug. She squealed, repeating the same things

I'd said in a higher pitch, her voice probably loud enough to alert the entire beach of their arrival.

Behind her, Austin smiled at the pair before turning to me. He waved awkwardly before shifting it into pushing his hair back.

I stepped towards him, smiling. "Hey, Austin."

"Isla," he greeted shortly.

I laughed, rolling my eyes, and opening my arms. "Give me a hug you big idiot. I haven't seen you in months."

He didn't have to be told twice. He stepped forward, scooping me into a big bear hug, his arms wrapping around my waist.

We pulled apart and I took a second to really look at him. Like Connor, he was tanner, his hair turning a lighter shade of brown. Or had it always been that brown? I couldn't remember anymore. He'd cut it shorter, like how he used to on the first day of school, when his mum would take him to the hairdressers and tell them to cut it inches shorter than he'd wanted. And he still wore his work clothes, neon orange with spots of dust and dirt splattered across it.

He must have caught me looking at his clothes because he dusted them off and said, "Sorry. Did I get your clothes dirty?"

I blinked, meeting his eyes. "Oh! No, no. I was just thinking ... It's so weird that you're, like, a proper working adult now."

He laughed, tugging on his shirt. "It is weird, isn't it?"

I nodded eagerly. "Yeah, it's like just yesterday you were this annoying kid who wouldn't stop bothering me in surf club."

"I was the annoying one?" He quirked a brow at me.

I grinned. "The most. The annoying-est, really."

"If you say so." He paused, shifting his position, glancing over my shoulder, then looking at me again. He cleared his throat. "So, how's Everett?"

I shrugged, looking at the sand for a moment. "He's good. He's busy with university—I mean, we both are—but he visited just the other week."

"Right, you texted me about that, didn't you? Sorry I didn't reply. Work's been so busy lately, I've just..." he sighed, running a hand over his face. "I've been exhausted."

"It's okay," I said. I offered him a small smile. "I get it. Really. Uni's kind of killing me. I just spent the past two weeks cramming for midterms. I have no idea what I'm going to do if I don't do well in them after all that."

Austin let out a laugh, shaking his head. "You'll do great, Isla. You've always been the smart one of the group."

"That's not really saying much when I'm stuck with you drop kicks who care more about surfing than studying," I teased.

He laughed, his eyes drifting over my shoulder. A grin erupted on his face, and he lifted a hand.

"River!" he shouted.

Behind him, Connor's head snapped to the side, watching as River strode across the sand. He reached Austin first, slapping hands and pulling each other into a short hug.

"What the fuck happened to your hair?" Austin asked, slapping him on the back of his neck.

River scowled, shoving his hand away. "I don't see or hear from you cunts for months and that's the first thing you say? Where the fuck have you been?"

"Work is busy," Austin said, shrugging.

Connor stepped forward. "We can't all have rich parents like you."

Normally, we would joke about River's rich parents as often as we breathed, but this—Connor's voice—it sounded almost like an accusation. The first thing he said to River in months, and it was this.

River frowned, turning to face him. They stared at each other for a moment until I cleared my throat, stepping between them.

"Well, you're here now," I said. "Can I grab you guys a drink?"

"Oh, no," Austin replied instantly. "I shouldn't. I have to wake up in, like, six hours."

"Same here," Connor said, waving a hand.

"Oh." I frowned. "Well, maybe a surf could cheer you guys up? Like our old bonfires in the summer, y'know?"

"No, I, uh—" Connor cleared his throat, fishing his phone out to glance at the time. "I actually need to get going soon. But, hey, it was great seeing you guys again. Maybe we could grab dinner tomorrow?"

"If I don't have to do overtime," Austin muttered. He shook his head. "I'll try finish early. Maybe we could take the Nauti Buoy up to Isla for it or something."

I glanced at River, gauging his reaction. He nodded curtly, his jaw clenching tight. There was a second of silence, where we could only hear the quiet music in the background, mostly drowned out by the rising shore and growing chatter, before Austin spoke.

"Well," he began, "I'd better get going. It was nice seeing you guys."

Connor nodded, stepping beside him. "Same here. I'll, er, see you guys soon. Yeah? Tomorrow."

I lifted a hand in a short wave, watching as the pair turned, disappearing almost as quickly as they had appeared. Once their silhouettes had completely faded into the night, I turned back to River.

Sky was watching him too, neither of us sure what to say. River looked away, lifting his drink to his lips. The fire flickered before us, reflecting in our eyes and on the glass bottles of our drinks.

We were in Shellside Bay, except everything had turned a little bit colder, a little bit quieter, and suddenly, it didn't feel much like Shellside Bay at all.

Chapter 13

L ast Summer

I laid down on Everett's mattress, letting the cold breeze from the overhead vents wash over me and my sun-kissed skin. Even at night, after the sun had long set, the Australian summer air remained thick with heat and humidity. The cold air was like a breath of relief, soaking through my bones.

A day on the beach had left my skin buzzing with heat and sun sleepiness, and lying here with Everett's body beneath me, his chest pressed against my back, only made my eyes heavier.

Except, I didn't want to sleep. I wanted to stay awake. I wanted to savour every minute we had together, every second. I couldn't let the time slip past us.

Everett shifted from beneath me, one hand resting loosely on my waist, the other tugging a curl that sat on my fore-head—an escapee from the bun I'd piled my frizzy curls into. I tilted my head up, meeting his eyes.

"Everett," I muttered. He hummed, looking down at me. "What were you like in high school?"

"In high school?" he echoed. "Why do you want to know?"

I shrugged, struggling to turn to properly face him. His hands slid over my back, holding me at my waist as I straddled him.

"I just figured that we never went to school together. We never will. I want to know what high school Everett was like." I poked him in his side, grinning. "Were you popular?"

"Oh, yeah. People turned wherever I went. Parted ways like the red sea. I was the Justin Bieber of my school, you know?"

I snorted, poking him even harder in the side. "Stop teasing me."

He chuckled, his hands sliding over my hips to rest on my legs. "I don't know. I had friends. It was high school. I don't know what to tell you."

"Tell me, like—where did you sit to eat lunch? What did you wear to school?" I paused, my lips twitching. "Were you a good student?"

"I sat in the cafeteria. There was like this one bench near the middle of the room that was right under the vents, so it had the best heating in winter. And then, after I—well, when I got back from Australia and online school, I started sitting on the bleachers. I wore a hoodie most days, which is why I have so many for you to steal. And yeah, I was a decent student. I didn't have the best influences around me, so I was in and out of trouble, but I got good enough grades."

I let my mind wander, imaging those bleachers that he'd sit on, imagining Everett sitting in a classroom, a textbook in hand, studying Pythagoras or something. It was hard to imagine an Everett that didn't live on the beach. His fingers squeezed my thighs and he grinned up at me.

"What about you?" he asked.

"Me?" I scoffed, my smile turning smug. "Oh, so now you're curious too?"

He rolled his eyes, but his grin grew wider. "Just tell me. In lots of detail. I want to imagine it."

He settled further into the mattress, closing his eyes theatrically and waiting for me to begin. I giggled, pinching his bicep, but he refused to give up.

"I'm..." I trailed off. "I don't know."

"See, it's harder than you think." He was looking at me now.

"It's harder for me because we have uniforms. And besides, Shellside Bay is so tiny. There's only, like, fifty kids in my whole grade. We don't have a cafeteria."

"I want to see you in your uniform."

"You weirdo," I teased, but his words made me warm anyway. I could imagine it for a minute, us going to high school together. Him teasing me for how high I would roll up my skirt. I imagined him ditching his blazer and unbuttoning his shirt collar, always getting into trouble by the teachers. Maybe we'd meet by the lockers and jig class together. I could almost imagine it. An Everett that was here, permanently.

"Do you think we'd be friends?" I asked.

"What do you mean? Are we not friends right now?" He gestured towards his lap, where I straddled his hips. "I'd say this is pretty friendly."

I snorted, whacking his chest. "I mean in school. If we met in high school, in class or something. Would we be friends?"

"We'd be friends," he said. He sounded certain. "I would've seen you on my first day and followed you around like a lost puppy. I would've enrolled into all the same classes and found a way to sit next to you in all of them. One day, you'd drop your eraser onto the floor, and I'd pick it up for you and place it on your desk and when you'd turn it over, you'd see my number scribbled on the back."

"You've really thought this through," I said, laughing. "I wouldn't call it. Your number, I mean. I'd think you were a total weirdo. I'd probably chuck it away."

"You'd call it," he said. "Extremely hot trumps total weirdo anytime. Besides, you have a thing for American guys."

"You're never going to get over that, are you?"

He shook his head, his fingers squeezing my legs as he looked up at me.

"Anything else you want to know?" he asked.

"I want to know everything possible," I said.

"I'll tell you," he replied. "Just ask, and I'll tell you everything about me, but you have to tell me too. Deal?"

I smiled back, dozens of questions already flooding my brain.

"Deal."

□□□□□□□□□□□

I sat on the sand, my knees drawn up to my chest. Sky and River sat on either side of me, Sky resting her head on my shoulder while River frowned out at the horizon.

The beach around us was empty. No beach towels lined the shores, no umbrellas stuck into the sands, no bobbing heads or surfboards dotting the oceans.

I never thought I'd miss the tourists that seemed to flood this tiny town in the summertime.

Further down the shore, a few school students tossed their uniforms onto the sands, revealing swimsuits underneath. They laughed in those squealing, high-pitched giggles that high schoolers always seemed to do before they turned, sprinting into the cold waves.

Sky sighed, leaning further into me.

"Remember when we used to do that?" she asked. "Skip school and just mess around on the beach?"

"You mean when there were more than just the three of us," River added.

I turned to him, frowning. "Austin and Connor aren't dead."

"They might as well be," he muttered.

"River!"

"Just look around, Isla!" he snapped. "We drove all the way here and where are they? We've seen them for, what? A total of five minutes? Face it. We're not how we used to be, and we never will be again. Everyone's busy with their own lives now."

He was right, but it still hurt. I turned away from him, glaring out at the ocean. It pissed me off.

It pissed me off that I had nothing to say to him, nothing to counter with, because he was more right than he knew.

I'd realised it the second Everett left Sydney the first time, then I realised it all over again when he left a few months ago.

As much as we tried, as much as we wanted it, we'd never be the same again. Our scattered phone calls, our late-night texts, our conversations where we held back our complaints, trying not to worry each other because let's face it, there wasn't anything we could do 10,000 miles away—they were nothing compared to our summers together.

The Nauti Buoys had officially died with the end of summer.

"You guys are such buzzkills," Sky chimed in. She pulled herself to her feet, sand sliding off her legs as she stood before us. "Yeah, maybe it sucks that we can't hang out as much as we used to, but we made it. How many other people can say they escaped this town? Moved to the city and got into university?"

"You say that like it's a good thing," River said.

Sky narrowed her eyes at him, her grin souring. "I know you're a city boy and take it for granted, so I'm going to let that slide for now."

"She's right, River," I said, nudging him. He turned to me, and I shot him a smile. "I'm living in the heart of the city with my best friend. Why are we complaining?"

His lips twitched and my smile grew. I jabbed him in the ribs.

"I mean, other than the fact that you're hell to live with, it's pretty great," I added.

"Me?" he scoffed. "You leave stuff everywhere."

"I left my books in the living room one time."

"One time too many."

"I just went to the bathroom for a minute!" I narrowed my eyes at him. "And besides, you're the one bringing strange people home and throwing ragers every weekend."

"Which you love."

I rolled my eyes but couldn't help the grin that split across my face.

"I only love them because I love you," I teased, leaning towards him.

He shoved me away, laughing and scrunching his face in mock disgust. "Of course, you do. It's hard not to."

"Hey!" a voice shouted.

We all spun, finding Austin walking towards us. His hair was messy, and he wore his work clothes, stained with smudges of dirt and splatters of what I assumed to be paint.

"Austin!" Sky squealed first.

I scrambled to my feet just as he reached us, and I pulled him straight into a hug. He laughed, pushing me away and gesturing to his clothes.

"I'm filthy," he pointed out. "I don't want to get you dirty."

"Since when have I cared about a bit of dirt? Come here you big idiot."

He relented and I grabbed him into a tight hug. It was cut short as Sky pulled us apart, taking him into her own arms next. She squeezed him tight, pretending to try and lift him off the ground despite being half his size.

"What are you doing here?" I asked. "Aren't you supposed to be at work?"

"I'm on break," he said. He squeezed Sky's waist and lifted her up, eliciting a giggle from her. He grinned back at me, placing her on the sand. "Figured I'd find you guys here."

"Is Connor with you?" River asked, slapping his hand in greeting.

Austin shook his head, frowning. "I texted him, but he said he got held up."

The hope in River's eyes died and he glowered, sinking back onto the sand. I snorted, rolling my eyes. If it wasn't obvious that River was only here for Connor before, it certainly was now.

"I missed you," I said to Austin, shifting the topic away from River's depressing atmosphere. "We've barely been able to talk since we got here. No, since we left in the first place."

"Yeah, sorry," Austin sighed. "It's been crazy here. Connor and I are fresh meat so they're working us to the bone. It's like, I'm out the door before sunrise and home by sunset, and my brain and body are so fried I just go straight to bed."

I whistled lowly. "That sounds rough. I can't believe I was complaining about uni to you yesterday. Like, all I have to do is read a couple books."

He shoved my shoulder, chuckling. "Come on, Isla. Don't sell yourself short like that. There's a reason I didn't go to uni, and it's definitely not because it's easy."

He paused to glance over at River who had gone back to sulking on the sand and leaned in close to whisper. "What's up with him?"

I followed his stare, my frown mimicking his own. "He's depressed that summer ended. He just... misses what we used to be, you know?"

"Oh, believe me, I know," Austin muttered. He ran a hand over his face, sighing hard. "We used to run this beach. Bonfires, surfing, boating out to Isla. Now all I do is wake up insanely early, work until my eyeballs are sore, and then sleep until I have to work again. Like, I know I have texts I need to reply to, and phone calls I need to return, but I just—I get off work and have zero energy and—" he paused to release a tired laugh, shaking his head. "Look at me. I'm just ranting now. How are you? And Everett? Every time I pass your house, I miss you even more."

I shrugged. Really, I couldn't stop thinking about everything he'd just told me. I couldn't imagine Austin working his bones off every day, too tired to even glance at his phone. The Austin I knew was always full of energy, spending his days running from the sea to the sand. This Austin—his eyes seemed too dull to be the Austin I always knew.

He was busy with his own problems. I couldn't throw my problems on top of all that.

So, even if I was burnt out from uni and not understanding half my content, I wouldn't say it. Even if I was frustrated that Everett was 10,000 miles away, and he was probably asleep at this time, and the only time I could video call him was between classes and while I brushed my teeth at night, I wouldn't tell Austin that. Instead, I smiled lightly, and looked towards the ocean.

"I'm good," I said. "We're both good. We're making it work. He might come down in the summer and we can all be reunited again."

"Cool," Austin said. "That sounds cool. Maybe I could take some time off and we can pretend it's like the old days."

"That would be awesome," I replied. The thought of us all spending our summer just lazing around the beach was already exciting me. "I'll see when Everett's break matches up with mine and we can—"

I was interrupted by the sound of Austin's phone buzzing in his pocket. He jumped, pulling it out with an embarrassed smile, and glanced at the screen.

"It's work," he muttered. Suddenly, he looked ten times more exhausted than before. His entire face seemed to fall, and I wondered briefly if his body would fall with it. Instead, he shook his head and released a hard breath. "I'm sorry, Isla. I need to go. Talk later?"

I nodded. Before I could even say goodbye, he had turned, making his way back across the sand towards his car. I watched him walk away, his retreating back. It seemed to be the only thing I'd be seeing of him these days. Austin leaving. Everett leaving. Connor leaving. And soon, Sky would be leaving again.

The autumn breeze of Shellside Bay whipped at my hair and I wrapped my arms around myself, suddenly feeling a little colder, a little emptier than I did before.

CHAPTER 14

I woke up to my bedroom door slamming open.

I turned in my bed, squinting at the hallway light. A silhouette with choppily shaved head stood in the doorway. I frowned.

"River?"

"I'm leaving," he said.

"What?" I murmured, burying my head into my pillow. "I'm sleeping."

"I'm leaving, Isla. I'm sick of this shit. I'm going back to Sydney."

That woke me up.

I shot up, my hands rubbing the sleep out of my eyes. He didn't say anything more. Instead, he walked towards me, flopping limply onto the bed, his head hitting my lap over the blanket.

"What are you talking about?" I asked, my voice still groggy. "How did you get in here?"

"Your mum let me in."

"What?" I sputtered. My mum left for work early in the morning before the sun was even up. "What time is it?"

"Five," River replied. He turned his head, his voice muffling through the comforter. "I hate Shellside Bay."

"Don't say that," I said, returning my attention to him.

I'd worry about interrogating my mother later for letting a strange boy with a badly shaved head in mismatched clothes into our house unsupervised while I was sleeping. Knowing how much she loved River, though, it was unlikely to change anything.

I'd never seen River like this before. Sure, he moped and complained a lot, and he had a tendency to look on the negative side of things, but a River who hated Shellside Bay was unheard of.

Shellside Bay was his escape.

It was where he went to escape Sydney, to hide from his parents, to get away from school. I didn't know what life was like for River in Sydney before I moved in with him. He refused to talk about it, always shifting the topic to Shellside Bay.

If he was claiming to hate Shellside Bay now, something was very wrong.

"River," I said, my voice turning as stern as possible while still thick with sleep. "What's wrong? Did something happen?"

"No," he said, his words vibrating against the blanket. He rolled over to the other side of my mattress and glared at the ceiling. If I looked to closely, despite the darkness, I thought

I could see redness rimming his eyes. "Nothing happened. That's exactly the problem."

I frowned. "I don't see how that's a problem."

"You don't see how it's a problem?" he echoed. He twisted onto his stomach to glare at me. "I drove all morning to Shellside Bay only for all of our friends to be busy the entire time and for Shellside Bay to be—be shit. I mean, we haven't even visited Isla yet!"

"I'm right here, River."

His glare turned sharper. "You know what I mean."

"Of course, I know what you mean. It's not like I've been having the time of my life here either. It's like, Everett's too busy for me, Austin's too busy, Connor's too busy. I just—" I sighed. "It's not what it used to be. Nothing is."

River sniffed. It was quiet, but the whole room was. The whole town was. So, I could hear him. And I could hear the shaky breath he released right after it.

Abruptly, he sat up, the entire mattress shaking with the movement.

"I'm leaving," he said again.

"You can't leave," I replied. "You're my ride home."

"You can leave with me, or you can find another ride, but I'm going," he said, and I knew he meant it.

I'd never seen River like this before and I thought if he spent another minute in Shellside Bay, he might spontaneously combust or something.

"I can't stay here any longer," River said, his voice an almost-whisper. "Be honest, Isla. Is it really worth staying here for another day or two? What are you going to do? Sit on the cold beach? Wait around for Austin to free up five minutes of his time to grace you with a conversation?"

I narrowed my eyes at him. He was being unfair. Austin and Connor had jobs. They couldn't just up and leave whenever they wanted. It wasn't like they wanted to ghost us for our entire surprise trip.

"How about you be honest, River? Austin's not the one you're really upset about," I replied.

River's face hardened. He stood up and walked straight to my door.

"I'm leaving at noon. It's up to you if you're coming or not."

□□□□□□□□□□

In the end, River was right. I would never tell him that to his face because it would inflate his ego so much that his head would probably explode, but he was right.

As soon as the sun came up, I dressed and dug out my old bicycle to ride to Sky's house.

Sky's house was exactly what you'd think if you heard the words 'beach house'. Her porch basically stepped out onto the sand a little further down from the main beach, and its walls had chipped into a faded wood that gave it a sort of vintage charm.

Sky was sitting on the steps to her front door when I saw her.

"What are you doing here?" she called to me as a way of greeting.

I hopped off my bike, walking towards her. "What? Not happy to see me?"

"It's barely morning," she replied. "Shouldn't you be asleep?"

"Shouldn't you?" I asked.

I reached her and sat on the steps beside her. She shrugged. A cold breeze bit past us and I tugged my hoodie—Everett's hoodie—around myself tighter.

"My house is so noisy. I forgot what it was like with all my sisters around," she said.

Sky had five younger sisters which sounded like a nightmare to me, as an only child in a tiny house. I supposed having two parents and a big house didn't make it any easier on her.

"River's leaving," I said. I thought it would be best to rip the Band-aid off. "And I'm going with him."

She spun to me, her eyes growing wide. "Already? The weekend's not even over yet."

I shrugged. "He's having a shitty time."

"Because Connor's not giving him attention?" Sky asked. She gave me a knowing look. "He's such a teenage girl sometimes."

"Can't blame him, honestly. It's a bit dead here. It wasn't always like this, was it?"

"It's a small town," Sky replied.

We both frowned, staring out at the ocean. The tide was still high, creeping up towards us on the sand with each wave.

It wasn't much of an answer, but I knew what she meant. Maybe if we'd met in Sydney, everything would be different. But then, everything would be different.

"Sky!" a voice shouted from behind us, through the thin walls of her house. A string of words in Khmer followed and Sky sighed.

"I have to go help make breakfast," she said, standing and brushing the sand off her shorts. "I'm going to stay here until my midterm break is over. Is that okay?"

"Of course," I replied, standing with her. "Will you find a ride?"

She nodded and before I could turn back to my bike, she leapt forward, pulling me into a tight hug.

"I love you, Isla," she muttered. "We're still getting used to everything. It'll be fine in the end."

"I love you more," I replied.

We let each other go and I watched her walk back into her house before I left. I wondered when I would see her rusted fly screen slam shut again.

❑❑❑❑❑❑❑❑❑❑❑

When I got back home, my mum was there.

I'd stopped by a few shops along the way, sitting at cafes I used to study in back in school, dropping by to visit Everett's grandmother, buying snacks I could never find in Sydney.

I shucked my shoves off, dropping my bags of junk in my room before making my way through the living room. I wouldn't have noticed her if she hadn't spoken.

"Are you leaving?" my mum asked when she saw me.

I didn't know how she knew. That was the thing with mothers, they always seemed to know. I nodded.

"River's driving me back up to Sydney at noon. I just needed to grab a few more things from my room. Why are you home so early?"

"Clemente House is empty during off-season," she replied.

We looked at each other for a moment. She was sitting at our old, creaky dining table. It was strange. I'd only been gone for a few months and I could already see how she'd aged.

Lines dipped into the skin beside her mouth, marking her smile even when her lips were still. Her forehead had similar wrinkles. Even her hair had turned a little greyer. Had she always looked like this?

People seemed to age faster when you didn't see them every day. It was more sudden that way. It wasn't one or two grey hairs each day. It became a whole head, an entire streak of grey and white in the months that passed.

She must have been seeing the same in me because she suddenly opened her arms, silently pulling me into a hug.

I held her head to my stomach in a tight hug, still standing over her as she sat.

"Are you alright here, Mum?" I asked when we pulled apart. "You're not lonely or anything?"

She laughed lightly, shaking her head. "I've gotten used to being alone since your father died. Before that, really. He was different those last few weeks, you know? Quieter. Less lively. He wasn't him anymore. I should've seen it coming. Been more prepared."

"You could remarry," I suggested. I didn't really want a new stepfather, but Everett's dad seemed to be happy ever since he remarried, and all my mother deserved was happiness.

She shook her head again, this time with certainty.

"Your father was the only one for me," she said. She looked up and met my eyes. "I've been thinking about travelling."

"Travelling?" I echoed. I grinned, blinking at her. "You should. Of course, you should. Where would you go?"

She sighed, wiping her hands on her pants, and shrugged. "I don't know. I just—this house is so much quieter without you and now that I don't have to pay for your tuition or anything, I was thinking of touring the world. Maybe Europe. Your father always wanted to visit Germany."

"Germany?" He'd never seemed like a Germany type of guy.

"For the beer," my mother said, reading my mind. "I think I'll start there."

"You should do it," I replied. "And text me every day. Ten times a day. And three video calls."

"Alright, alright," she laughed. She reached up, tugging one of my curls before running her hand over my arm. "I'm so proud of you. You know that, right?"

"Of course," I said. I squeezed her should and smiled. "I'm proud of you too, Mum. You have no idea how much I've missed you."

"You have to tell me before you visit next time. I might not be here."

I laughed. "In that case, I'll meet you in Europe somewhere. Germany. Italy. You name it."

"It's a deal."

At that moment, a car horn sounded outside. I jumped.

"That must be River," I said, checking my watch. "He's almost an hour early."

"Go pack," my mum said. She stood, pulling me into another tight hug before covering my face with kisses. "I'll see you soon, okay? Be good at school."

"Always," I replied.

I ran into my room, gathering all my grocery bags into the one duffel I'd brought with me before digging through the rest of my drawers.

I'd forgotten a lot of things when I left for Sydney—my favourite hairbrush, my pack of floss, candles to burn in my new bedroom—but the most important thing was in my bedside table, buried deep in the drawer there.

I shoved my hand inside, digging around old notebooks and tangled jewellery until my fingers closed around it.

My seashell.

Outside, the car horn honked again.

My favourite hairbrush and vanilla scented candles didn't matter. I tightened my fist around my seashell and grabbed my bags.

And I left Shellside Bay again.

CHAPTER 15

L ast Summer

Austin had a summer fling.

It was kind of becoming his thing. Every other month, he'd show up to the beach with a new girl; one from our grade, one from the year above us, one from out of town. Always someone new.

He'd always been popular, and short-term girlfriends seemed to follow wherever he went, but he'd never had as many as this past year.

I wasn't sure what it was all about. Before Everett appeared and turned Shellside Bay upside down, Austin would tell me everything. Even without telling me, I could read him. I knew his every thought. I could tell how he'd react to something before he even knew himself. Every twitch of muscle in his face, every slight drop of his eyelids—I could read it all.

Last summer, everything changed. Now, I didn't even know his coffee order, much less about why he was seemingly dating every girl that breathed near him.

Maybe he wanted to prove he was over me. Or maybe he was still trying to move on. Maybe he was just having fun before we graduated and officially became adults.

Whatever it was, he was always with a new fling, and this one was no different.

Diane was a tall, local girl just two years older than us who liked to go by Dia—which, with an Australian accent sounded a bit too similar to 'dire' and had the same number of syllables as her full name, so it wasn't really a nickname, but we went with it anyway.

They'd only been together for a month, but one day she showed up to the beach with a gold necklace shining on her collarbones.

"Pretty," Sky said, leaning uncomfortably close to scope out the infinity pendant. "Where'd you get it?"

"I got it for her," Austin jumped in, smirking proudly. He wrapped an arm around her waist, pulling her closer, and she giggled, tugging on her necklace. "Nice, isn't it?"

"I love it," Dia said. "Isn't he the best?"

Sky and I nodded in agreement, and she giggled again. For the rest of the day, she kept tugging on her necklace, her fingers unconsciously wrapping around the metal every time I looked at her.

That night, I lay on Everett's mattress beside him, soaking in the air condition of his room. His arm was wrapped under my back and around my waist, his fingers tracing patterns on my stomach as we stared at the ceiling.

"Do you regret choosing me?" he asked.

I frowned. "What do you mean?"

"Choosing me over Austin," he clarified. "Do you regret it?"

I spun, my heart sinking into my stomach. "What? Why are you asking that? Have you always thought I'd regret it or something?"

He shrugged. "I don't know. I mean, you liked the guy for years. He was your first love. And he liked you back. Why didn't you choose him?"

"You're insane if you think there is any universe where I would choose Austin over you," I said. I leaned down to kiss him. "And besides, you were my first love. He was just—I don't know. He was comfortable."

"Am I not comfortable?" he teased.

"You're... I don't know how to explain it. It's like my life was still and then you came into Shellside Bay and suddenly everything was moving so quickly, and it was all moving towards you, you know?"

"I think so," he said. He paused, his eyes flittering away before returning to mine. "I just think that Austin could've treated you better. He's a local. He could get you nice gifts and take you on dates whenever you want. I can't do that for you."

"First of all, I'd love you whether or not you bought me things, Ev," I chided. "Secondly, you give me hoodies all the time. And you spend your money on expensive flights just to see me throughout the year. That's more than I could ever ask for."

"But I didn't buy you a necklace," he said. He frowned, his voice growing low. "I bet if I didn't spend all my money on plane tickets, I'd be able to buy you a necklace. I'd buy you ten."

"I don't need a necklace," I replied. I kissed him again, this time slowly. When I pulled back, he leaned up towards me. "I have you."

His lips twisted and he looked away. "Are you sure you don't mind?"

"Of course."

"I just—I want to spoil you, you know?"

"You spoil me enough just by being here," I said.

His expression soured, his lips pulling into a frown, eyes flittering away for a moment. Then, his eyes widened slightly with an idea, and he was reaching past me, the mattress bending beneath us as he pulled something off his bedside table.

He looked back to me, something hidden, clutched into his fist.

"What's this?" I asked.

His eyes glittered at me. "It's a gift."

"A gift?" I inched closer.

He took my hand, opening my fingers to rest his fist in my palm. Something cold touched my hand and he moved his fist away, revealing a seashell.

"It's not necklace, but—"

"It's a shell," I muttered. I turned it over in my hand, running a finger along the chipped edge. "From Isla."

"You remember it?"

"Of course, I do, I'm the one who found it last week," I replied.

It was nothing special but seashells weren't common on Isla and so I'd gotten excited when I found it half-buried beneath the sand. That was, until I'd seen that it was chipped on the corner.

"I threw it back," I said, awed as I turned it again. It was as if it had reappeared in thin air, re-emerging from the corners of my memory.

"I picked it back up," he said. "I wanted to keep it as a memory of you and of Shellside Bay, but now I want you to keep it. Not much of a gift, I know..."

"It's better than a necklace," I replied. I squeezed my fingers around the shell, memorising the curves and ridges and that sharp, jagged edge where it'd been chipped.

I imagined him watching as I threw it back into the sand then, when my back was turned, kneeling down and digging for it again. I imagined him wiping the sand off the shell, cleaning it, turning it over his fingers and placing it on his bedside table, thinking of me the entire time.

I smiled. "I love it."

□□□□□□□□□□

I had about four assignments and one week to do them all. I hadn't started yet.

Instead, I was lying on my bed, staring at the ceiling, pretending the assignments might get done themselves, or the ten lectures I had to catch up on would absorb into my brain as I lay there.

What I really wanted to do was talk to someone, hang out with someone—hang out with Everett.

Even thinking about it upset me. I turned, my eyes landing on my seashell that I'd set on display beside the rest of my sentimental junk—the melted piece of plastic Austin had given me, my dad's snow globe, and my photographs.

Groaning, I turned the other way, grabbing my phone in the process.

Everett couldn't talk. He was busy. We were always busy. I didn't want to think about it. So, I called someone else.

By the time I got to the coffee shop, Lachie had already ordered himself a coffee and gotten us a table.

It didn't take me long to start ranting.

"I just don't understand. It's like, I'm paying them thousands of dollars and for what? For professors to read off of slideshows for an hour? How am I supposed to learn anything from that? How am I supposed to feel motivated to watch them? Or worse, attend them? I just—I have no idea what I'm doing. I can't work up the motivation to do anything now. There's just so much, I don't know how to start."

Lachie listened to me silently. He lifted his mug, taking a slow sip before placing it back onto the table with a clink.

"None of us know what we're doing," he said simply. "I just did a quiz for a subject I forgot I was taking."

I snorted, rolling my eyes, and shoving his shoulder. He laughed, shrugging.

"What? I did. I actually passed too. Can you believe it? One of the questions asked something about gravity and I drew a hot dog for my answer."

"You're an idiot," I said.

"Point is," he replied, "Nothing ever makes sense. Yeah, it's pretty shit, but that's uni. Trust me, half your class haven't started their assignments yet either. Don't sweat it."

"You think?"

"I know. Hell, half my hallway hasn't attended a lecture since week one," he said. He smiled at me. "Isla, you're doing fine. Relax."

I sighed, my shoulders sagging in relief. Lachie was my only friend in university, other than River who barely counted considering how much time he spent in his room rather than in class or with me, and so I hadn't realised that other students were in the same boat as me. It was different from high school. It felt like they'd taken an entire year of high school and shoved it into a term of uni, and I was drowning beneath the waves of assignments that only built up every week.

"Look," Lachie said, drawing my attention back to him, "how about this—start with the assignments that are due first. There's still a few weeks until our finals so you have time before you need to catch up on all lectures. Just take them slowly. And look, for our class, I'll send you the notes I've got so far. How's that?"

I narrowed my eyes at him. "You've been taking notes?"

"Well, not yet, but I was planning to catch up this weekend."

"The key word being planning."

"I'm a very organised person, thank you very much. It's definitely going to happen."

"In that case, it sounds good," I said, smiling. "Seriously, Lachie, you're saving me here."

He raised his mug to me in a mock cheer before lifting it to his lips and draining the last big of his coffee. He stood then, fishing for his wallet in his pocket.

"I should get going, then. I have work in an hour, and you can never trust Sydney trains," he said. "I'll just go pay for this and walk you back?"

I nodded. "I'll wait outside."

I pushed out of the café doors, feeling the bite of cold wind hit my bare shoulders. People seemed to rush past me, crowding the streets. I shrunk back into the window of the café, hoisting my bag in front of me. At that moment, my phone began to ring.

I jumped, digging through my purse to find my buzzing phone, my heart instantly beginning to race as I spotted Everett's name flashing on the screen.

"Everett," I answered chirpily.

His voice came raspy through the other end. "Hey, Isla."

"What are you doing? Shouldn't you be asleep?"

"I'm about to sleep. I just wanted to hear your voice first," he replied. There was some shuffling in the background, and then he said, "You never told me how your trip to Shellside Bay was. Did you get to see Connor and Austin?"

I almost snorted. Our trip to Shellside Bay had hardly been anything to talk about.

"Not really. They were both busy with work the whole time." I paused, smiling. "But guess what? I brought your shell back with me this time. It's next to my bed at home."

"The shell? I thought said you'd keep it in Shellside Bay, so you don't lose it."

"I won't lose it," I said.

He laughed lightly. "Not that I don't believe you, but what if you do?"

"Then I'll just find another shell," I replied without pause. "Next summer, when you come to visit."

When—never if.

"Or I'll buy you that necklace after all," Everett said.

I snorted. "I don't want a necklace."

I just want you here.

I didn't say it. I couldn't. Everett went silent on the other end, and I wondered if he was thinking of the same thing. Or if he was picking out a necklace in his mind.

Beside me, the glass door to the café opened and Lachie stepped outside, his eyes on his wallet as he pocketed his cash.

"Alright, I paid, should we get going—" he cut himself short as I turned to him, my phone pressed against my ear.

"Oops," he whispered, smiling coyly. "Sorry."

He gestured me to continue my call as he stepped back, giving me privacy. I turned away, tuning back into Everett's voice.

"Who was that?" he asked. "Was it that Luke guy?"

"Lachie," I corrected. My voice lowered. "Yeah. We're just grabbing coffee."

"Coffee? Since when do you drink coffee?"

"I don't really. Lachie does. I just came with him."

"And he just needed you there to drink coffee?"

"Why are you getting jealous?" I scoffed. "I was just stressed about uni. I needed to rant to someone."

"You could've called me."

"No, I couldn't have," I snapped. "It's night-time there. I thought you were asleep."

"Before that, then."

"When? When you were in class? When I was asleep? When Everett? When should I have called you?"

He fell silent and guilt tore through me. I wanted to swallow my words. I sighed, breaking the silence first.

"I didn't mean that," I said. "I'm sorry. I was just—I didn't mean it."

"No, I'm sorry. It's stupid of me, being jealous," he replied. I couldn't tell based on his voice whether he was upset, but my guilt only grew anyway. There was no way my words hadn't hurt him. I shook my head, frowning.

"It's fine," I said. "I know you just want to be here. I want to be with you too. It's just—it's out of our control."

"Yeah."

We both fell into silence again, tension drifting between us through the form of unspoken words—words that didn't need to be spoken, because we'd spoken them a million times. How much we missed each other, how much we wanted to see each other—how impossible that would be.

Behind me, a few steps away, Lachie waited, his hands deep in his pockets.

"You'd better get to sleep," I said eventually.

Everett took a second to reply. "Yeah. Yeah, I should. Do you have class today?"

"Yeah, statistics," I said. "And about a billion assignments to work on."

"Well, good luck. Text me, yeah?"

"Of course."

We both paused.

"I love you, Isla," he muttered. "A lot."

"I love you more," I replied.

I hung up first.

CHAPTER 16

T he next day I woke up to banging on the door.

Loud banging.

I shot up in my bed, my eyes wide as I glanced at my phone. Barely sunrise. Who was at our front door?

The knocking didn't stop, not even for a second, so I groaned, forcing myself out of bed. River was already in the hallway when I opened my bedroom door.

"Expecting someone?" he asked me in an indignant drawl.

I narrowed my eyes at him—at the accusation. "No. Are you?"

He shook his head and we both turned back to the shaking front door. The last time this had happened, it was Everett, surprising me from New York.

I blinked hard. I couldn't get my hopes up. There was no way he'd be able to visit me again so soon. And yet my pulse quickened as I stepped up to the door.

Just as I was about to yell out, who is it? A voice shouted from behind the banging.

"River let me in!"

My eyes widened and I ripped the front door open without a second thought.

"Connor?"

He stood in front of me, his expression softening for a moment before his eyes landed on River behind me. Just like that, the anger behind the banging returned.

His eyes flashed and nostrils flared as he pushed past me to reach River, who he shoved with two hands planted against River's chest. I inhaled sharply, my hands flying to my mouth as he pushed him again.

"Where did you go?" Connor spat.

River's expression seemed to drift between confusion and fear. Connor seemed to tower over him, but River refused to back down. His chest puffed as he glared back at him, in his usual River fashion.

"What do you mean?" he asked. "What the hell are you doing here? Did you drive all the way up from—"

"Where did you go? I looked everywhere for you; I've been texting you. You left Shellside Bay without telling me! Without saying goodbye."

"Oh, like you've never ignored my texts?" River was shouting too now. "You were too busy to see us, even when we drove all the way to see you, you big dumb arse! You have no right! You have no right to act all high and might and—and—"

"Me?" Connor sputtered, interrupting him. "I have no right? That's fucking rich. You just—after last year—" he cut himself off and shoved River again until his back was against the wall. "You're the one bringing shirtless boys back to your bedroom!"

The two fell silent. I froze, still trapped at the front door, too scared to slip past them and go back to my room.

River released a breath, so shaky that I could see his chest move from where I stood. The tension had grown so thick, I felt as though I could barely breathe. My mind raced. Was he talking about Alistair? Why would Connor care about Alistair?

"You knew?" River murmured after a long pause. "Is that why you never replied to my texts?"

Connor's eyes fell. He shrugged, then reluctantly, he nodded.

"Sky told me," he said.

River snorted. He lifted his chin, challenging Connor.

"So what, then? I can't fuck around with other guys? You're not my boyfriend, Connor. We barely even kissed."

Kissed?

I held in a breath before I could say something stupid, my eyes widening. River hadn't mentioned anything about a kiss. What was this about a kiss?

Whatever had happened, the memory of it was making River angry now. He shoved Connor hard on his chest, moving closer to size him up.

"You never replied to my texts," he spat. He shoved him again. "You never answered my calls!"

"That doesn't give you the right!"

"You don't have the right!" he shouted back.

"You don't think I wanted to? What was I supposed to do? You were gone! You kissed me and then did nothing for a year! And then Sky tells me there's a shirtless guy in your apartment? What the fuck River? What was I supposed to do?"

"You're not my boyfriend," River repeated, and it sounded like his words held more weight than he was trying to let on.

Connor must have heard the weight in his voice too because he shoved him back, his hands slamming against the wall beside his head as he leaned into him.

"You think I care about that shit? You think I'm worried about what people think? About who knows? The whole world can know, River, I don't care about that. That was the last thing on my mind since you—since we—"

River was unaffected.

"You're not gay, Connor. Don't do this shit." His words were scarily calm. Connor shook his head.

"How would you know? You kissed me and then disappeared."

"What did you want me to do?"

"I wanted you to—to—"

He groaned and shook his head, his jaw clenched so hard that I thought his head might explode.

And then he kissed him.

I gasped, my hands flying right back to my mouth, then over my eyes before I hunched over and finally ran passed them towards my room. I slammed my door shut behind me, my back hitting the wood as I processed what just happened.

Connor kissed River.

And it wasn't the first time that they've kissed.

Holy shit.

I had to tell someone.

Squealing, I jumped onto my bed, grabbing my phone, and typing in Everett's number.

He answered almost immediately, his face appearing on my screen.

He looked tired, with bags lining his eyes and his hair messy like he rolled out of bed and went straight to class. It seemed like he was in his dorm room. When he'd first moved into his dorm room, he'd given me the grand virtual tour and now I could recognise his shabby bookshelf in the back, his roommate's faded poster on the wall.

"Hey, Isla," he said, grinning. His voice snapped me back to the reason I'd called.

"Everett, you'll never guess what literally just happened two seconds ago."

"Should I try?"

"Okay. You've got one guess."

"Did... your professor get arrested for tax fraud?"

I blinked. "Why would you guess that?"

He shrugged. "You told me to guess."

Shaking my head, I turned onto my back, holding the phone above my face as I kicked my legs in the air. "Connor just appeared at our door, and he was so angry and banging on the door that it woke us up, and River came out and Connor was angry at him—"

"Wait, River came out?"

"Not that kind of out," I chided. "Anyway, he came out of his room and Connor saw him and got so angry about him leaving Shellside Bay without saying goodbye, and then they were arguing about how Connor doesn't respond to his texts and about how they kissed—"

"Kissed?"

"Yeah, right! And then, you'll never believe it." I paused, grinning at the camera for dramatic effect before saying, "He kissed him."

"He what!"

"He kissed him!" I was squealing now.

"Who kissed who?"

"Connor!"

"What?"

"I know."

"I just can't believe—" he cut himself off, his eyes widening as he tilted his head slightly, listening for something I couldn't hear. "Hold on, Isla. Someone's at the door."

He turned his attention to the door behind him, placing his phone upright on his desk. At that moment, I glanced at the time, realising I was probably interrupting him, guilt beginning to tear at me. I would've been just after six in the evening for him. Had he eaten dinner yet?

"Come in," Everett called.

Beyond his head, I could just make out the door creaking open, a boy poking his head through the gap. His voice was quiet, but just loud enough for me to understand his words.

"What's happening, Ev? You coming to Zack's party tonight? We're starting pre-drinks soon."

Everett nodded towards the camera. "I'm on the phone with my girlfriend."

The boy glanced at the camera, stepping further into the room.

"The mysterious Isla," he said. He waved at the camera, and I waved back. "I was beginning to think Everett made you up. I mean, a mysterious girlfriend who lives in Australia? It's a bit of a classic."

I laughed. "Nope. Real and ten thousand miles away."

"So, it seems," the boy said. He turned back to Everett. "So, what? You're not coming then?"

"Nah, I'm going to stay here."

"To talk to your long-distance girlfriend?" the boy scoffed, his tone turning accusatory. He turned back to me. "No offense, Isla."

"We don't get to talk as often as I'd like," Everett replied in a way of explanation.

"Seems to me you guys talk constantly," his friend muttered. He must have thought his voice was quiet enough to avoid being picked up by the phone, because then he said, "Dude, you know there's real girls at the party? Like, live and in the flesh?"

Everett's face turned red, and I couldn't tell if he was angry or embarrassed. Or both.

"I don't give a fuck," he said. "I'm not going."

"You never come. Are you ever just going to live your college life? We only get this chance once, you know."

"How many times do I have to tell you? I'm fine staying here."

"It's fine Everett," I interrupted.

Both boys turned to the camera, blinking as if they'd forgotten I was there.

"What?" Everett asked.

"You heard her," his friend said.

I ignored him, focusing on Everett. I wished he had headphones in, but it was unavoidable. I was the one who called him on a whim. I was the one who had intruded on his evening. On his college life.

"It's fine," I repeated. "Go to the party. I want you live the full experience. You can call me afterwards."

"Isla, I don't understand. I'm fine not going. I don't need to go."

"I don't want you to miss out on anything." My voice quietened. "I don't want you to regret it. Go. Have fun while you can, yeah? Just not too much fun. Obviously."

"Isla..."

"You're awesome, Isla!" his friend cheered, suddenly stepping even closer to the camera. Now I could just about make out his dark features and boyish smile. He seemed the friendly type. He reminded me of Lachie in that way. He patted Everett's shoulder. "Let's go, man. You heard her."

"But what about River?" Everett asked, still ignoring his friend. "And Connor? We were talking about them."

"It's fine. I'll update you later, yeah?"

Not that either of us knew when later would be. It seemed later barely arrived these days.

He seemed unsure so I mustered up my brightest smile yet.

"You know what? I think I can hear them calling me outside. I'd better go check in on them, but you have fun at your party, okay? Come back with lots of stories."

"Alright... I love you, Isla. I'll call you. When you're free, I'll call you, okay?"

I nodded, smiling. "Love you too, Ev. Have fun at the party."

He waved and I hung up, watching as the screen turned to his contact number before slowly fading to black. My reflection frowned back at me, and I groaned, tossing my phone onto my pillows.

If I listened really carefully, I could still hear Connor and River outside, and I knew it'd be a scene I didn't want to walk into, so I turned over on my mattress and stared at the ceiling. And I imagined Everett, halfway across the world, getting ready for a party that I wouldn't be at.

<h1 style="text-align:center">CHAPTER 17</h1>

The next morning, I sat at the kitchen counter, picking apart an old croissant while revising my notes. In high school, revising notes was simple. I'd re-read my old notes, flick through a textbook, answer some questions. Sure, there'd be topics I didn't understand but a few hours of studying normally sorted that out.

Now that I was in university, revising notes only reminded me what I didn't know—which was everything. It felt like I was getting nowhere. It seemed like I'd just filled pages and pages with nonsense; words that blurred together for me, and no one else.

Sighing, I flicked to the next page of my lab manual, frowning at yet another page that I barely understood.

Behind me, a door clicked.

"Morning, Isla."

"Moning, Riv—" I cut myself off, realising it hadn't been River's voice that spoke. I spun, my eyes widening to find Connor walking out of River's room.

Shirtless.

My face must have shown the pure shock I was feeling because Connor smirked, leaning against the back of the couch as he pulled a shirt over his head—the same one he'd worn yesterday.

"Connor," I corrected myself after a moment. "Morning."

River was out next, except unlike Connor, he was fully clothed.

"Don't go walking around shirtless like you own the place," River scolded. He smacked Connor's chest with a wrinkled shirt and Connor laughed, grabbing it from him.

"Oh, so Alistair can, but I can't?" He cocked his head before leaning towards River, pressing a kiss to his cheek. "I'll do what I want."

River pushed him away, fleeing to the other end of the kitchen and filling the kettle. He turned towards the sink, yet I could still see the pink at the top of his ears. Whatever had happened last night—and I was pretty sure I could guess what that whatever was—it had really knocked River down a peg.

He'd gone from his arrogant, confident self into a blushing mess overnight. Only Connor could ever do that to him.

Beside me, Connor pulled the shirt over his head. He yawned, mussing up his hair and glancing over my shoulder at my notes.

"What the fuck is an osmosis?" he muttered.

"You tell me," I replied with a groan. I leaned forward until my head was resting on the counter and Connor laughed, reaching over to ruffle my hair this time.

"I take it uni isn't going so well?" he asked.

"I don't understand anything," I mumbled, my face smushed against the table. "I hate not knowing things."

"It'll come to you," he said easily. "It always does. You were my tutor for a reason."

"We were nine and you didn't know your two times tables," I droned. "It was hardly tutoring."

"Yeah, but now I know that two times twelve is twenty-six."

"It's literally not."

"Twenty-five?"

"One more."

"Twenty-four?"

"Got it."

"See!" he exclaimed, grinning. "I never would have gotten that without you!"

I couldn't help but laugh, sitting back up to match Connor's smile. "Thanks for the confidence boost, Connor."

"Was it a confidence boost?" River's sarcastic voice came from the kitchen.

"At least I tried," Connor replied. Judging by the expression on his face, I could only guess that River had sent him some kind of sour look. He turned back to me, his smile fading.

"Sorry I can't stick around," he said. "I didn't tell work that I was leaving, and I need to get back before my dad finds out."

"That's okay." It was. I understood why he needed to leave. But for the five minutes he'd been here, things almost felt normal. Except now he was leaving again. I didn't want him to leave, but I knew I couldn't stop him. Not even River could get in the way of Connor's responsibilities. I knew that feeling more than anyone.

"I'll come again soon, and we can hang out more, yeah?"

I nodded and he grinned widely, leaning down to pull me into a tight bear hug. I let him take me into his large arms, hold me against his chest. For a moment, I pretended we were children again, saying goodbye on the warm sands of Shellside Bay before our next stupid adventure in the morning. Before he pulled away, he pressed a quick kiss to my forehead.

"You'll be great," he whispered.

I nodded again, letting his words sink into my skin, through to my heart. I needed him to be right. He smiled one last time before stepping past me to reach River at the kitchen. He pulled him into a brief hug, pressing a kiss to his cheek before squeezing his hand.

"I'll call," he promised.

And just like that, he was gone.

The door shut behind him with a quiet click and the room fell into silence. River stood with his back turned to me, putting all his attention and effort into pouring hot water into a mug.

I stared at his back, taking in the redness of his ears, the edges of a hickey poking out of his shirt collar, the wrinkles that zigzagged across the back of his clothes.

Slowly, a grin spread across my face. I leaned onto my elbows, lifting my brow at his silence.

"So," I started. "What was that all about?"

His body tensed and he turned, shooting me a glare. "Shut the fuck up."

"Oh, my God!" I squealed, rounding the table to stand beside him. "What the hell, River? I didn't even know you guys kissed—did you guys... sleep together?"

"Yes, Isla. We slept together. Just slept. We didn't do anything more," he replied lowly. He spoke with annoyance thick in his voice, but his face betrayed him, and his lips twitched into a small smile. He turned away from me, carrying his mug to another counter, hiding his face from me—hiding his growing smile. "We kissed the summer Everett came to Shellside Bay."

I almost choked on his words. "What?"

"We kissed."

I sighed at his nonchalance. "I heard that part, River. When? How? Details? I didn't even know." I followed him across the kitchen, forcing him to face me.

He groaned, rolling his eyes. "Do we have to talk about it?"

"Yes, River! We have to talk about it! It's like—when did you stop telling me these things?"

"I was just—" he sighed loudly. "I was embarrassed, okay? It was after that bonfire party, before you found us hungover at the Shack. I was jealous and too drunk to hide it, and Connor—I don't know. He just kissed me."

"Holy shit," I muttered. I remembered that night. I'd left early. How had I not noticed the next morning? Or the rest of the summer? "And you kissed him back?"

River nodded. Then, quietly, he added, "It was my first kiss."

"Your first? So, then Alistair..."

"Was my second," he filled in. "We went to school together so when I came back after that summer... I don't know. I kept thinking about Connor. And then I kept thinking about all of Connor's girlfriends and flings, and I kept imagining him in Shellside Bay without me. We were never serious, but Alistair was there, and so was I. It just happened."

I frowned, processing his words. So much had happened between River and Connor, and with River in Sydney, by himself. I hadn't even realised. I'd never even asked. River hated talking about his life in Sydney, but it was suddenly occurring to me that it was a whole other life—a whole other River that I didn't know about.

"So, what now?" I asked after a pause. "Connor's going back to Shellside Bay."

He nodded. "We talked it all out. He promised to reply to my texts for once. We're not dating or anything." He paused, eyeing me carefully. "We decided long distance would be too much."

The words struck me hard. Shellside Bay was only a few hours away from Sydney, I'd never even thought of it as long distance.

"Sorry," River said immediately. "I don't mean that it's too much. I'm sure you and Everett—"

"No," I interrupted. "You're right. It is too much."

River said nothing and I laughed, shaking my head at how tense the room had become, all from the mention of two words—long distance.

"It's hard enough not being able to see him when you want, you know?" I said, "But then seeing how guilty he feels about it, hearing the sadness in his voice on the phone... I feel like I can't even complain about things because I can tell he's sad that he can't be here for me. And I know he's doing the same to me. I know he's keeping it all in. I just wish… I don't know." I let out a bitter laugh. "It's almost like the messed-up time zones are the easy part."

"I'm sorry, Isla," he said. He stepped forward, pulling me into a hug. I squeezed him back before we pulled apart.

"It's fine. I'm getting used to it."

"You shouldn't have to. Neither of you deserve it."

"What can you do?" I smiled at him, squeezing his shoulder. "I've missed you, River. You've been so distant since we moved to Sydney. I'm glad Connor came here. You seem… different now. A bit more like the River I knew before."

"I'm sorry," he repeated. I'd never heard River apologise so many times before, especially with no sarcasm laced in his words. "I hate it here. This place reminds me of my parents and then with Connor on top of all that—I was in a shitty mood. I shouldn't have ditched you like that."

"It's fine," I said. I jumped onto him, squeezing him in a quick hug again. "Just don't do it again or I'm moving out."

"Like you can afford rent elsewhere."

I raised a brow at him. "I'm sure I can find another rich friend to leech off of."

"Go ahead and try. You'll come crawling right back to this apartment."

I laughed, rolling my eyes. He was right. This apartment was pretty unbeatable. Never in my life had I imagined living in a luxury apartment in the heart of the city, but here I was. Sometimes I wondered what my dad would have thought about it all.

The thought made River's words hit me again and I frowned. I didn't know his situation with his parents, but if living in his family apartment put him into such a bad mood, I knew it had to be bad. River was always appearing at Shellside Bay in the middle of the school term, escaping something here in Sydney, but he'd never told us about it. He never spoke about it.

I reached out, taking his hand. "You know you can talk to me about anything, right?"

"Oh, please. Don't go getting all sappy on me, Monroe," he teased, ripping his hand away from me and taking his mug, rounding the kitchen table. He paused, meeting my eye with a small smile. "I know. Thanks, Isla. Same goes to you, yeah?"

I nodded and he turned back around.

"You tell anyone about this talk, you're dead."

I laughed, watching as he started walking back to his room. "Love you, River!"

"Whatever!" he called back, and with a slam, his bedroom door was shut.

Smiling to myself, I moved back to my seat where my lab manual and half-eaten croissant sat waiting for me. Nothing had really changed in this apartment, but it was feeling a whole lot warmer than it had felt last night.

I could suddenly envision the next two years and a bit that I'd be spending in this place.

My eyes flickered to my phone, and I unlocked it, instinctively pulling up Everett's messages with the urge to tell him everything I'd discovered.

River could threaten me all he wanted, but one thing he'd learned in the past year was that his secrets with me were also Everett's by extension.

I grinned at the screen; my fingers ready to type out every thought that had slipped into my mind. Except, I'd sent a barrage of messages last night, ranging from 'Have fun at your party!' to an entire ramble about the noises I could hear between River and Connor in the living room. And yet, the messages sat there, unread, not replied to.

I frowned, staring at them as if their read status would change any second.

When they didn't, I clicked my phone off, placing it face down on the counter before dragging my lab manual over it, covering it completely from my sight.

River had been right with what he'd said, no matter how hard he tried to take it back, no matter how hard I tried to avoid saying it—thinking it.

It was too much.

CHAPTER 18

My midterm results were released the next day.

It had barely been over two weeks, and yet it felt like it had been an eternity since I took my midterm exams. It had gone past in a blur of anxious days until I woke up to the blinking notification that stuck a lump into my throat—a manifestation of all my anxieties rolled into an immovable ball.

I sat on my bed, my laptop tilting on the mattress in front of me, cursor hovering over the link to my grades for the exam I'd been most worried about; the biomolecular subject I had with Lachie.

My pulse quickened but I sucked in a deep breath. I'd worked hard for this exam. I studied every day. Even when Everett showed up, ready to spend every waking minute together, I still studied. I put my all into this.

It would be fine.

No, it would be more than fine. It would be good. I'd get an amazing score, and I wouldn't have to worry about my last assignment and final exam. My hard work would pay off. The rest of the semester would be a breeze.

It was going to be great.

Breathing out, I clicked onto the link, watching the link turn purple, waiting as the page loaded.

Waiting.

Waiting.

My eyes fell straight to the numbers, flashing on my screen in bright red. Bright red that blurred suddenly as my eyes began to water. I blinked hard, re-reading the screen. The numbers that were impossible to misinterpret.

Forty-five.

Forty-five out of one hundred.

I hadn't even passed. I hadn't even scraped a pass. No. I failed.

I froze, staring at the screen. This had to be some sort of joke. This had to be a prank, or a mistake. They must have switched my paper with someone else's. They must have misread my name. I must have typed my student number in wrong. It was impossible.

I'd spent hours studying—days. I wasted my nights hunched over my laptop, the screen straining my eyes. I spent calls with Everett, my eyes glued to my notebooks. His entire visit here, I spent most of it flicking through my lab manual. And for what? Failure? I'd never failed an exam in my life, and yet here I was, the bright red forty-five laughing at me from my laptop screen.

I didn't realise when I started crying, but by the time the screen flickered into blackness, my cheeks were already wet, salty tears dripping over my chin and onto the keyboard. I huffed, slamming the laptop shut and moving it to my bedside table, grabbing my phone instead.

It was like the room was spinning around me. Nothing made sense. How could this be possible? After all that? I had been so confident that I was prepared, and I couldn't even scrape a pass?

Now—now, my report due next week was vital. My final exam—I had to pass it. No, I had to do well in it to make up for the lost marks.

My mind was whirring, already calculating how many more marks I'd need for an overall pass. It was too many.

I needed Everett.

My phone was ringing before I could even wipe my tears away. It didn't matter, though, because it rang, and rang, and rang, and he never answered.

My eyes flickered to the time, and I realised it was two in the morning in New York. I laughed, the bitter sound coming out harsh between my sobs.

Instead, I shot him a text, apologising for calling him so late, asking him to call me when he woke up. Maybe it'd worry him. Maybe I wanted him to worry so that he'd call me sooner.

I just wanted to hear his voice.

Except, that wasn't true, was it? I wanted his arms around me. I wanted his words by my ears, whispering comforts so closely that his breath filled the air. I wanted him here. Not that I'd admit it to him.

I sighed, flopping back onto my pillow, and pulling up Instagram. I needed a distraction. I didn't want to think about my marks, about my assignments that had been piling up—about university in general.

What I hadn't expected was Everett's profile picture to pop up at the top of my screen, for him to have a story posted since the last time I'd opened the app.

Frowning, I clicked on it and immediately, my screen was illuminated with bright flashing lights, the camera pointed on Everett as pounding music played in the background. He was with the boy I'd met the other day, as well as some others I didn't recognise. A few mouthed to the lyrics in the background while Everett tossed back a shot, grinning at the camera.

He was at a party.

Before I could process what I'd seen, his face appeared on my screen again, except this time it was his contact number. He was calling me.

I answered without thinking and Everett smiled at me through the screen.

"Hey, babe—" he cut himself short, his smile morphing into a deep frown. "What's wrong?"

"What?" I looked at myself in the corner of the screen, noticing my watery eyes and teary face. I sniffed, wiping at my face. "Nothing. Allergies. Where are you?"

He hesitated. I knew from his story that a few minutes ago, he was taking shots at a party, but now it was quieter. He must have found a room to call me in when he got my text.

"I'm with some friends," he replied eventually. "What happened? You don't have any allergies. Did something happen to you?"

He lied. Why would he lie? It wasn't like he was trying to hide the fact that he was at a party a few minutes ago. He knew I had him on Instagram. Hell, half of his followers were the Nauti Buoys—the only time he used Instagram was to show us what he was up to, halfway across the world.

But now he was covering it up?

This was a mistake. I had called him again without thinking. I interrupted him. If I listened carefully, I could still hear the music in the background, laughter, shouting, singing. And here Everett was, hiding in a room to talk to his crying girlfriend all the way back in Australia.

And what was I crying over? An exam? It was my own fault. I had been too stupid to answer the questions properly. I had been too arrogant, thinking I deserved to go to one of the most prestigious universities in the state despite coming from a tiny, sheltered school in the middle of nowhere.

I was an idiot.

But Everett didn't have to deal with this. Not while he was having fun—finally living the college life.

So, I shook my head and put on my best smile.

"I didn't think I had allergies, but we just don't have that much pollen in Shellside Bay, you know? Sydney's, like, next level pollen. I'm dying here," I said.

Everett didn't buy it. "You texted me. You said to call you as soon as I got your message."

I shrugged. "I've never had allergies before. I thought it was so weird and wanted to show you it, but I'm realising now that you've probably seen allergies before, huh? I should leave you to what you were doing, sorry, Ev. I'll just—I need to take some—what are they called? Antihistamines? Maybe River has some—"

I was rambling. I had to stop. I could already feel that burning behind my eyes again, the promise of more tears to come. Everett frowned at me.

"No, Isla, you're not—I don't mind talking."

I shook my head, waving a hand. "It's fine, I have to get to go anyway. I have class soon. Don't want to be late/"

"Class? Isn't it almost night-time in Sydney?"

Shit. He was too good. Even when he was tipsy, he knew what time it was here. He could read me too well. My smile grew and I forced a chuckle.

"Oh, yeah. It's, like, a non-university class. I'm part of this club at uni that offers extra-curricular classes. They're in the evening so more people can attend. You know, after their compulsory lectures."

"Club? What club?"

"Spanish club," I said quickly. "Well, I should get going. Have fun with your friends, yeah?"

"Oh. Alright. Buenas noches, Isla."

"What?"

His frown deepened. "It's good night in Spanish."

"Oh. Right. I haven't attended that class yet, so..." This was becoming too convoluted. I shook my head, waving to the camera. "Night, Ev."

Before he could reply, I hung up, sighing and holding the phone to my chest.

Spanish club? I didn't even know if my university had a Spanish club. I'd never taken Spanish in my life!

It was all too much. First, I failed my midterm meaning I was on thin ice when it came to passing the subject this term, but now I was lying to my boyfriend? What was happening to me?

When had all of this become so complicated?

Picking up my phone, I turned to the next person I could think of—Sky.

Sky always knew what to do. She would cheer me up. And unlike Everett, we were in the same time zone, so I didn't have to worry about it being past midnight for her.

Before I could change my mind, I tapped onto the call button and waited as it rang. It rang five times before I decided she wouldn't pick it up. She did have a thing for leaving it on silent.

My room was dark. The sun had set since I'd checked my midterm marks and I felt like the darkness was eating me alive. River had gone out for dinner, Everett was at a party, and Sky wasn't answering her phone.

Now what?

I stared at the screen, the brightness straining my eyes in the dark of the room, but my body too lazy and worn out from crying to get up and turn a light on.

Austin's name stared up at me, but our conversation in Shellside Bay was still fresh in my mind. He was probably tired after work. I couldn't burden him with my problems too.

Besides, we hadn't spoken in so long, and Austin probably wouldn't understand. He never cared about his marks in school. He'd probably just tell me it was only a number and that I could do better next time.

Yeah, right. I'd studied until my eyes were droopy. I'd gone over every prescribed reading, and optional reading. I'd watched every lecture twice. And yet, I still failed. I didn't even fail by one mark, or half a mark. Even if I'd gotten another question or two right, I still would've failed.

Calling Austin was out of the picture. Even my mother was overseas. She was supposed to fly to Italy last night. There was no way I was going to impede on her first day of travelling like that. She needed to destress and enjoy Italy, not sit on the phone listening to my problems.

Groaning, I threw my phone onto the floor, listening as it landed on the carpet with a thud before turning over and burying myself under my bed sheets. The mattress dipped with the movement, and I wished it would open up and take me whole.

I couldn't imagine going to class tomorrow, seeing Lachie, admitting that I'd failed while the students around me probably bragged about their high marks and amazing scores.

No, I wanted to lay here forever.

I don't know when the tears came back, but bythe time I fell asleep, my pillow was soaked.

CHAPTER 19

I woke up with swollen eyelids, my dried tears sealing them shut. I groaned, rubbing at the tender skin with a wince, and squinting through the brightness of my room.

Immediately, the events of last night hit me. My failed midterm, Everett at his party... I wanted to go right back to sleep and pretend none of that had ever happened.

Except, there was a knocking at my bedroom door, and I realised why I'd woken up in the first place.

I squeezed my eyes shut, trying to drown out the banging. I had a killer headache, and the noise wasn't helping whatsoever. Dehydration, probably. I must have cried a litre worth of water last night.

I felt like an idiot. I was never really one for crying, but when I was driven to tears, it became difficult to stop.

The banging continued, and I slapped my hands against my eyes, silently begging for whoever it was to leave me alone.

"Isla?" It was River's voice shouting as he knocked against the door. "Can you open the door? You've been in there all day. Are you alright?"

I frowned. All day? What time was it? I turned, looking for my phone where I normally left it, charging beside my bed. My hand met empty sheets and my eyes swept across the floor as I remembered that I'd flung it across the room in frustration last night.

With a huff of annoyance, I forced myself out of my bed and searched the carpet for my phone, finding it in the corner of the room. I turned it on, realising my phone was about to die. I had dozens of missed calls and unread messages from Everett, Sky and River.

I glanced at the time—almost two in the afternoon. I had missed my class. My stomach growled and I realised I hadn't eaten since lunch time yesterday. I'd missed dinner, crying in my room until night, and then missed breakfast when I didn't set an alarm this morning. I had been so exhausted from crying all evening that I'd slept right through the morning.

Worse, I had dozens of missed texts and calls from Everett, all the way from the time I'd hung up on him. I groaned, turning the phone off and leaning back against the wall. What was I supposed to say to him now? I probably ruined his entire night. And for what? A stupid midterm?

"Isla?" River repeated. I could hear him sigh through the door. "Can you just open the door, please? I heard you get up. I know you're in there. I'm kind of sick of knocking on this door."

I opened my mouth before shutting it again. I didn't feel like talking. I definitely didn't want him to see me like this. I knew my eyes were red and swollen, and I could imagine what a mess my hair was.

I might have fooled Everett over a video call but avoiding River's questions when I looked like this would be borderline impossible.

"Isla." His voice was full of complaint now. He banged against the door again, his knocks becoming lazy and slow. "You'd better open the door, or I'm going to start charging you rent."

I snorted. He could threaten me all he wanted but underneath that evil exterior, he secretly loved me.

"Isla," he whinged again. I pursed my lips. No matter how much he complained, I wasn't in the mood for talking. All I wanted was to be left alone to sulk in my bed. "Alright, that's it. I'm going to call Everett and make him drag you out of there."

That got my attention.

I bolted up, pulling the door open. "Please don't call him."

River's eyes widened as they flickered from my face to my hair, to my clothes, then the room behind me. His brow creased in a deep frown.

"What the hell, Isla?"

I ignored him. "I don't want Everett to worry. Please don't call him."

"I won't. I wasn't going to. I just wanted you to open the door," he said, shaking his head. "What happened? Are you okay?"

I sighed, my shoulders sagging, and I turned back to my bed, flopping onto my mattress. I didn't have the energy to deal with anything today. I was still reeling from last

night—from everything. My midterm. My assignments. Eve
rett...

I wanted to go right back to sleep and stay there until
everything vanished.

I wanted to vanish.

"Isla." The mattress dipped as River sat beside me. His hand
rested awkwardly on my back. "Don't make me comfort you
because you know I'm not going to do it well."

I laughed drily, turning my head to meet his eyes. "I hate
university," I said.

"Who likes it?"

"Ha. Ha. Very funny. I hate it. Like, would this all be a waste
if I just dropped out right now?"

River's expression soured. He sighed, moving closer to
nudge my shoulder. "Stop talking like that. You don't actually
want to drop out. You've been working towards this your
whole life. What happened that's got you so torn up about
university?"

"I just—" I huffed, turning so that I lay on my back. "Promise
not to laugh?"

"I would, but I couldn't lie to you like that, Monroe."

I narrowed my eyes at him. "Just promise."

"Alright, jeez. I get it. I will... do my best to sympathise with
you."

It was the best I was going to get. I sighed, covering my face
with my hands. I had to force the words out, but I figured it
was like ripping a Band-aid off.

"I failed my midterm."

It was embarrassing to admit. I'd never failed anything before. In high school, I'd excelled in all my assessments, even the ones I didn't study for. But for this? I'd studied for days. Weeks. And it hadn't been enough. I'd never be enough.

River was silent for a minute before he spoke. "That's it?"

I peeked through my fingers. "What do you mean that's it?"

"You failed a mid-term. So what? What was it worth, ten percent?"

"More like forty."

He whistled lowly. "Alright, now I'm starting to see why you're so upset. What did Everett say?"

I frowned. "He didn't say anything."

"Wow, he's worse at comforting than I am."

"No, he didn't answer his phone. Well, I mean, he did answer, but he was at a party, and I didn't want to interrupt, so..."

"Isla..."

"I'm just—I'm so lonely." My eyes watered and I squeezed them shut, embarrassed to be seen like this in front of River. "I miss Everett so much, and it's like I can never see him or speak to him and—I don't know. I wish... I don't even know what I wish. Everything is impossible. There's just no solution. If he made more time for me, I'd feel guilty for cutting into his sleep, or his studying, or his partying. If he visited, I'd feel bad for him wasting his money on me. There's just nothing we can do at this point. I can't even wish anymore."

The mattress creaked and River was lying beside me, pulling me into his arms. I sobbed, letting him hug me, letting him wrap his arms around me as my tears stained his shirt and my shoulders shook.

"I don't know what I'm doing here anymore," I cried. "Nothing's going right."

River rubbed my arms, squeezing me tight. "I know," he muttered. "I know. It sucks. All of this sucks, but you can't just give up on everything. What happened to the girl that literally pined over Austin for, like, a decade?"

I scoffed. "That was stupid."

"It wasn't stupid, it was just you. You're not the type to give up on something so easily. I mean, look at you. You moved all the way to Sydney just to go to university. You worked your arse off at the Shack for years, saving up money for this." His arms tightened around me, and he rested his chin on my head. "You can't just give up now."

"I don't know," I murmured. I leaned into him, letting him hug me tighter.

My phone was still on the floor across the room, my unread messages and missed phone calls weighing on me. Everything felt heavy. Though he remained silent, River's hands rubbed my back, his form of quiet comfort.

"I don't know," I repeated. "I don't know anything anymore."

"That's okay," River said, his voice almost a whisper. "It'll be okay."

"Will it?"

"What, you think I'm a liar?"

I let out a watery laugh. Even without looking at him, I could tell he was smiling. I squeezed him tighter, letting him gather me against his chest. "Thanks, River."

His grip tightened around me, and I closed my eyes against his chest. With my eyes shut, I could almost pretend it was Everett. Except, River didn't smell like him. His arms weren't as big as Everett's. His chest was too bony. It only made me feel worse, remembering what wasn't here.

But if I closed my eyes and I really tried, I could almost pretend. Just for a second.

□□□□□□□□□□□

I dreamt of my high school graduation. I knew it was a dream immediately because that was the only place that I saw Everett these days.

Except it wasn't a dream. It was a memory from last September.

Everett had visited me. He'd spent his summer working to make extra cash and, in his first week of college, he flew to Australia to attend my graduation ceremony.

In my dream—my memory—I was lying next to him. When he visited Shellside Bay, he usually stayed at Clemente House with his grandmother, but that night, we snuck him into my room and my mum kindly pretended not to notice.

The light of dawn slanted over his face as we faced each other. I wondered how long he'd been awake. I had half-expected him to leave during the night, to vanish as he always did.

He lifted a hand, his finger sliding down my cheek like a whisper of his breath.

"You're a really heavy sleeper, you know?" he muttered.

"Only when you're here," I whispered back. His lips twitched as he continued drawing patterns across my cheek.

"Your eyes are so swollen," he muttered. His finger reached my eye, and he traced the skin there. It stung with his touch and I remembered how much I'd cried that night, sobbing into his chest as he held me.

"Do you have to leave?" I replied, my voice croaky from both sleep and last night's crying.

He pursed his lips. Neither of us would like his answer.

"I can't miss my first week of college," he said.

"But you just got here. You're still jetlagged. Your flights—it's not worth it to go back yet."

There was no point arguing. He'd heard all of my excuses last night, my reasons for him to stay longer. There was no changing his mind.

I knew there was no changing his mind. I remembered the feeling of him leaving, watching him walk away into the airport, and yet, there in my dream, I continued to beg. I continued to hope.

He released a hard breath, his hand moving to my hair as he pulled me into his chest.

"I'm sorry, Isla," he said. "I can't. I have to leave."

"You don't have to," I replied. I looked up at him with teary eyes. "You can stay. You can—You can go to college here. In Australia. In Sydney!"

"I can't do that."

"Yes, you can! You can. You can stay with me and River! He's in Sydney right now, you can go and drive up there tonight. You just need to—"

"I can't," he interrupted with a soft murmur. He stroked my hair, looking away. "I'd need a visa first. I'd need to talk to my dad and my grandma. I'd need to pack and—and visit my mother to say goodbye—"

"We'll do all that!" I said quickly. "And then you can come here. Just take a few months off from uni. Start at the same time as me."

"Isla, I can't afford it right now."

"I'll help you. How much is it? Ten thousand a semester?"

"Fifty thousand a year," he replied.

My mouth snapped shut. Fifty thousand a year... that was more than my entire degree would cost, in total.

"And that's just for the subjects," Everett continued. "Not including my student services fees or living expenses, and that's all assuming I pass all the subjects on my first go."

"You will," I said immediately. "And you can... you can get a scholarship. Get a loan. We'll figure it out."

"I already did," he said. "I applied for every fucking scholarship under the sun. None of them accepted me. I have no credit. Who's going to give me a personal loan for two hundred thousand dollars? My dad... he's not going to pay for me to study halfway across the world. He was very clear when he said that it was NYU or nothing. I just—I've thought of all this a million times, Isla."

"And there's nothing?"

My voice sounded so small in my memory. Had it really been like that?

He shook his head. His hand cupped my cheek, his thumb stroking just beneath my eye, still red from crying.

"We'll be okay, Isla. It'll be no different from these past few months, yeah? We can get through it."

□□□□□□□□□□□

When I woke up, River's arms were still tight around me.

I sighed, leaning further into his hug. My eyes stung as they rubbed against his hoodie. They were already sore and red when I first woke up but crying even more after that—I could imagine how swollen and puffy they must have been at this point.

No wonder I had that dream.

His arms squeezed me, alerting me to the fact that he was awake, and I rested my face against his chest as my body slowly woke up. I was a little embarrassed that I'd fallen asleep from crying in River's arms, but I had to admit that I was feeling better after letting it out. I hadn't realised how lonely I'd been, how badly I'd needed a hug.

What time was it? My eyes strained open against his hoodie. It was still light outside, meaning it was probably still—I froze.

His hoodie rubbed against my cheek.

River wasn't wearing a hoodie when I fell asleep.

His arms were tight around me.

River's arms didn't feel like that. River never hugged me like this, with his arms around my waist, his hands settled on my lower back.

I inhaled. River didn't smell like this.

I bolted upright, my head colliding with his chin in the process. He cried out in pain, hands flying to his chin, my own head throbbing from it, but I didn't care. I couldn't believe what I was seeing.

"Everett?"

"Isla," he replied simply. "You just beat the shit out of my chin."

"What are you doing here? Did I just manifest you? Am I still dreaming?" I sputtered. My eyes fell to the red spot on his chin, and I frowned, reaching for it. "I'm so sorry."

"It's fine," he said, his fingers resting over mine. He met my gaze and sent me a tiny smile. "You're a really heavy sleeper, you know?"

"You just said that."

"What?" He smiled incredulously at me.

"In my dreams. I was dreaming of my graduation night."

His smile slipped slightly, his eyes darting between my own, but he then pulled a smirk on and said, "Of course, you were dreaming of me."

"Don't be so arrogant," I scolded. "Why are you here? Did—Oh, God. Did River call?"

"Yes." I frowned, ready to kill River, but Everett continued. "And no. By the time he called me, I was already in my layover, on my way here."

"What?"

"He called me a few hours ago, right before I boarded my last flight."

"You were already coming to Sydney? For what?"

"For you, idiot. You called me and hung up so quickly, and then you weren't replying to any of my texts or calls. I was freaking out, Isla."

"Oh." My heart sunk. I turned away from him. "I'm sorry for worrying you. I didn't mean to. When I saw you were at a party, I just—I felt bad for interrupting, and I mean, I wasn't calling for any major reason—"

"Isla," he cut me off. He pulled me closer. "Don't apologise. I was only at that party because my friends dragged me there. After you told me to go on that call, they took it as permanent permission to go to every party ever. I've had to come up with a million other excuses to avoid them. And, I mean, look at you, Isla. It doesn't matter what the reason is, if it makes you cry this much, it's reason enough to call me. I'm your boyfriend."

"I know," I muttered. "I just—I saw your story and then you lied to me. I felt like—it was like you didn't want to talk."

"Isla." His voice was so quiet, almost a whisper, and I could hear his heart shatter in the way he said my name. "I'm so sorry. I didn't—I wasn't lying because I didn't want to talk, it was more like the opposite. I just felt guilty. I was at a party, and you were calling me—I didn't want you to think you were interrupting me."

"You mean—" I released a shaky breath, an almost-laugh. "You mean, I wasn't?"

"Of course not." He ran a hand over my hair, frowning. "You could never. Especially when you feel like this. I mean—what was it anyway? The reason?"

"It's... It's stupid," I said, suddenly embarrassed again. "I just—I failed my midterm."

"You failed your midterm?" He scanned my face. "Is that all you were upset about?"

"Yes," I said. I paused. "At first."

"But then?"

I sighed. I'd been a blubbering mess when River found me in this room, sputtering everything on my mind in between sobs. But now—I sat up, straightening my back to meet Everett's eyes.

"I guess... I've been lonely," I said. "It's like—uni has been so much harder than I thought. I haven't made many friends, and the work is so much harder than I'm used to, and now, after all my hard work, I still managed to fail. And then River's been distant. I mean, everyone's been distant and busy with their own things, but with both of us busy with uni now, I miss you. I miss you so much, and I can't even tell you without the guilt eating me alive."

"Guilt?" he echoed.

"Guilt about making you worry. About making you feel guilty for not being here for me. About making you miss out on college life because of me."

"Isla," he muttered. He shook his head and ran a hand over his face before meeting my gaze again. "I'm not... Is that what you've been thinking all this time?"

I nodded. "It's like... I'll feel the urge to call you or text you but then I'll remember that you're busy, or sleeping, or whatever, and I just—I feel guilty. I can't—I don't want to burden you with anything else."

He sat up at that, leaning forward and taking my face in his hands as he looked me directly in the eyes.

"Isla," he said. "Listen to me. You are never a burden on me. I don't care if you tell me about a dog you passed on the street, if I'm the one you thought of telling, then I want to hear it. If I just get to hear your voice or see a notification on my phone from you, my day is already ten times better. I would—you know I would do anything to stay here with you instead. I think about you every second we're apart. Every second we're together."

"I just—we're both in uni now. I don't want to cut into your sleep, or make you miss out on parties. I don't want to interrupt."

"Interrupt?" he scoffed. He shook his head, smiling at me. "Isla, I'll take you anyway I can get you. A second. A summer. A text. I want you. Wholly and completely. You."

I couldn't help the smile that grew across my face, remembering the same words he'd told me a year ago, when he'd left me the first time.

"You're such a dork."

He laughed, pulling me into a hug. His head settled in the crook of my neck and he pecked the skin there, causing me to squeal and giggle. His arms locked around my waist, preventing me from squirming away. Instead, he held me closer, kissing my neck loudly, all the way up to my jaw before capturing my lips.

I smiled into the kiss; my eyes fluttering shut. His tongue swiped over my lip hungrily, and I realised I hadn't kissed him in weeks—hadn't seen him, held him, touched him in weeks.

But before he could deepen the kiss, I jumped away, rolling across the mattress and out of bed.

"Stay away from me!" I squealed.

Everett frowned, crawling across the bed towards me. "Why?"

"I haven't brushed my teeth." My voice lowered. "Or.. . shaved in a while."

"Shaved?" He raised his brow, a smirk beginning to pull at the corner of his lips. He sat at the edge of the bed in front of me. "You think a bit of hair is going to stop me from kissing my girlfriend after weeks without her?"

"Kissing? No. But, other things..."

He laughed, grabbing the hem of my shirt and tugging me closer until I stood between his legs. "What other things are you suggesting?" he asked.

"I have a few ideas."

His fingers skimmed beneath the material, drawing a line of heat across from my hips to my lower belly, just above the drawstring to my shorts. He paused there and tugged on the elastic. "Like what?"

"Like," I started, smirking down at him. His fingertips grazed my skin, his eyes wandering where they touched. I let him wonder for a moment before stepping back. "Brushing my teeth for starters."

"Isla!" he complained.

I threw him a grin over my shoulder as I made my way into the bathroom. "How long are you staying?"

"As long as I want," he replied.

"Well then." I spun, smiling as I faced him. "We'll have plenty of time for all my ideas after my shower."

I could hear him groan through the closed door.

Chapter 20

L ast Summer

I lay on the bed, my skin hot and slick with sea water and sweat. The sun had been scalding all day, followed by a sun shower, which meant the night was humid. The air stuck to me like a cloth of heat, and no matter how many times I took a cold shower or jumped into the ocean, it only stuck to me hotter.

"We should've gone to your place," I groaned.

Everett lay beside me, inches away. The mattress wasn't big enough for the two of us to lay spread eagle the way we were, but I took measured care to keep my arm a millimetre from his. Even with the distance between us, I could still feel the heat of his body mingling with the humid air and invading my skin.

"I like your room," he replied. "It's got character."

I sighed, fanning my face with a hand, but it only blew hot air onto my sweaty forehead. "Your room's got an aircon. I'd argue that's better than character."

"You're being a big baby. It's not that hot," he replied. He shifted, turning to face me and I tilted my head, meeting his eye. His hair stuck to his face, the sweat on his skin making him glow. I scowled.

"Easy for you to say. You can take your shirt off."

He looked down at his exposed chest before smirking at me. "Hey, be my guest. No one's going to stop you here."

I rolled my eyes. He was teasing me, but I didn't care. I wriggled on the mattress, grabbing the hem of my shirt, and pulling it off my skin, tossing it onto the floor.

When I looked back at Everett, he was staring wide-eyed at my chest.

"Eyes up here, mate." His eyes flashed up to meet mine and I grinned. "Or maybe another punch to the face will remind you?"

"I think I remember it pretty vividly." He rubbed his jaw in memory of our first meeting. He pouted at me. "I forgot that you were wearing a bikini."

I snorted. I knew he'd forgotten, or we wouldn't have teased me so arrogantly. I tugged at the bikini string holding it all together. "I can take that off too if you'd like."

"Oh, I would like."

Laughing, I flopped back onto the bed, decidedly keeping my bikini on. "Of course, you'd like."

"Not my fault you've got amazing—"

"Everett!"

"What? I was going to say eyes. They're just so compelling."

"Of course, they are."

His hand traced up my bare stomach before stopping at my waist in a hug. I groaned, shoving his arm off of me.

"What?" he whined.

"It's hot."

"I want to cuddle."

"It's too hot to cuddle, you big baby."

"It's never too hot." His hand trailed over my skin again and I pushed it away, turning to glare at him. He smiled back. "Well, if it's too hot to cuddle, maybe we can do some other things."

"It's too hot to do anything."

He was silent for a moment. Outside, cicadas sang, a signal of summer's arrival. Beyond the chirping, the washing of waves cut through the night, almost lulling me to sleep. Almost.

"It's a shame you don't have an aircon in here," Everett said.

I frowned at him. "Yeah. We established that."

"Well." His hand returned to my skin, sending butterflies all through my stomach. "I have an aircon back in my room."

We met eyes.

In an instant, both of us were off the bed, pulling our shoes on.

"I'll get my bike," I said.

"I'll grab my keys."

We missed the sunset that night. In the silence of his room, all I could hear was the low buzz of the vented aircon, and the mix of our breathing in the air.

□□□□□□□□□□

"Isla, can we slow down a bit?"

My expression soured as I glanced at the time on my phone. "No. Hurry up, we're already late."

I grabbed his hand, dragging him down the steps and into a building on the right. The doors had already been shut, so I quietly weaselled them open and stepped into the lecture hall. My professor was halfway through a slide about protein in cells when I led Everett to an empty row in the back.

He settled in beside me as I pulled out my laptop—as if I'd be able to concentrate on my lecture with Everett beside me.

"Why is the lecture hall so empty?" he muttered, leaning over to whisper in my ear.

"It's nearly the end of the semester. Everyone's probably just going to watch it online."

"Not you, though?"

I shrugged. "I wanted to see what it felt like going to a lecture with my boyfriend."

He blinked at me. Then, a smile crept onto his face, and he leaned back against his seat, his hand finding mine beneath the small desk.

For once, I was glad my lecture was late in the afternoon. It had given me time to take Everett to all the tourist-y sites in Sydney and stop at my usual café before dragging him to my university.

If I sat here, with him beside me, here in my lecture hall, I could almost imagine what life might have been like for us. I could imagine a world where Everett and I went to the same university, attended the same classes, saw each other after class.

Maybe we would've gone on dates on campus. We could've had study dates in the library. We could've snuck into each other's' lectures, and caught lunch between courses, sneaking kisses on the way to class.

Summer could've lasted forever.

Everett's hand tightened around mine and I smiled, leaning onto his shoulder. Maybe we didn't have forever, but we had right now, and I was going to take what I could get.

I listened to the professor, not bothering with rushing to take notes for once, simply enjoying the way Everett's thumb stroked the back of my hand as we both learned about cell structures together. Weirdly enough, it felt like I was absorbing more information than the lectures where I spent every second transcribing notes onto my laptop.

At that moment, my phone buzzed. I frowned, pulling away from Everett for a moment to check who had messaged me. Lachie. I hadn't spoken to him for a few days now. He was probably wondering why I'd missed class yesterday.

I'd worry about coming up with an excuse for that later. I was still dreading the inevitable question. "What did you get for your midterm?"

No. For now, it was just me and Everett. Everything was perfect.

I ignored his text, placing my phone back beside my laptop when it buzzed again with two more texts from Lachie.

Huffing, I swiped my phone up, setting it to silent.

By the time I leaned back against Everett, he was frowning at me.

"What was that all about?" he asked.

"Nothing," I whispered back. I didn't feel like talking about Lachie or my midterms. I wanted to pretend the last few days—months—didn't exist.

He didn't push it, instead turning back to face the lecture.

The next forty minutes felt like seconds and the lecture was over before we knew it.

Everett turned to me as I packed my laptop away, despite barely using it.

"Where to next?" he asked.

I grinned back. "Why do I get to decide?"

"Aren't you my tour guide?"

"Is that all I am to you? A free tour guide?"

"Hey, your words, not mine."

"The last time I gave you a tour, I left you stranded in the middle of Shellside Bay."

Everett chuckled at the memory. He'd insulted me, teasing me at the fact that Austin didn't return my feelings at the time, and I'd kicked him out of the car in the middle of nowhere.

He deserved it, really.

"I really got my steps in that day." He leaned back in his seat, throwing an arm over my shoulders. "Your lecture halls are way comfier than mine."

"You should just stay here, then."

He smiled at me. "I think I will, then."

I shoved his shoulder, rolling my eyes. "Don't tease me like that. You'll get my hopes up. New York's waiting for you to return. Speaking of which, you haven't told me. How's uni life?"

"College life is going great," he replied. "Well, as great as it can go without you. Meaning, not great at all."

"What? Come on, you seemed to be having a good time."

"Good. Great. Shit. It's all the same," he said, shrugging. I settled him with a patient stare, and he sighed, explaining. "I've made some friends but they're not as cool as you. I feel like everyone I meet, I just compare them to you, you know? And everywhere I go, it's just like—Oh, Isla would like this place. Oh, Isla would like this restaurant. Oh, if Isla was here, she'd definitely do this."

"At least I don't have to worry about you cheating," I teased.

He rolled his eyes at me. "Come on, that's the last thing I'd do."

I knew it was true. I'd never even worried about it. When I met Everett, he was still torn over his ex-girlfriend cheating on him with his best friend. He knew how it felt to be betrayed in that way.

"I don't know about you though," he teased.

I raised a brow. "Not to alarm you, but I did fall asleep in River's arms yesterday."

He laughed, shaking his head. "Don't even joke about that. If you told me that a year ago, I probably would've knocked him out."

"Oh, please, River would've had you on the ground in seconds."

Everett flexed a bicep. "Are you sure about that?"

We both laughed and I turned to properly face him in my seat. The lecture hall had emptied by now and since no one else had entered since, I assumed this had been the last class for the day.

"What about everything else?" I asked carefully. "Outside of uni?"

"You mean my evil stepmother?" When I didn't laugh, he cracked a smile and continued. "She's fine. I mean, she's annoying, but I only see her at family dinners when I have to be there. And I guess she feels the awkwardness too, because she avoids me as much as I avoid her now—Are you going to answer that?"

I followed his gaze to my phone. Despite being silenced, the screen still lit up with an incoming phone call, Lachie's photo flashing brightly.

I frowned, turning the phone off.

"Not friends anymore?" Everett asked.

"Huh?"

He nodded towards the phone. "That... Luke guy. Are you guys not talking or something?"

"Oh." I sighed, shaking my head. Just what I was trying to avoid talking about. "No. Nothing happened. I just—I really don't feel like talking to him right now. He'd just ask about my midterm results and talk about our labs and classes. Besides, I'm busy. I'm with you today."

Everett watched me for a moment. "I wish I could be with you every day."

"Me too."

"Maybe..." He paused, running a hand over his face. "Maybe I could."

I turned to him, frowning. "What do you mean?"

"Well, I—I wasn't going to mention it until I knew it could actually be possible, but I'm applying for an exchange program. To come here. To study here, in Sydney, with you."

I thought I was hearing things. I shook my head, blinking hard. When I looked up, meeting Everett's hopeful eyes, I knew I wasn't imagining this. He'd just said what I thought he said.

"Are you being serious?"

He nodded, then paused, pursing his lips unsurely. "I mean, it's not certain. All I've done so far is apply."

"When did you apply? How long have you known? I mean—What do you need to be accepted?"

He laughed, grabbing my hands. I realised I was halfway out of my seat and smiled meekly, sitting firmly back down.

"I need good grades. I've known about this program since before I even got accepted to study at NYU. It's just—my first semester; it was so much harder than I expected. My grades were alright, but not good enough to be accepted into the program. So, this semester, I've been studying like crazy—"

"Is that why you've been so busy?" I paused, the pieces beginning to connect as I recalled the past few months—the past year—with this new perspective. "Is that why you were skipping out on all those parties? Not just to talk to me, but to study?"

He shrugged. "I needed those grades."

"And do you have them?"

He hesitated. "I think so. But we won't know until I get all my grades back."

"Holy shit."

"I know."

"Holy shit, you might come to Sydney. You might—" I paused, cutting my excitement short and meeting his eyes. "Everett, you're doing this because you want to, right? You're not—it's not just because of me, is it?"

He shook his head, his fingers intertwining with my own.

"I want to be here. I mean, I would be lying if I said it wasn't partially for you, but I like it here. I like being able to see you when I want. I like being in the same time zone as you. But I also like the weather here, the city, the beaches, the culture. I like being able to visit Shellside Bay and my grandma when I want, instead of being stuck in New York with my dad and stepmom. And I'd rather see River every day than hang out with my college friends again, or have to bump into my ex and act civil.

"I've thought about this a lot—since before we even started dating officially. I've thought about it from the first day I kissed you, and I want to stay here."

My eyes watered and his jaw fell slack. He reached up, cupping my face. "What's wrong? Did I say something wrong? I don't have to study here if you don't want me to."

"No," I said quickly. I shook my head, blinking back my tears through a watery laugh. "You didn't. I just—I'm so happy. I can't believe it."

"Well, it's not confirmed or anything—"

I interrupted him by pressing my lips to his. His eyes widened briefly before fluttering shut, kissing me back with a newfound passion. His hand slid across my jaw, his fingers burying in my hair as his tongue slipped into my mouth.

I sighed into the kiss, leaning towards him, letting him pull me in.

We pulled away at the same time, our eyes heavy and chests rising and falling in sync.

"Imagine your professor walks in right now," Everett murmured.

I laughed, shaking my head. "Way to kill the moment, Ev."

"Kill?" he repeated. His hand fell to my waist, pulling me closer until the arm rest stopped me from coming any closer. "You're going to have to get used to this when I'm going to college here."

I raised a brow at him. "Am I? Well, you're going to have to get used to calling it uni, or you're going to get mocked relentlessly."

"I'm not scared of you Aussies."

"You should be."

He snorted and I grinned at him before turning to my backpack and digging through the front zipper.

"This calls for a celebration," I said as I searched.

Everett leaned closer, trying to peek into my bag. "I haven't been accepted yet, Isla. Don't get your hopes up."

"I already know you'll be accepted. And besides, I was planning to share these with you. I just never had a chance today."

"Yeah, because you've been dragging me all over the place like the world is gonna end tomorrow."

"It kind of is," I said.

I intended it as a joke, but he fell silent, his brow creasing. The world wasn't ending, but this world was. When Everett left for New York, this world—this invented world where

Everett and I were a normal couple, doing normal uni things together—would be over.

My fingers finally grasped the plastic edges of what I was looking for and I whipped it out with a grin. "Here!"

His eyes fell to the chocolates in my hands. Slowly, a smile crept onto his face.

"How did you know I missed Australian candy?"

"Candy," I mocked in a bad American accent. "This is a Picnic bar."

"Picnic?" he asked taking one from my hands. He turned the packet over, frowning at the image. "Why is it called Picnic?"

"I don't know. Why would I know that?"

"Aren't you Australian?"

I rolled my eyes. "Just try the stupid chocolate."

He smirked at my reaction before ripping the plastic open and taking a large bite. He chewed for a moment before frowning.

"It's so chewy."

"Yeah, it has nougat," I pointed out. His frown deepened. "What, you don't like it?"

He swallowed hard. "I mean, it's no Flake."

I laughed. "I can't believe you remember what a Flake is."

"Of course, I do. Except, with the Flake, I don't remember eating it like this."

He gave me a pointed look which I didn't understand for a moment until it hit me.

Slowly, I took the chocolate from his hands, instead holding it up to his mouth. He smiled at me, leaning closer until he took the bar into his mouth, his lips grazing my fingertips.

My face warmed as I watched him lean back, chewing the chocolate and swallowing it.

"Delicious."

CHAPTER 22

"Everett! My man!"

As Everett and I stepped foot into the apartment, we were greeted with blasting music and flashing lights. River was right at the door, a red cup in hand with sweet smelling liquid sloshing around inside. He tossed an arm around Everett's shoulders and tugged him away from me.

"Guest of honour is here!" he shouted into the crowd. A wave of cheers responded, strangers raising their cups and whistling for him.

"River!" I scolded, grabbing him by the neck. "What is this?"

"Isn't it obvious? It's Everett's going away party." He shoved his cup into my hand. "Drink."

I rolled my eyes, watching as he vanished into the crowd before taking a long swig and shoving the cup into Everett's hand. I screwed my nose up, the taste burning its way down my throat. Whatever River had mixed into the cup, it was already beginning to buzz through me.

"I'm sorry," I said once the taste passed. "I didn't realise he'd throw one of these stupid parties tonight. I'll go tell him—"

Before I could walk away, Everett grabbed my arm and took a swig out of the cup himself. He wiped his mouth with the side of his wrist and grinned at me.

"It's alright," he shouted over the music. His thumb rubbed over my skin and my heart swooped in response. "It's just his way of saying goodbye, you know? Let's just pretend we're on Shellside Bay and there's a bonfire in front of us."

His hold dropped to my hand, and he pulled me closer until our chests were almost touching.

"Besides," he said, "this is my favourite song."

The speakers were blasting a song I'd never heard of and judging by the way Everett bopped his head to the complete wrong rhythm, I guessed he'd never heard it either. Nevertheless, the way he nodded to the music and grinned down at me, I was beginning to catch his energy.

Relenting, I smiled at him. I had to admit, River's parties had always been dull without Everett, but now that he was here...

"I guess I could have a little bit of fun before you go," I replied. I took the cup out of his hands and swallowed the remaining alcohol. "But you can't get too drunk, or you'll be hungover on your flight."

Everett shrugged. "So, I'll sleep the entire flight. It'll be fine."

"You're going to sleep for a whole twenty-hour flight?"

"Do you know how many times I've flown out here, Isla? You're lucky my dad sold his soul to the corporate world and my grandma likes it when I visit. I've probably slept on a plane more than I have in my own bed. I think I can handle one plane ride with a bit of a headache," he teased.

I shoved his shoulder. "Well, sorry for living half-way across the world."

He caught my hand and leaned closer, his smile growing. "Hey, I never said I didn't like it. I'd fly anywhere if it meant I could see you. Even for a second."

I couldn't help it. My lips twitched and I fought a smile before rolling my eyes and pushing him away. "You're so cheesy. Let's get drunk."

I didn't know what River had put in the drink I'd downed, but I was already feeling more alive. We found our way to more alcohol—beer bottles and plastic cups knocking against our llips.

It didn't take long for the room to start spinning.

We stumbled through the kitchen, squeezing between dancing bodies and other thirsty souls. Everett blindly grabbed for a glass bottle, procuring an almost-empty bottle of vodka. He grinned at me, his entire body tipping as he poured it into cups for us, the alcohol swishing against the edges of the plastic.

He raised his cup to mine and smiled.

"Cheers, babe."

Clinking our cups together, we knocked back the shot—or shot and a bit—the alcohol burning its way down our throats.

I gagged, sticking my tongue out at him.

"Where's your teen spirit, Monroe?" Everett teased, leaning in close so that I could hear him over the music.

I rolled my eyes, turning my head so that my lips brushed his ear. Even then, I had to shout, the music and chatter too loud to hear my own voice. "That was much more than a shot."

"Hey, I'm here for a good time. You want another or what?"

I settled him with a glare but lifted my cup anyway. I could complain all I wanted, but the buzz of alcohol was lighting my veins and I wanted more.

He filled it with even more vodka than last time. Again, we cheered and threw it back. This time, the burning bothered me less.

The next time he filled it, he added some soft drink to help wash it down. Vodka and cranberry Red Bull—my favourite. How long had it been since our last Shellside Bay bonfire? And yet he remembered. He always did.

One song faded into another and soon the room seemed to be screaming, girls squealing and dragging their friends and partners to the centre of the room. I gasped alongside them, dropping my cup onto the table, and grabbing Everett's arm instead.

"Oh, my God! This is my song!"

"Is this Taylor Swift?" he shouted incredulously.

I barely heard him, already screaming the lyrics with the rest of the room as I dragged Everett towards the edge of the dance floor.

Soon, we found ourselves squashed between bodies, Everett's chest to my back. I swayed my hips, grinning over my shoulder and yelling along to the song as Everett's arm wrapped around my waist, his hand gripping his own drink over my stomach.

His lips settled near my ear. "I don't know why you like this song so much."

"Are you crazy?" I shouted back at him.

"Possibly."

His lips brushed over the tip of my ear, his breath fanning over the skin there, cool over the sweat that lined my neck. They trailed down, sliding behind my ear and down to the place where my jaw met my neck, gently biting the skin there.

I gasped, leaning further into this touch, Taylor Swift long forgotten.

My hand slid up to grab his hair, holding him to my neck as I pushed my body closer to his. Around us, people continued screaming to the music, dancing, drinking, but to me—we were the only ones in the room.

And Everett—Everett was here. If there was anything that could prove it to me in that moment, it was his hard body against mine, his lips on my skin, his hands trailing over my stomach and lower, lower, until his fingers reached my upper thigh, curling around the flesh there.

"Everett," I mouthed, my voice drowned out by the music, but he seemed to hear me anyway. He pulled back to smile at me, a smirk in the very sense of the word before I'd had enough. I turned to him, pressing my lips against his.

He fell into me immediately, his mouth moving against mine, his tongue eagerly seeking my own. With my body facing his, I could press our chests flush against each other, his arms wrapping around my waist, his cup knocking against my lower back as he held me close.

One hand trailed lower, tugging at the hem of my shorts and I pulled back to shoot him a look.

"When did you become so—"

"So what?" he challenged.

"Such a tease," I finished.

"Since I got some alcohol in my system." To prove his point, he lifted his cup, tossing his head back to take another drink. He leaned closer and I could smell the sweetness of the drink on his breath. "Why? Do you like it?"

"Hmm. I don't know. I might need to test it out a bit more."

His smile grew. "I'd be happy to help with that."

Before I could respond, he was kissing me again. His fingers were roaming over me again. His body was pressed against mine again. And I couldn't breathe. My heart was pounding against my ribcage, the noise buzzing in my ears along with my blood.

All I could hear, feel, breathe, was Everett.

And when his fingers crept under the hem of my shorts, pressing beneath the curve of my bum, I pulled away with gasping breaths.

"Maybe we should go back to my room," I muttered against his lips. His chest rose and fell as quickly as his lips twitched in response.

"Is that a direct invitation?"

"Would you like me to take it back?"

He shook his head immediately and it was my turn to grin. I trailed a hand down his chest, pausing at his stomach.

Through the thin cloth of his shirt, I could feel the heat of his body, the fast rise and fall of his breaths.

"Follow me," I said. He didn't have to be told again.

We turned together, only to stop in our tracks.

"Isla!" Lachie shouted. He was already halfway towards us by the time we'd met eyes, and within frantic seconds of searching for a hidden path to my room, he closed the small gap between us, lifting a hand in greeting.

My smile fell, then returned as I smoothed my hair back. Everything was spinning. I could feel Everett's hand tensing against the back of my thigh. I wondered if Lachie could see it. I hoped my shorts hadn't ridden up.

"Lachie," I said. "Hey."

"I knew that was you!" he yelled back. "I was calling you!"

"She was a bit preoccupied," Everett murmured, too low for Lachie to hear, but just loud enough for me. I elbowed him in the ribs, keeping my smile steady.

"I didn't hear you," I shouted.

Lachie shrugged, his eyes falling to Everett beside me. His eyes landed on his face, then fell to his hand, wrapped around my thigh. His gaze flickered back to Everett's face.

"Good to see you again, man. How was the flight? Wasn't expecting you to be back so soon."

"My girlfriend lives here, obviously I'd be back." His voice was curt, and I frowned, looking up at him over my shoulder. His entire focus was on Lachie. It seemed as if every muscle in his body had tensed up. "How's college going, Luke?"

"Oh, it's Lachlan. Or Lachie." He paused to crack a smile at me. "Or Lachlan Lachie."

I forced a laugh, my eyes flicking to my bedroom door, just out of reach. "I almost forgot about that."

"You know, for a second, I thought you really believed that was my real name."

"I would never! I'm not that dumb."

"Really?"

"Positive."

"Because I seem to remember a blank lab manual that day we met in the library..."

I scoffed. "I was—well, that was because—I just hadn't started working on it yet."

"Really? Because you were sitting in that library for a while. Staring at your blank pages."

"How did you—I was not."

"She was top of her grade," Everett jumped in. We both turned to him. "Valedictorian," he added.

Lachlan met my eye, then snorted. "Valedictorian? I think that's an American thing."

"I was dux, yeah," I said. Everett's fingers tightened around my thigh, and I leaned back, hoping my touch would calm him down. Lachie was joking. It was who he was. He couldn't get through a conversation without teasing.

"Well, you have to admit, that's a stupid name," Everett replied, smiling down at me.

"Stupid name? Like valedictorian is any better," I shot back.

"It is better. By miles." He raised a brow at me, challenging me. I was never one to turn down a challenge. I lifted my chin defiantly.

"You literally say dick every time you say valedictorian." Not my strongest argument, but my head was still foggy with alcohol and the feeling of Everett's fingers on me. All I could focus on were his lips, just there, centimetres from mine.

"It's a Latin word," he replied.

"Because so many people speak Latin these days."

"And what language does dux come from?"

"A... language. That everyone speaks."

He smirked down at me. "Oh, really?"

"I think it's Latin too," Lachie said.

We both spun, suddenly remembering our persistent guest still standing in front of us. My whole face warmed as I realised just how close Everett was leaning towards me now. I shifted slightly away from him, but his grip on my tightened and he refused to move back.

"See?" Everett said, his voice tight. "Latin. Such a useful language."

We fell into an awkward silence, although Lachie didn't seem to be bothered. It felt as if every person that passed knew him and patted his shoulder or slapped his hand in way of greeting.

Everett's fingers seemed to be massaging me now, his other hand moving to hold my hip, as if urging me to keep walking—to reach our final destination. I shook my head slightly, waiting for Lachie to finish talking to the latest passer-by so that I could wrap up this conversation and drag Everett against me again.

Beyond him, the rest of the room continued to bounce. If I narrowed my eyes, I thought I could see River—except it wasn't him.

No, this person was taller, and distinctly less Asian. The only reason I'd mistaken him was the buzzcut and the fact that Alistair had him pressed up against a wall, his fingers palming across the not-River's skin.

I warmed, turning back to Lachie who was finally saying goodbye to his friend.

"Alright, well..." I started, but Lachie interrupted.

"Actually, I've been meaning to ask. How'd you go on your midterm?"

My smile fell. "Oh. The midterm. Yeah. It was—uh—not bad. I mean..."

"Isla," Everett interrupted. "I need to use the bathroom. Can you show me the way?"

I turned to him, my mind whirring. He knew where the bathroom was. He knew the way. He—I swallowed hard, catching on as he sent me a sharp look.

Lachie, however, did not catch on.

"It's just down the hall, mate."

Everett paused. He settled Lachie with a glare, then slowly said, "I think I need clearer instructions."

"Clearer? Mate, it's an apartment. You'll know it when you see it."

Everett's jaw twitched.

"Listen, mate, I said that I need clearer fucking—"

"It's fine!" I shouted. "I'll take him. I needed to go too, so... yeah. I'll see you at uni, yeah?"

Lachie frowned but nodded. I nodded back, taking Everett's hand and continuing through the crowded room until we reached my room. I lead him through the door, shutting it behind me.

As soon as it clicked shut, he had me against the door, one hand on the wood beside me head, the other on my hip as he pressed his lips against mine.

"Never thought that fucker would shut up," he muttered against my mouth.

I laughed. "You need to be nice. He's my only friend."

"You really couldn't find anyone else?"

"Stop complaining you jealous idiot and kiss me again."

He did. His hands slid down, tracing my body until he reached my thighs. He lifted me easily and I wrapped my legs around his waist, sighing as our hips met.

"Fuck," Everett murmured. "I missed this."

"I missed you," I replied.

I could feel him smile as he kissed me again, this time his lips parting and his tongue sliding into my mouth. Before I can wrap my mind around what is happening, he spun, dropping me with a rush onto the mattress.

I blinked, my eyes still adjusting to the darkness of my room compared to the party outside, when I realised, he was pulling his shirt off. He leaned over me, and I took advantage of his bare chest, running my hands across his skin, loving the feeling.

His lips moved to my jaw this time, trailing down to my neck where he sucked hard. My grip on his bare shoulder tightened and he pulled away a moment later, staring down at his handywork.

"Don't tell me you left a mark," I chided.

He smiled back. "Was that against the rules?"

"Very. River will never let me get over it."

"Well, that's too bad for you. I need to leave you with something that'll last when I'm gone tomorrow."

I frowned. I'd been trying very hard all night not to think about the fact that in a few hours, he'd be gone again. Vanished to the other side of the world.

Back to intermittent phone calls and scattered texts.

For now, I reminded myself. For now, until he transferred here. Until he was mine permanently.

"You're lying," I teased. "You're just upset about Lachie."

His eyes settled on me, and he grew serious. "I am upset. I'm fucking devastated that he gets to keep talking to you and looking at you while I'm gone. I just gave him something to look at."

I rolled my eyes. "Jealousy isn't a good look, Everett."

His smile returned, this time softer. "Will you forgive me?"

"That depends," I said.

"On what?"

"On how I'm feeling."

"Oh?" he hummed. His hand slipped down, tracing down my chest until it reached the hem of my shirt. His fingers slipped under, laying flat against my lower stomach. "And how are you feeling?'

"Impatient."

He laughed, leaning back down to kiss me. My clothes were gone in seconds, tugged from my skin until his bare body was pressed against mine.

Outside, we could still hear the party going, music blasting, people shouting.

But in here, it was just us. It was just Everett and me. And our breaths mingled into one, our voices blended, and our chests pressed against each other, rising, and falling in sync.

He held me in his arms until the sun began to brighten the sky and leak into my room. Until the sky turned into orange clouds dotted against deep purple.

Until the promise of his flight home became sealed, and tears began to well in my eyes.

"I don't want you to leave," I whispered into the dawn.

Everett's hand slipped across my bare waist as he tugged me against him. "I'll be back soon."

"I can't—" tears fell freely now and a sob choked my words—"I'm not sure if I can see you go. I don't—I can't—"

"You don't have to," he murmured, pressing a kiss against my forehead. "Go to sleep. I'll leave when you're not awake anymore."

I couldn't deny that I felt tired. My whole body ached to sleep, my eyes refused to open, but I refused to let go. I clung onto what little consciousness I had left, my hands gripping Everett's. My voice came out quiet.

"But... I don't want you to leave."

"Sleep," he whispered. His thumb stroked my hand, and I felt my breathing turn heavier.

"Sleep," he repeated.

The world seemed to fade in and out. I swore I could feel Everett's lips on my forehead again. His hand left mine.

And I knew, when I woke later and the sun turned the sky its pale blue, he'd be gone.

And I'd be alone.

CHAPTER 23

L ast Summer

Everett had to leave at some point.

He always did.

Except this time, I had an extra few days—this time, we'd be driving up to Sydney together. He was going to help me move in with River.

Maybe I could convince him to stay too.

Except, I knew NYU was waiting for him back in America. He never spoke about it much, but I'd seen enough movies to assume it was a pretty famous university. He'd be mad to leave it behind for some girl.

I hugged my knees closer to my chest, watching the waves wash over the shore—wash over Everett's body, a dot on the horizon.

He'd gotten better at surfing with all the time he was spending at Shellside Bay. Pride swelled in my chest every time he managed to catch a wave, even more when he suggested surfing himself.

It was like I'd given him a part of me, and he'd accepted it happily. He'd taken that piece of my soul and connected it to his own. Surfing had become our thing.

He waved at me from the distance, and I grinned, waving back.

Beside me, someone fell to sit on the sand, and I turned to find River, still scuffing out a cigarette in an empty can of soda.

"Don't tell me you're sooking about leaving for Sydney in two weeks."

I shrugged. "I always thought it was what I wanted, but now that my room is half packed and the others are already buying new work uniforms... I don't know. It feels..."

"Wrong."

"Different," I replied. I would never admit it, but wrong was exactly what had popped into my mind at first. "It feels different."

"It feels like we're growing up," River replied.

I stared straight ahead. Of course, he was right. It didn't mean I had to like it. Everett was standing on his board. A wave hit and seconds later he was falling back into the ocean. The sun had begun to fade already, turning the ocean darker. Everett would have to come back to shore soon.

The day would have to end.

"Shellside Bay isn't the reason you're upset though, is it?"

I turned at River's voice, frowning. He looked at me for a moment before sighing, looking back at the water. Everett was beginning to swim back to shore, but I knew it wasn't him that River was looking at.

Connor's head bobbed beside his surfboard, just metres away from Everett.

"I know," River said. "It won't be the same again."

I could only sigh in response.

□□□□□□□□□□

When I woke up deep in the afternoon, he was gone, leaving an Everett sized dent in my mattress and a sweater that smelt of his cologne.

I bolted upright, my eyes searching the room for his familiar smile and his messy morning hair. But he had held true to his promise. He'd vanished in my sleep, taking his bag and my heart with him.

I frowned, stretching in the empty bed before reaching for the sweater he'd left me. It was one I only recognised from blurry video calls; the letters NYU embroidered along the chest. I held it to my face, breathing in his scent, silently praying that it'd stick longer than it usually did.

What an idiot. He'd left me a jumper, but I hadn't given him back his last one. Now he was two sweaters down.

Smiling to myself, I pulled his jumper on and turned to search for my phone. I was sure that I had been drunk last night—my pounding headache was a testament to that—but my phone was there, on my bedside table, plugged in and fully charged. I knew I had Everett to thank for that.

Turning it on, I found a flood of texts from Everett already waiting for me, ranting about his delayed flight, complaining about his seat mate, wishing me good morning. He was probably just a few hours into his twenty-something hour long flight by now.

I typed a quick reply, wishing him a safe flight and asking him to call me as soon as possible before forcing myself out of bed. I found my shorts discarded on the floor and tugged them on. No matter how much my head pounded, or stomach turned, I needed to see the damage we'd done last night.

Pushing the door to the living room open, I found River already awake, a bag of rubbish in his hands.

"Good morning, Princess," he said as I entered the room.

I yawned widely, gazing about the place. It was mostly cleaned—at least, by River's parties' standards. All the furniture had been placed back in their rightful spots. Most of the rubbish was picked up. No stray guests were draped over the couches.

"I already kicked out the strays," River said, reading my mind. "You want some paracetamol?"

"You know me so well."

I followed him to the kitchen where he poured me some water and popped some painkillers into my hand. I swallowed them, watching him carefully.

"Why aren't you as hungover as I am?" I asked.

"I didn't drink much last night."

I scoffed. "You? You didn't drink much last night?"

"Hey, I'm a changed man," he replied with a shrug. "That, or you're just an absolute light weight."

I snorted, draining the rest of my water before standing again. River's eyes fell down to my jumper, then back up again.

"I saw him leave," River replied. "He seemed... okay."

"That's good," I said.

"Are you?"

"Am I what?"

"Are you okay?"

I huffed, pushing off the kitchen counter with a bitter smile. "That's a loaded question, River."

"You know what I mean."

"I'm fine. We're halfway through the semester now. Everett will be back again soon. We'll call. It'll be fine." I rounded the kitchen counter to pat him on the shoulder. "Thanks for putting yourself through that emotional torture to check on me, though."

He rolled his eyes at me, a smile still twitching at his lips. "Never make me do it again."

With my help, the rest of the living room was cleaned within the hour, leaving me with the rest of the day to study.

With the midterms done, I knew exactly where I had to practice now. It was a lot of areas, but at least now I knew in time for the next one. I knew where to begin now.

Everett's first text came in the late afternoon, when I was already deep in my studying. When my phone buzzed, I jumped, fishing through my pockets to check my messages.

Everett: Hey, just landed for my lay over. How's the damage?

I responded immediately.

Isla: Not bad. Hangover's sorted, and River cleaned most of the living room before I woke up.

Isla: How was the flight?

Instead of replying, Everett's face popped up on my screen, requesting a video call. I answered it, finding his face grinning up at me.

"Good morning, gorgeous," he said.

I laughed, rolling my eyes. "It's actually past five now."

"Well, it's morning for me. I slept through that whole flight. Woke up for the food though."

"Was it worth it?"

He scrunched his nose. "Absolutely not. Fish stew? Whose idea was that?"

I snorted. "I thought you liked fish."

"Oh, I don't know what that was, but it was definitely not fish. Misleading name, really." He grinned at my laughter and his eyes softened. "Nice sweater."

"Thanks, my boyfriend left it for me."

"You have another boyfriend?"

I rolled my eyes, smiling. "Everett."

"Well, he has pretty good taste."

"He goes to NYU."

"Must be smart too."

"Sometimes. He's transferring to Australia soon, though. We're going to be... what's the opposite of long distance?"

"It doesn't matter. As long as I can wake up to you every morning, you can call it whatever you want."

I smiled back, shifting how I was sitting to move my laptop further away, instead making my videocall full screen to cover my study notes. Everett seemed to notice because he asked, "Are you studying?"

I nodded. "I got the feedback for my midterms now so I figured I should use it."

"Oh, well, don't let me stop you," he started,

"But I want to talk to you," I said quickly.

"I wasn't going to hang up." He laughed and shifted slightly, leaning closer to the camera to rest his jaw on his hand. "Teach me."

I scoffed. "What?"

"Teach me. Whatever you're studying. We can study together."

"Seriously?"

"Yeah. I have a four-hour layover, Isla. I'm willing to do anything at this point."

"But—I barely know what I'm studying. How am I supposed to teach it to you?"

"Just try it," he said, "trust me."

I frowned, unsure, but pulled my laptop back onto my lap anyway.

"Alright," I said, scrolling to where I'd left off. "So, there are a few different types of glial cells."

"Glial cells?"

"Yeah. They're, like, supporting cells."

"What do they do?"

"They support neurons. You know, they transport waste out and nutrients in. Stuff like that."

"Right. So, they're only in the brain then?"

"Well, sort of. They're in our nervous system."

"What were the different types?"

"In the central nervous system, there are astrocytes, oligo-dendrocytes and microglial cells. Astrocytes are called that because they look like stars."

I blinked, realising Everett was grinning widely at me. My face warmed.

"What?" I asked.

"Nothing," he said. "You just said you barely know what you're studying but you answered all of my questions."

I frowned. He was right. I did. I cleared my throat.

"Well, I've got my laptop right here and—I mean, how do you even know I got them right?"

"I know," he said. He smiled and my chest grew warm. It was probably a good thing he was off in some faraway country. My eyes moved back to my laptop screen. "So, what's the next one?"

"Right. The myelin sheath."

By the time Everett's layover was done, I'd finished revising and fixing half of my notes with him as an eager listener.

We'd eaten dinner together—or whatever meal Everett was on in his mixed-up schedule. River popped in and said hello, and then Connor did too—from the screen of River's phone.

Somehow, our apartment had turned into a hostel for long distance relationships. Luckily, River's parents had valued a strong Wi-Fi connection in their home.

And then the sun had gone down again, and Everett was off on the next leg of his flight; this time, until he was actually home, halfway around the world.

But it set the tone for the rest of the week.

And suddenly, my call log was filled with Everett.

It was like that first month we dated—we called in between classes, during meals, while he was at the gym, while I was lying in bed before sleeping. Everett flooded my life.

But most of all, we called while studying. If I wasn't talking to Everett, I was revising my notes and doing assignments—or both. I had always been good at multitasking. And with Everett as a motivator, I was finding studying more appealing than usual.

Even River joined us sometimes, our phones set up beside each other, Connor on one screen and Everett on the other.

It was certainly a sight to see—Everett walking through New York at odd hours of the day, Connor dressed in his fluorescent vest on some worksite; and River and I's books laid out in front of them. An odd mixture that somehow worked.

With the increase of improvised study dates, River seemed to stop throwing parties as often as he used to. Instead of groaning coming through the walls of his room, now I could hear laughter, stolen in the quiet hours of the night. Sometimes I wondered whatever happened to Alistair. Most of the time, I didn't care. I liked seeing Connor more often, with Austin sometimes waving in the background, but most of all, I liked seeing River happy.

It wasn't until two weeks after Everett left that I had another quiz due. I'd called him as soon as I hit submit, the tab minimised and my score was hidden from me until he answered.

"Just click on it, Isla," he said through the line. I could see his camera shaking slightly as he walked through dark streets this time.

Dark for a different reason. For me, it was just after sunset. For him, he had just woken up and was getting an early start before his first class.

"Get it over and done with. Like ripping off a Band-Aid. You know?"

"I'm scared," I said. "It's a quiz, but it was worth like 30% of my grade."

"You have nothing to be scared of. You worked hard."

"That's exactly why I'm scared! I studied so hard for this. If I fail again, after all that work—it's like, what do I even do now?"

I sighed dropping my head into my hands. With all the studying I'd been doing, and with Everett occupying most of my time, I had barely given myself time to stress over this quiz. It was all hitting me at once—the what-ifs. The possibility of failure.

"Isla." His voice was stern, forcing me to look up and catch his eye. "You studied hard, and that's why you should have faith in your score. Whether it's what you hoped for or not, you know that you gave it your all. You can't change the past now."

"But I can ignore it."

He laughed, rolling his eyes. "Or you can ignore it."

I hummed, considering it. "Maybe I can just close the tab and find out after my final exam when marks are released."

"Isla, just open it."

"But what if I did really bad?"

"What if you did really good?"

I huffed. He had a good point.

"Fine," I said. "But if I failed, I'm dropping out. For real."

"If you say so."

"And it'll be on your conscience forever."

"I mean, you're the one who took the quiz."

"Still!" He grinned at me, and I sucked in a deep breath, nodding. "Okay, on three."

"One," Everett started.

"Two," I continued.

"Three."

My results flooded the screen, my eyes immediately landing on the numbers.

My heart fell into my stomach.

A gasp caught in my throat.

Everett said nothing. He only watched me as my hand flew to cover my mouth.

A smile grew beneath my fingers.

"I passed," I whispered.

CHAPTER 24

L ast Summer

Everett sat beside me. His laptop lay propped open beside him on the mattress, his lap completely occupied with me laying in it. One of his hands toyed with my hair, the other idly scrolling through his notes.

I turned, shifting slightly so that I could see his screen more clearly.

"What are you doing? Aren't you supposed to be on break?" I asked.

He snorted, pausing his scrolling to smile at me. "There's no such thing as a break in college. I still have assignments due."

I sighed, leaning back to look up at him. His hand moved, sliding over my forehead, and brushing my hair back, out of my face, as he met my eyes. It was only the start of December, so the weather was still warming up. It wasn't quite summer yet, but I'd savour our time together as much as possible before he left again for university.

Before I left for university.

"That sucks," I muttered. "You deserve a break."

"It's only for a few years," he said, smiling. He leaned forward, pressing a soft kiss just above my brow. I melted under his lips. "Besides, I'm trying to get my grades up. I need to ace this assignment."

"Is it going to be like this when I'm at uni too?" I asked. He didn't have to answer me. I already knew what I'd signed up for. "How will we have time to do anything else?"

"We'll find time," he replied easily, like it was nothing. Like the thought of going long distance again didn't weigh on his shoulders. Our shoulders. "We've always found time before, haven't we?"

"You're right," I said. I offered him a small smile. "You're always right."

"I try," he hummed, his eyes veering back to his laptop screen.

He resumed his scrolling, occasionally pausing to highlight certain sentences or bold words. I watched him in silence for a few minutes, observing the layout of his notes, watching the way his hand slid across his keyboard.

For a moment, I wondered. What would it have been like if we'd met like normal teenagers? If we'd gone to school together and bumped into each other in a classroom instead of in Shellside Bay. What would it have been like then?

The thought fleeted and I shut my eyes for a moment. There was no point in thinking about those things. They would never happen. But what we did have, it was more than enough. It was perfect.

I opened my eyes again to find Everett already staring at me. We locked eyes and his lips twitched in a smile.

"What are you thinking of?" he asked. His hand drifted through my hair again, combing strands back from my forehead before tracing a path down the edges of my face.

I smiled back at him, memorising the feel of his fingerprints on my skin.

"Nothing," I said.

□□□□□□□□□□□

"You know, if you started earlier, you would've been done by now."

I rolled my eyes, not bothering to look up and see Everett's smirking face through my screen.

"What was that you told me last time? Can't change the past? Besides, I was busy studying for my final exams."

"Not sure why you bothered. You did amazing on that quiz last time," Everett said.

I looked up, finally, and smiled arrogantly at him. "I did, didn't I?"

"Don't make me take it back."

My grin grew as I turned back to my laptop, continuing my final touches on the last report I had due this semester.

My first semester at university, and it had flown by so quickly. There had been bumps along the way, but I felt I had redeemed myself in the second half. And now the semester break was approaching, and I'd have two months of freedom before I had to subject myself to the same torture all over again.

But first, I had a report due tonight, and my last exam of the semester tomorrow.

"So, what time are you leaving?" Everett asked between bites. He was eating something—lunch? Breakfast? Brunch? I wasn't sure at this point—while talking to me. Multitasking, the most important skill in a long-distance relationship.

"Three," I replied. "Tomorrow, right after my exam."

"And when's your report due?"

"Seven."

"So, that's, what? An hour from now?"

I blinked, my eyes flittering to the time in the corner of my screen before I looked up from my report. "Look at you, you're so good with your Sydney time zone knowledge."

"What can I say? I'm just such an incredible boyfriend."

I deadpanned. "Don't make me take it back."

"One hour," he said, ignoring me. "That's not much time to finish your report, submit it, study for and take your exam, and then pack before you leave."

"Oh, please. River said three, but knowing him, he won't even be packed until six tomorrow."

"Actually, I'm already completely packed."

I spun at the sound of River's voice, finding him leaning against the doorframe to my bedroom.

I frowned. "I'm going to start closing my door."

"Would you, please? I'm sick of hearing you and Everett's 'You hang up!' 'No, you!'"

"We don't even do that."

"Well," Everett inputted.

"We don't," I cut in. I narrowed my eyes at River. He'd gotten a haircut, buzzing his hair down to a neat buzzcut—the kind he always had when he used to visit Shellside Bay. "Why are you already packed? You're not even busy tomorrow."

"He's got someone waiting for him down in Shellside Bay," Everett teased.

River scowled, yet his blood betrayed him, rushing to his cheeks.

"Shut up," he spat. "I just pack light. Unlike somebody."

He gestured meaningfully towards my overly large suitcase spread out on the floor between us.

"Oh, come on. I have to bring back souvenirs for everyone. And I didn't pack any winter clothes when we moved here. I need to bring a lot of jumpers back from Shellside Bay, okay?"

"What, my sweaters aren't enough?" Everett asked.

I frowned at him. "Everett. I love you, but no. Two sweaters are not enough for an entire semester."

"How many do you need? I'll bring you more next time."

"Everett!" I exclaimed, half-laughing. "Stop. You've already given me so much."

"I want to do this for you. I like seeing you in my sweaters."

"No, we have an agreement. I don't want to take more of your stuff from you."

"Screw the agreement, Isla—"

"Gross," River interrupted. He gagged at me, rolling his eyes. "You two are so fucking disgusting."

"Oh, please. You and Connor aren't any better. I hear you at night. 'I miss you, Connor. I can't wait to see you, Connor.'"

"I have literally never said that before in my entire life."

"If you say so."

River blushed, looking away, and I knew I'd caught him in his lie. "Whatever. Just—be ready tomorrow or I'm leaving without you."

"You wouldn't."

"Wanna bet?"

We stared at each other for a moment before I sighed, closing my laptop.

"Change of plans, Everett. I'm packing now. The report and exam can wait."

River smirked, nodding before pushing off the doorframe and leaving. Everett chuckled through the screen.

"You're really going to let him boss you around like that?"

"Hey, I don't have a car, okay? And petrol is expensive."

I knelt down beside my suitcase, leaning my phone against it as I carefully folded my clothes to put inside. We'd be staying for three weeks, and I needed to pack accordingly.

"How many bras do you think I'll need? Six?"

Everett's expression twisted. "What do you even need six different bras for?"

"Well, this one's my comfy daytime bra, this one's a push up, this one's more of a bralette—"

"I don't know what any of those words mean."

I smirked at him. "Do you want me to model them for you?"

"Yes," he replied instantly. "Wait! No. I'm at the cafeteria. Anyone could look over my shoulder and see you. In fact, maybe you should turn your camera off completely. I don't want any passers-by stealing you from me."

"I don't know. That brown-haired guy behind you looks pretty cute."

Immediately, he spun, his eyes growing wide only to meet his reflection in the mirrored column behind him. He turned back to send me a look through the camera.

"Good one, Isla."

"I'm such an adorable girlfriend, aren't I?" I teased.

"Completely adorable," he replied, monotone.

I narrowed my eyes at him. "You're just jealous that I'm going to Shellside Bay while you're stuck in stinky New York."

"New York is not—okay, it does smell occasionally. But Shellside Bay will smell worse once you're there."

"You're such a bully. A jealous bully."

He laughed. "Alright, you got me. I'm jealous. Extremely jealous. You're going to be having fun beach hopping and surfing while I'm attending classes at eight in the morning."

"Hey, I won't be having that much fun. I'll be too busy missing you." He scoffed, shaking his head with a small smile as if I'd told a joke. I persisted. "Seriously, though. I wish you could come."

"I wish I could too, but I have class. Besides, I've spent most of my money visiting you these past few months and my stepmom won't give me anymore until I visit for dinner next month," Everett grumbled. "As if it's her money to lend."

"Play nice, Ev. Your dad likes her."

"I know, I know. But it doesn't mean I have to. And now she's holding my dad's money hostage so that I'm forced to see them more often—as if that'll make me like her any better!"

"Maybe she just wants to motivate you to visit more often."

"I hate it when you're rational."

"One of us has to be." I shrugged. "And it's not like I want you to spend any more money coming here after all. I don't want you wasting it like that. You're supposed to be funding your education or saving for your future."

"You are my future."

My whole face warmed, every neuron in my body lighting up. But I steeled my face and settled him with a serious look.

"Everett."

"Alright, alright," he said, sighing again. "I just miss you. All the time."

"I can buy you a ticket? You can spend a few days here and re-energise, and—"

"Absolutely not," Everett cut in. "No. You need your money. I'll see my—ugh—stepmom for dinner next month. I'm getting a job soon anyway. Just—just have fun at Shellside Bay for the both of us, yeah? Say hi to my grandma for me."

"I will," I replied before quickly throwing in, "And I'll use my savings to visit you this summer."

Everett didn't miss it. He shook his head, huffing. "Isla, what did I just say?"

"I want to, though! I've never been to New York and—I don't know—my mum is travelling the world. A winter Christmas sounds amazing. I want to visit. Truly."

His lips twitched and I knew he couldn't deny it anymore. "Fine. But you have to bring me Tim Tams."

A smile erupted on my face, matching his, and my folded clothes sat on the floor, long forgotten.

"Okay, I'll bring Tim Tams."

"And Flakes. Oh, and Freddo Frogs!"

"Flakes and Freddo Frogs, added to the list. Anything else?"

"Nothing," he replied, "Just your cute self."

"Oh, that's all, is it?"

"It's all I need, really. If I don't have chocolate to eat, I'd be happy to eat—"

"Everett!"

"I was going to say dinner with you." He smirked. I wasn't buying it.

"Oh, really?"

"Really."

"Me and my cute self?"

"That's what I said, wasn't it?"

Seconds later, River's voice came from the other room.

"You both are fucking disgusting!"

Everett and I shared a smile before laughtererupted from both of us—simultaneous laughter on opposite ends of the globe.And in that moment, it felt good enough. It felt perfect.

CHAPTER 25

"We're officially done!"

I squealed as Lachie pulled me into a hug, spinning me outside the exam hall. Around us, students turned, sending us looks as they flooded out into the open air, but I didn't care. I was officially free.

"Freedom, at last!" Lachie cheered, setting me back onto the ground. "Let's go wreak havoc. Let's burn our notes and lab manuals to ash."

I laughed, waving my notes in the air. "I know our first semester is officially over, but as much as I would love to burn these notes, I feel like we'll need them for next semester."

"God, don't remind me that we have another semester," he groaned.

"And another after that, and another, and another..."

"Go to university, they said. It'll be fun, they said."

I rolled my eyes, whacking his arm with my loose papers. "You're such a dork. Don't pretend you aren't having fun. I see you, with your millions of friends on campus and parties every other night."

"Hey, that's on you for living off campus. Campus is where the fun's at." He paused to grin. "You know, because I'm there."

I scoffed. "Right, because you're such a blast."

"I really am," he replied. He shrugged his backpack higher onto his shoulders and turned to me. "So, what are your plans now that you're free? You down for dinner?"

He blinked at me hopefully, a charming smile pulling on his lips. I shook my head.

"Nah, I'm off to Shellside Bay," I said. "River's picking me up from here and we're heading straight down to the beach."

His smile faded with a nod. "Right. Of course. That sounds amazing. I'm sure you'll enjoy yourself."

"Hopefully." I turned the conversation back towards him, suddenly feeling bad for turning him down for dinner. "What about you? Aren't you heading home for the holidays?"

Now that I thought about it, I'd never asked Lachie where 'home' exactly was. I knew he lived on campus, which usually meant home was probably too far to just catch a train or drive each day, but that was just an assumption. I had no idea where he'd really come from.

"No, not me," Lachie said. He looked away from me, a forced smile pulling on his lips. "It's—uh—a bit too far. My parents live out past Dubbo, actually."

I frowned. I knew Dubbo was pretty far from the city, but it couldn't be that far. It was probably just a few hours longer than a trip to Shellside Bay. Surely, he'd be okay with the distance for the chance to spend a month with his family—especially after not seeing them for so long.

He seemed to sense my thoughts because he quickly added, "Besides, I'm sure they've got a lot on their plate right now. I'd rather stay here instead of making the trip. More to do anyway."

"Right," I muttered. We met eyes and he shrugged slightly, as if waving the subject off. I couldn't help it. I felt sorry for him. Even if he seemed to have a lot of friends on campus, how fun could it really be sitting on an empty university campus all break? And how many of his friends would be leaving for home themselves?

He'd be here, alone, for weeks until everyone returned.

The words came tumbling out before I could stop them.

"Hey, why don't you come down to Shellside Bay with us?"

His brows furrowed. I resisted the urge to smack my hands over my big fat mouth. Had I really just invited him on a three-hour road trip with me and River? That would probably evolve into an almost month long stay with us?

Where would he stay? What would he do the whole time?

What would River say? He'd either laugh or murder me in my sleep. Both were terrifying prospects when it came to River.

But worse—what would Everett say?

God, I really hadn't thought that through.

Everett knew Lachie wasn't a threat. Really, no one was a threat against Everett. Except for maybe Tom Holland, but that was highly improbable.

No, he knew Lachie wasn't a threat, but that wouldn't stop his heart from breaking when he discovered that Lachie would be spending a few weeks in Shellside Bay with me while Everett was stuck on the other side of the world. The thought would eat him alive.

It was too late, though. The words were out, drifting in the air between us. I couldn't put them back in. It was like my entire body was frozen, waiting for a reply as Lachie opened his mouth and his answer came out—

"Is Everett coming?"

I blinked. "What?"

"Everett. That's your boyfriend's name, isn't it? Is he going to be there?"

"No," I said slowly. "He's back in New York."

It was a perfectly normal question, and yet it felt strange somehow. Why was he asking that? Why did he need to know that to answer me?

"Right. Well, I'd have to check with work. See if I can get time off so suddenly," Lachie replied.

"Oh, of course!" I rushed out, waving a hand. "I mean, no worries if it's a big deal. I wouldn't want you to get into trouble or anything."

Part of me felt entirely relieved. He had to check with work. There was no way he'd be able to find out if he could come before River arrived.

I glanced towards the road—where was River? What was taking him so long? I tapped my foot against the pavement, anxiously waiting for him to help me escape this conversation and the consequences of my own fat mouth.

Right on time, a car pulled up on the road beside us. Any normal person would have called or texted, but instead, River honked loudly, grabbing the attention of everyone on the street.

When I refused to acknowledge him, he rolled down the window and started yelling.

"Come on, Monroe, or I'm leaving without you!"

I rolled my eyes, flipping him off, keeping my eyes on Lachie.

"Well, I need to get going. Maybe next time then, yeah?" I spoke quickly. Lachie smiled, glancing towards River.

"Oh, well, I could always drive down myself," he said. He waved at River who only glared in response, slowing rolling his window back up. Lachie turned back to me. "Look, I'll call my work and let you know, yeah?"

"Oh," I said, words escaping me. Right when I'd thought I got out of it. I cleared my throat, forcing my lips to move. "Sure! Of course. Right. Let me know."

"And, have fun on your trip, yeah? Enjoy the freedom and your three-hour car ride with River," he said. He leaned forward, whacking my back in the form of a brief hug before turning away.

I snorted, my feet already moving towards River's car as I waved goodbye. "I'll do my best! Have a good break! I'll see you next semester."

"Or sooner!" he hollered back.

My smile felt forced. "Or sooner."

I entered River's car with a slam of the door and a heavy sigh. He only stared at me, his face emotionless.

"What was that all about?" he asked. I sighed, my entire body slouching in shame as the words escaped me,

"I may have accidentally invited him to Shellside Bay this vacation."

"Accidentally?" he sputtered, chortling in disbelief. "How do you accidentally invite someone on a trip?"

"I don't know! It was like—he was telling me about how he's staying here for the break, and his family is, like, busy or something, and I just—my mouth kept moving! I couldn't stop myself! It was like—like when Mrs Clemente asked me to babysit Everett. The words just slipped out!"

River seemed to struggle in holding back his laughter. He clapped a hand over his forehead, shaking his head at me. "God, Isla, you're too nice for your own good."

"Sorry for having a heart. You should try it sometime, you know," I shot back.

He lifted a brow at me. "Yeah, well, based off the trouble it gets you into, I don't think I will. He's not coming is he?"

"What do you have against Lachie?"

He glanced at me, narrowing his eyes as if he'd caught me in a lie. "Oh, so you want him to come, then? It wasn't an accident?"

"No, it's just—he's—I don't know. He's nice."

River snorted. "Sounds real charming."

I rolled my eyes as he reached forward, starting the engine and the three-hour journey back home.

☐☐☐☐☐☐☐☐☐☐

Two hours into the road trip, Everett called me.

"God, don't tell me you're going to have phone sex for the rest of the drive," River complained.

Everett laughed through the phone. "You can relax, River. I'll save the phone sex for later."

"Everett!"

"Gross," River gagged.

Everett only laughed some more. "I've only got fifteen minutes before my next class anyway."

"More than enough time for you," I teased.

"Double gross," River gagged again. "At least Lachie isn't here to make it triple."

"Lachie?" Everett asked. "Why would he be there?"

"Oh, you won't believe it. Isla here accidentally invited Lachie to spend the break in Shellside with us."

"What?" Everett frowned through the camera.

Great. I glared at River. He just had to open his mouth.

"I felt sorry for him," I explained. "Anyway, it's no big deal. He said that he would have to call work first, so he probably won't even come."

"You mean, he might still come?" Everett asked.

I hesitated. "I mean, possibly, I don't really know... We didn't talk about it, I just left as soon as River pulled up!"

"Isla."

"If it's any consolation, I regretted it as soon as the words left my mouth. But, I mean, I couldn't just take it back!"

"Oh, the struggles of having a heart," River teased wistfully.

"It'll be fine. Even if he does manage to come, it'll be like a friendly hangout, you know?" I justified.

"I still don't want him to go," Everett whined.

"You and me both," I replied.

"Well, I want him to come," River said. I turned to look at him and he grinned. "It would be funny."

"You know, I'm starting to second think that phone sex idea," Everett said.

"I take it all back."

"That's what I thought."

"Everett," I said, drawing his attention back to me. "It'll be fine. Besides, how would he get time off work so last minute?"

He paused, his face twisting into a sour frown before he nodded slowly. "Yeah. Yeah, I know you're right. And I trust you so... How was your exam?"

I smiled. "Amazing, but only because it's over. Did I do well? Questionable. Is it over? Hell yeah."

"I'm sure you did incredible. You taught me lots about cell biology," he said. He paused, lifting a brow in a teasing smirk. "And other forms of biology."

"I will not hesitate to swerve this car into a tree," River threatened.

Everett laughed. "Okay, okay! I'm done! Please don't murder my girlfriend."

"I won't," River said. "For now."

"For now?"

"Make one more sexual innuendo, Everett. I dare you."

"I'm suddenly feeling very uncomfortable in this car," I said.

River grinned. "Good. Only an hour to go. And then you're stuck with me all month."

I forced a smile. "I'm so excited."

My voice was dry, filled with sarcasm, but the words themselves were true.

If I craned my neck to peak through the trees, the cliff dipped into the ocean—an ocean that connected to Shellside Bay.

An ocean that would lead me home.

CHAPTER 26

Watching the sunrise in Shellside Bay had become something I took for granted for all those years I lived there. But visiting for my autumn break, it was a luxury that I'd soak up as much as I could.

I sat on the sand, just metres from the water, watching as the clouds turned pink. Orange flames licked the sky, slowly stretching towards the horizon. Even looking at the water, I could tell it was freezing. There was some icy quality about it in autumn—or maybe it was the chill breeze messing with my mind, making the water seem more silver than usual.

I willed the ocean to rise higher, for the water to creep over the sands and step over my toes. I missed the feeling of salt water on my skin, and yet I was too cowardly to take the step into the icy waves.

When I lived here, autumn in Shellside Bay was a time for staying indoors, hiding from the cold wind and colder water.

Now, I would take what I could get. I would recharge at the beach and take in every last second until I was forced back into the city.

I loved the city. I loved living with River and all the opportunities it brought with it. I loved being able to buy a carton of eggs downstairs at two in the morning. And I really loved being able to get a cheeseburger for Maccas at any time of day.

But Shellside Bay owned a corner of my heart; and staying away for this long had drained it empty. It was time to refill.

I counted the waves as they lapped over the sand until my counting was disturbed by footsteps shifting the sand behind me.

"Isla!"

I spun at the sound of River's voice. He raced down the sand, his feet almost slipping, sand piling into his sneakers. Yet, he didn't stop. His face looked frantic.

"Isla!" he shouted again. His voice was eaten by the wind and the waves, barely reaching me on the final syllable.

"What happened?" I yelled back.

He reached me, bending over his knees, and sucking in air as I waited for the news. He shook his head, like shaking the exhaustion away, and met me with wide eyes.

"Results are out."

"What?"

"Results. They're out."

"Already?" I sputtered. How many weeks had it been? It didn't feel long, and yet, it felt like months at the same time. A thought occurred to me. "Have you checked yours yet?"

He shook his head. "Want to check together?"

I nodded, fishing in my pocket for my phone. I'd turned it to silent, deciding to spend my entire morning surrounded by only the sound of the ocean and the light of the sunrise. And yet, there it was.

An email waited for me in my notifications.

Subject line: Term 1 Results.

"Holy shit," I muttered.

"What, that bad?"

I shot River a glare. "No. I haven't opened them yet. I just—I don't know. What if it's like last time?"

What if I failed again?

What if, after all of that additional effort, it still wasn't enough?

What if university was all a big mistake? And I wasn't made for this life. And I was destined to live in Shellside Bay forever—take over my mum's waitressing job, throw out my textbooks, shut down my laptop.

What if all this was for nothing?

"What if it's not?"

I turned to River, frowning. "What?"

"What if it's not like last time? You'll never know unless you look, right?"

I blinked down at my phone, the words on the screen glaring up at me. "I guess so."

"Let's find out then," he said.

He pressed my finger down and the email opened before I could react. The screen flashed white, and then the numbers appeared.

75, 87, 61, 86.

I read them again.

"Holy shit," I whispered again.

River's chin rested on my shoulder as he read my results aloud. He whistled, the sound cutting through the crashing of waves.

"Isla, that's pretty good."

"Good?" I echoed. "I used to get 90's in high school. I could get full marks without breaking a sweat. All that studying, and I could barely scrape a sixty?"

"Oh, come on Monroe," he sighed. He shifted, moving to sit beside me. He flashed his phone in front of my face, showing me his marks; all between fifty and seventy.

"This is university," he began. "Obviously you're not going to get marks like you did in high school. Shit gets hard. So what? You passed, didn't you?"

I exhaled a laugh, turning to smile drily at him. "Has anyone ever told you you're amazing at comforting people?"

"No."

"I can see why."

He rolled his eyes, yet a smile pulled at his lips. "Oh, shut up. I tried my best, okay?"

I grinned, leaning towards him until my head rested on his shoulder. "And I love you for that."

"Yeah, yeah. Whatever."

His voice was thick with annoyance, and yet he leaned his head against mine, his arm wrapping around me in a half-hug. I lifted my arm behind him, landing my hand on his buzz cut.

"I missed this River. Shellside Bay River," I said, running my fingers over his shaved head. "He was gone for too long."

He snorted. "What can I say? The city corrupts."

A smirk tugged at my lips, but I kept my voice steady. "I think it has more to do with your boyfriend than the city itself."

Immediately, River's walls flew up. "He's not my boyfriend."

His voice was completely flustered. I glanced his way to find his cheeks splotching red and had to fight the urge to burst out in laughter. River? Blushing? Those two things rarely went together.

I couldn't help it. A giggle exploded from my lips and his half-hug turned into a half-tackle as he pushed me into the sand. It didn't stop me from laughing.

"You're in such denial," I teased.

"He's not!" he complained, pushing me over. "Shut up."

"Oh, come on. You guys talk every day."

"Yeah, well, so do you and Lachie," he shot back.

My face warmed and I shoved him away, my mood turning sour. I felt the intense need to defend myself. "I do not!"

"Oh, please."

"I don't! Especially since the semester ended."

He was not convinced. "But before that?"

"Only because we had class all the time." I shoved him hard, catching what he was trying to do. "Stop deflecting. I have a boyfriend." I paused, kicking sand towards him. "And so do you."

"I'm telling you, he's not my—my boyfriend. He's never used that word before."

"Do you want him to be your boyfriend?"

"Do we seriously have to have this conversation right now? Can't we just enjoy the sunrise?"

He glared at me, and I matched his look for a moment before relenting.

"Fine," I said, settling back into the sand and watching as the sun continued to lift above the horizon. "But as soon as Sky gets here, we're talking about this. For real."

□□□□□□□□□□

Sky made it to Shellside Bay before lunch. She'd been spending the last month in Perth, so after flying back to the east coast, her first stop had to be Melbourne to visit her pregnant cousin and official cousin-in-law Josh. They'd held her up for longer than she'd anticipated, and so here she was—two weeks later, but here.

She found us at the Shack and sprinted across the sand to reach us.

"Isla!" she squealed, throwing her arms around me. I squeezed her back, burying my face in her neck.

"I missed you so, so much. How's the Gap Year 2.0 going?"

"Amazing," she replied. Her shoulders sagged as she pulled back to smile at me. "But it's so good to be home."

"What, you travelled all around Australia just to figure out that Shellside Bay is the best?"

She laughed. "I never said that. But you're not entirely wrong. I mean, what other town or city has a Shack like this?"

She nodded towards the Shack beside us. My old boss, Tom Buckner, stood under the shade, scribbling in his notebook. He looked up at her voice and smiled sarcastically.

"Good to see you too, Sky," he said.

"Tom, you know it's autumn, right? Take the day off! Relax a little," Sky said, grinning as she leaned over the counter towards him.

He ignored her, only continuing to fill out his notebook. "Just because it's a little colder than usual doesn't mean we need to shut down. People still drink water in autumn."

"Right, because $4 bottles of water are what run your business."

"Sky, leave him alone," I interjected before shooting Tom a cheeky smile. "He's an old man, you don't want to raise his blood pressure."

Tom narrowed his eyes, pointing a finger towards me. "Don't forget, I'm still one of your job references."

My mouth snapped shut. Sky giggled, throwing her arm around me, and pulling me closer.

"How were your finals?" she asked.

"Fine," I replied. "I mean, I passed everything."

"Yes!" she cheered. Her hug became tighter and, combined with her shorter height, I found myself bending over, my face growing closer and closer to the sand as her arms squeeze tighter around me. "I knew my best friend was a genius."

"Alright, alright," I said through my laughter, prying her arms off of me. "I said I did fine; I didn't do amazingly."

"Oh, please. Fine to you is beyond amazing to me." She paused, looking around the beach. "Where's everyone else?"

"Austin and Connor are working," I replied. "River's out there."

Sky's gaze followed mine towards the water where River was already looking at us. He was shirtless, walking slowly from the ocean to the sands, a surfboard dragging behind him.

"What the hell is he doing? It's freezing out there!" Sky frowned, watching him as he tried to hide his shivering, keeping his usual nonchalant 'River' expression on settled on his face instead.

By the time he reached us, he couldn't hide his shivering any longer. His entire body shook as water dripped off his shoulders and down his bare chest.

"It's fucking cold," River said.

I scoffed, reaching behind the counter of the Shack to grab his towel and throw it over his head.

"No shit. I told you it was a bad idea," I replied.

He grabbed the towel, running it over his body with quick movements before throwing an arm around Sky in a half-hug. She shoved him away immediately.

"Get away. I don't want to get wet," Sky chided.

River cracked a smirk. "Don't worry, you're not my type."

"Gross," Sky and I said in sync.

"Don't do that again," I added.

River's smirk fell and he rolled his eyes. "Whatever. Pass me my shirt, yeah?"

I threw it at his face. He peeled it off, settling me with a glare as I stifled my laughter. Before he could say anything, though, my ringtone went off. I grabbed my phone, instantly answering it without looking.

"Ev," I said.

"Hey, Isla," he said. Except it wasn't Everett's voice.

I glanced at the screen, frowning, before pressing the phone back to my ear. I stepped out of earshot from the others before saying, "Lachie?"

"Hey," he replied. "Sorry, were you expecting a call from someone else?"

"No. No, I just—I didn't look properly. What's up?"

"Did you see the semester results are out?" he asked. "I was wondering how you went."

"Oh! Good. I did good. Passed everything. What about you?"

In front of me, Sky and River were exchanging strange looks and mouthing words to me that seemed a lot like, who are you talking to?

I shook my head, turning so that they would stop distracting me.

"Good," Lachie said through the receiver. "Could've been better, but hey, P's get degrees, right?"

"Exactly."

Lachie was silent for a moment before saying, "Sorry I couldn't come to Shellside Bay, by the way. I didn't realise all my co-workers had blocked out their schedules for the break. Maybe next time though?"

"Oh, yeah," I sputtered. "Maybe."

I wondered if my maybe sounded convincing enough. Really, my maybe was more like a never.

It wasn't that I didn't want Lachie to come to Shellside Bay. It was just—Shellside Bay was almost like a little secret for the Nauti Buoys and I only. And bringing someone from the city into home territory, especially when Everett wasn't around—it felt almost treasonous. It felt wrong.

It was like when Everett first appeared, and he seemed to taint the bright sands of Shellside Bay with his outstandingly city attitude.

Maybe one day, Lachie would visit.

My phone beeped and I frowned, noticing I'd received a text from River. I spun, shooting him a glare as he shrugged, grinning at me.

"Sorry, Lachie, I think I have to go," I said, still glaring at River. "I'm being pestered by someone who can't figure out what 'I'm on the phone' means."

"Let me guess, River?"

"Yep."

"I'll leave you to it then," he said, laughing. "Congrats on the results! See you next sem?"

"For sure."

He hung up and I stepped forward, slapping River on the back of his neck.

"What was that for?" he complained.

"Disrupting my phone call," I said. I pulled up River's text, reading it out loud. "Tell Lachlan that it's not normal to call up girls who have boyfriends to ask about their exam results."

River chuckled to himself. "Am I wrong?"

"We're just friends, you dolt."

"Does he know that?"

"Of course, he does. He's met Everett." I paused, frowning. "How'd you know I was talking to Lachie?"

He laughed, meeting knowing eyes with Sky. "Isla, you're from a small town. You don't know how to talk to people outside of Shellside Bay. Your face goes all stiff and shit."

"Gee, thanks, River. Good to know I'm frigid."

"Anytime," he replied. "Besides, it's not like Lachlan is any less frigid than you are. You should've seen him in high school."

I narrowed my eyes at him. "Why do you say that like you knew him in high school?"

"Because I did," he said, as if it were obvious. "We went to the same school."

"What? He told me he's from the countryside."

"We had dorms, Monroe. He was a boarding student."

"And you guys were in the same grade?"

"No shit."

"So, you knew him."

"No shit."

The news hit me and turned the world lopsided for a moment. It was like everything I knew about River and Lachie had been erased and replaced with this new piece of information. It was like realising once again that River outside of Shellside Bay was a River I never knew. It was a reminder that, other than the people I grew up with—Sky, Austin, Connor, and to some extent, River—I would never know their lives, who they were before they met me. Not really. Not in the same way.

I wondered what I didn't know about Everett. What things I'd never thought to ask him, things he'd never thought to mention; things I'd never thought to mention.

"Why didn't he say anything?" I asked.

River shrugged. "I was barely at school. I don't think I ever said a word to him. Besides, he was only there for our final year. He was super introverted. Never would've expected him to be such a popular guy on campus. I guess he's trying to change his reputation now or something."

"What, like go from an introvert to an extrovert?"

"Yeah," River said. "Not that he knows how. I don't think he knows how to talk to girls—even the ones he's just friends with."

"What do you mean? He's not, like, strange or anything."

"That's because you're strange, Monroe."

"What! No I'm not!" I frowned at him and when he didn't react, I turned to Sky. "Sky, defend me!"

"He's not wrong," she said, betraying me in three words. Catching my glare, she explained, "I mean, it's a bit weird that he asked if Everett is coming to Shellside when you invited him."

"Oh, come on. He just wanted to be prepared," I said.

"Or," River began, "he doesn't know how to talk to girls. Probably just didn't realise what a question like that suggests."

I was silent for a moment, turning this new information over in my head. Really, it was kind of nice to know that Lachie acted this way with everyone—that our friendship wouldn't have to be tarnished by any potential presence of a crush. Because he didn't have a crush. Apparently, he just asked questions like that to everyone.

I shrugged, turning away. "Well, it doesn't matter. He's my friend. He's nice."

"If you say so," River replied, ending the conversation and immediately preoccupying himself with his phone. He never did care much about other people. That was, until he met Connor. Really, Lachie probably found River equally as strange.

Suddenly, my phone buzzed, ending my train of thought.

"Oh, who's that? Lachie, begging for more?" Sky teased.

I rolled my eyes, unlocking my phone to find a notification from Everett. Without thinking, I opened the message, my heart jumping out of my throat as a picture appeared, three words flashing beneath.

Everett: Just finished gym.

Too slow, I turned the screen off and pressed it against my chest, but not before River caught a peak of skin and a dirty mirror. His eyes popped out of his head and my face grew hot. Very hot.

"Oh, my fucking God," River said. He pressed his eyes shut, covering his face with his hands. "I saw nothing."

"What?" Sky asked, clueless. "What did I miss? I want to see."

"You really don't," I said, my face turning hotter and hotter.

"Why not?" She frowned, looking between us.

River and I met eyes. I groaned covering my face with my hands and River snorted, shaking his head.

"You need to teach your boyfriend how to send a warning," River chided.

"He wasn't that naked!"

"He was naked enough."

"Oh," Sky said. Her lips twitched and she looked at River. "Oh."

My phone dinged again, vibrating against my chest, except this time I didn't dare to look.

"Not going to get that?" River teased.

I narrowed my eyes at him. "Don't make me check my phone, River. I know you won't be able to look him in the eye anymore."

"Oh, yeah, nah. If you guys ever break up, send him my way."

It was my turn to gag.

CHAPTER 27

We sat together on the sand. Sand that was usually too hot to touch; that was now so cold it felt damp. Wind whipped my hair into my face, raising goosebumps on my exposed skin. The sun had vanished hours ago, fading into a cloudy night marked only by the harsh waves crashing on the shores nearby.

I pulled my sweater tighter around my arms, cursing the autumn weather of Shellside Bay.

The only light that guided us were the lights that lined the path nearby. Even the houses across the bay seemed to flicker in and out, half-hearted, sleeping until the promise of summer was fulfilled.

I wanted to join them. I wanted to curl against my mattress and close my eyes until December. Until Everett returned and refused to leave.

Sky sat beside me, her head resting on my shoulder as we listened to Austin talk about his day at work. Across from us, Connor laid on the sand, his head on River's lap as River toyed with his hair, smoothing it across his forehead and sliding his fingers down, across the slants of his cheeks.

We didn't talk about the things we used to.

It wasn't like when I was seven, and sat on these sands, arguing with Austin about who was the better surfer.

It wasn't like when I was twelve and Sky appeared out of nowhere and our group was officially formed, sitting on these sands, just talking about cartoons and surfing and sharks and whatever else popped into our pre-teen brains.

It wasn't like when I was seventeen, and Everett burst into my life in a series of colours and curses, and we sat on these sands, just holding each other until we were forced to let go.

This was different.

This was eighteen and sitting on the beach in autumn because it was all I could get now.

This was eighteen and stealing weekends at home to recharge after long months in the city.

This was eighteen and Shellside Bay being both home and as far away from home as possible at the same time.

Eighteen and sitting on these sands, waiting for the morning to send us apart again, only to reunite on the sands another day and fall back into our spots like nothing has changed—and yet everything had changed.

"When do you guys leave, again?" Austin asked when he was finished with his story.

"Next week," River answered. Connor frowned at him, and River's hand flattened against his face. "We'll come back for summer, though."

"Will Everett come too?" Sky asked. I could feel her eyes on me, feel everyone's eyes on me.

My face warmed. I looked down at my sleeves—Everett's sleeves—and nodded.

"He's coming as soon as his semester ends and he's moving in with me and River," I said. I couldn't help the smile that pulled on my lips.

Everett would be here in less than a year, and this time, he wouldn't be leaving. He'd be finishing the final year of his degree here, in Australia, with me.

And, by the end of the summer, Sky's gap year would be over. She'd be in Sydney with us. The Nauti Buoys, reunited.

At least, most of us.

Across from me, River's fingers were running through Connor's hair again, as if comforting him, reassuring him. We'll be back in no time. We'll call each other every day. We'll be fine.

Promises I'd made with Everett a million times, so often that I'd memorised that look on River's face. I could feel the ghost of it still on my own.

"Not long now, then, hey?" Austin asked. He smiled at me. Working in construction had made Austin look older. His face was darker. He carried wisdom in his skin and bones now. He didn't look like that eight-year-old boy I grew up with anymore.

"I'm happy for you, Isla," he said.

I smiled back, nodding. "Just a bit longer now."

It was only a few months, less than a year. And yet, the weeks seemed to stretch into months, the months into years.

It felt like I hadn't touched Everett in months, when it had only been a few weeks.

But I'd be okay, because summer would be here in a few months, and I'd have Everett's arms around me again.

This time, forever.

EPILOGUE

"Where should I put my mugs?"

I turned to find Everett entering the kitchen, a box labelled 'kitchen' on his hip. I smiled coyly at him, watching as he placed the box on the counter and pulled out his 'I heart Sydney' mugs.

"Right in the front," I replied.

He hummed. "I don't know. Maybe I should hide them in the back with the rest of your 'I heart NYC' mugs."

"Oh, come on. These are classics." I leaned past him, taking the mugs from his hands and placing them gingerly into the kitchen cabinet, right in the front beside my cat shaped mugs. "Look at that. Perfect."

"I don't know. I'm not really 'hearting' Sydney right now."

"Hey!" I spun to him. "Where's your Australian pride? You're a student here, now. This is official. Soon, you'll have to get a citizenship and everything."

He grinned, stepping towards me, and wrapping a hand around my waist. He pulled me closer until our chests were touching, and he looked down over me.

"What? Are you going to help me get my green card?"

"Is that a proposal, Ev?"

"Is that a yes, Isla?"

My lips twitched. I couldn't help myself. I leaned up, pressing a hard kiss against his mouth. He smiled into the kiss, his grip around my waist tightening as he held me against him. His hand slid beneath my jumper, sliding over my bare skin. His mouth opened, his tongue sliding into mine, and I—

"Gross."

We pulled apart, turning to find River walking into the room. He wrinkled his nose at us, gagging. Everett snorted, pulling me closer as his eyes settled on River. I clicked my tongue, pushing him away. I was not about to make out with Everett in front of our landlord.

"Keep that up and I'm going to have to charge you rent, Everett," River chided. "You and any little babies you produce along the way."

"River!" My face turned hot, and I stepped around the kitchen counter. If I didn't put some distance between myself and Everett now, River might be right about us producing little babies anytime now.

After over a year of long distance, this whole in person relationship thing was new to the both of us. Sometimes I just found my hands drifting towards Everett, like my skin had a magnetic reaction to being near him—like my body was only just learning that it could touch him at any time now.

And sometimes, I'd look up to find Everett's eyes already on me. To find him watching me, in the most mundane of moments, his fingertips angled towards me, catching any brush of skin he could manage.

I was glad I wasn't alone in feeling that way.

The weirdest part of it all was that now I could steal a hoodie whenever I wanted. Now, I could wander the hallways and I'd find Everett right there, in the flesh. Sometimes I still found myself reaching for my phone, ready to call him and tell him about my day before remembering I didn't need to do that. Not anymore.

"What?" River smiled his usual teasing smirk. "I'm only speaking the truth."

He paused to drop the box he'd been carrying onto the kitchen counter beside the rest of Everett's kitchen items. The items inside clattered as they hit the marble countertop, but River didn't care. He turned to face us, his hands on his hips.

"We need to set some ground rules," River began.

Everett paused his cup stacking to turn towards him. He nodded, suddenly growing serious. "Yeah, no. Of course. I'll keep things clean, put things back where they belong. No unexpected visitors, no parties, no—"

"No sex in the kitchen," River continued.

My hand flew to my mouth. "River!"

Everett froze, stunned for a moment, before his lips twitched teasingly and he lifted a brow. "Even if I really want to?"

"Everett!" I scolded.

"On top of that, no sex on the couch, in the hot tub, in my room, in the shared bathroom—"

"Where are we supposed to be having sex then?"

"Why are we pretending this is a totally normal conversation to be having?" I interjected, bewildered. "River, we've got it, okay?"

His face twisted and he seemed unsure. "Really?"

"Really!"

"So, just to be clear, the boundaries of having sex include—"

"Everett!" I shouted, interrupting his train of thought. "We are not discussing me and Everett's... physical relationship here, okay?"

River smiled. "We can take it to the living room if you'd like—"

I cut him off with a glare. "You know what I mean."

He shared a look with Everett, both of them fighting teasing grins. I only rolled my eyes, moving towards the next box to start to unpack.

"I have no idea how I'm going to survive in this apartment with the two of you," I muttered.

Everett appeared behind me, his arm snaking around my waist as his other hand moved to take a water bottle out of my hand.

"Get used to it," he said, lifting a brow at me, "because it's going to be for the next two years."

"Or so," River added, "you know, what with the marks you lot have been bringing in lately."

I narrowed my eyes at him. "Tell me again, what did you get for your Financial Management course?"

"Hey, I passed!"

"By half a mark!"

"That's still a pass!"

"Barely!"

"Point is," he said, flipping the box in front of him open, "I don't have to repeat. So, let's keep that up and we won't have to be stuck with each other for longer than necessary."

"He says that like he's not letting us live here for free," Everett murmured in my ear.

I giggled, elbowing him gently in the ribs, and he laughed, his grip on me tightening. I leaned back against him, savouring that feeling of just Everett. Here and with me. Laughing in a kitchen like a month ago we weren't video calling between meals just to get a word in.

Across from us, River gagged, dropping his box. "You guys are disgusting. You can unpack by yourselves."

And with that last word, he turned, leaving the kitchen directly out the front door.

"We were barely touching!" Everett exclaimed, releasing me, and throwing his hands up.

I laughed, turning to face him. "He's just jealous that you're here, and Connor's three hours away working his little butt off."

"Remind me again why Connor can't just move in too? I mean, River's already got two strays."

"Connor loves his job," I replied, shrugging. "I'm sure one day he will but for now, it's a three hour drive each way. Speaking of which, did you notice River grab his keys before he left?"

"No way."

I nodded, my smile growing. "Yes way. That's at least six hours of freedom in this apartment."

I slid out from behind the kitchen counter, trailing to the front door where I secured the lock and bolted the deadlock, just in case.

"So," I said, leaning against the wall. "What should we do first?"

□□□□□□□□□□

We sat in the hot tub, letting the bubbles massage our backs after a long day of unpacking.

Really, we'd only spent about an hour unpacking—Everett was a light traveller, after all—but we'd done... other strenuous activities in the past few hours so the hot water and bubbles were a welcome comfort.

Everett threw an arm around me, and I allowed myself to lean into his bare chest, my body relaxing with a heavy sigh.

"This is amazing," I said, my voice almost drowned out completely by the bubbles.

"It really is."

I tilted my face up to find him already looking at me, his eyes soft, his lips slanting in a quiet smile. We watched each other for a moment. And then, his hands were sliding over my bare waist, slipping through the water, fingers sliding beneath the strap of my bikini.

I shivered, drifting closer to him until I was straddling his hips. His fingers moved to massage my back, his wide palms laying flat against my skin. He leaned close, pressing a slow kiss to my lips.

"I still can't believe I get to hold you like this," he murmured. His hands moved higher to my shoulders, then back down to the small of my back, like trying to relearn the map of my skin. "It's like I'm dreaming."

"Would you like me to pinch you?"

He smirked at me. "Is that an offer?"

I rolled my eyes before kissing him back. Once. Twice. I pulled away to take in his face, his darkened eyes and blood red lips. His freckles were long gone now, and I lifted a finger to brush over his face where they used to live. His hair—it was darker. Longer. This was what American Everett looked like. New York Everett.

Shellside Bay Everett was all golden skin, brown freckles, streaks of sunlight through his hair, curled from the salt of the ocean.

Sydney Everett—what would that look like, I wondered. Would we walk around campus together? Sneak into each other's lectures? Maybe we could take a class or two together. Would we meet up for lunch dates and study dates, and go on coffee dates in the city? I couldn't imagine it. Soon, I wouldn't have to imagine it.

My hand trailed over his cheek, across his jaw, and down his bare collarbone. I let my fingers dawdle, drifting over the jutting bone there, lifting to his Adam's apple. He swallowed as my fingers touched his throat and my eyes flittered to his.

He watched me carefully, his breathing quick, like mine. I moved my hand down to his chest, feeling his heartbeat. Fast. He smiled, his hand covering mine, like he knew what I was feeling for.

"I will never get used to you," he said, as if explaining his quickened pulse. I leaned in, my lips hovering over his, and his hands fell to my hips, tightening there.

"Promise?" I muttered.

"Of course," he whispered. "Isla."

I grinned. "Everett."

"I missed you."

"How much?"

His fingers squeezed the skin at my hips, and he shifted a miniscule closer. He pressed a kiss to my lips, hard, as if accepting my challenge—as if to say this much. His tongue slid over mine and I lifted my arms, wrapping them around his neck, holding him against me.

When we parted, Everett moved downwards, his lips grazing over the skin of my jaw and across my throat.

"Don't leave me again," I muttered when he reached the spot beneath my ear. I felt his teeth scrape against my skin, his lips stretching in a smile.

"Is that another proposal, Isla Monroe?" he spoke against my skin.

I laughed, rolling my eyes. Of course, he had to take this moment and make a joke out of it. It was one of the reasons I loved him.

"If it has to be," I replied. He tilted his head, meeting my eye. "If that's what it takes to keep you with me. I'd move to New York for you."

"You don't have to," Everett said. "I'm here for good. Whether you like it or not. Although, I really hope you like it."

I grinned. "I love it."

"Good." He kissed me again. "Now, remind me, did River include the hot tub in his list of banned zones?"

"Hmm." I pretended to think. "I can't seem to remember."

"And how much time do we have left?"

"At least three hours."

Everett smiled. "Perfect."

He wrapped his arms around my waist and lead my lips to his. The bubbles of the hot tub broke against our skin. It wasn't quite the sea foam of Shellside Bay, but it'd do for now.

At the very least, Everett was here now. And this time, he wasn't leaving.

THE END